Mary Jane looked out the car window for a while, thinking about her dad

Mom had told her a long time ago who he was. That big new building downtown was her dad's. And she was glad he didn't know about her. If a man came to live with them, it would just mess things up. Still…

"Do you think Blake Ramsden woulda wanted me if you'd told him I was born?"

"He wasn't anywhere I could've told him," Mom said. "You know that."

"But when he did get somewhere, do you think he woulda wanted me?"

Mom was quiet for a while. "I believe that if he knew you, he'd love you as much as I do," she finally said.

That was good. "But would he *want* me?"

"I can't speak for him, sweetie," Mom said. "But I don't see how he *couldn't* want you. I've told you before that I'd contact him for you if you'd like," she added. "Would that help?"

"No!"

D0048120

Dear Reader,

I started out to tell you a story about a precocious little girl and her relationship with her forward-thinking and very competent mother (with a big dash of a classic romance theme—the secret baby—thrown in). I should've known better. What follows is what happens when I try to write a lighthearted, make-you-smile story. It becomes emotionally intense—for me, and I hope for you—with all kinds of surprises and unexpected challenges. I also hope you'll take these people into your heart, recognizing that while they may be larger than life, they're really there as representations of you and me and all our possibilities. You're still going to get the precocious child. The competent mother. And a secret-baby romance. And the rest... I hope it speaks to you in some way, maybe brings a little understanding, a new way of looking at something, or perhaps lightens a burden. Most of all, I hope to give you an experience you won't regret. A valuable return on the investment of your time.

As always, I love to hear from you. I reply to and keep each and every letter I receive. You can reach me at www.tarataylorquinn.com or by mail at P.O. Box 7434, Chandler, AZ 85246.

Tara Taylor Quinn

TARA TAYLOR QUINN

What Daddy Doesn't Know

HARLEQUIN®

TORONTO • NEW YORK • LONDON
AMSTERDAM • PARIS • SYDNEY • HAMBURG
STOCKHOLM • ATHENS • TOKYO • MILAN • MADRID
PRAGUE • WARSAW • BUDAPEST • AUCKLAND

ISBN 0-373-71225-1

WHAT DADDY DOESN'T KNOW

For my mother, Penny Gumser, and aunts Phyllis Pawloski,
Toni Wager and Evelyn Wessley—who taught me by
the example of their lives how to be a strong,
competent woman. And that, as a woman,
I can do anything I put my mind to.
(I want a Vegas trip *every* time I finish a book!)

Books by Tara Taylor Quinn

HARLEQUIN SUPERROMANCE

HARLEQUIN SINGLE TITLE

*Shelter Valley Stories

MIRA BOOKS

CHAPTER ONE

"Ms. McNeil, your daughter spit at her teacher. We don't tolerate things like that at Tyler Elementary."

After one quick exchange of glances with her eight-year-old daughter, Juliet McNeil understood that Mary Jane's story was different from the principal's. She fought the feeling of dread seeping through her. If Mrs. Cummings kicked Mary Jane out, Juliet's child would be facing the fourth new school in her brief, three-year educational career.

"Mary Jane will apologize to her teacher," she said for the third time that Friday morning. "And she and I will speak more about this when we get home."

The woman leaned forward, not a strand of her clearly dyed reddish-brown hair moving out of place. Probably didn't dare to. "I hesitate to say this in front of the child, Ms. McNeil..."

Juliet looked at the raised face of her simple but elegant gold watch, trying to distract herself from the panic that threatened to make her sound harsher than she intended.

"Anything you have to say to me regarding Mary Jane can be said in front of her," she said calmly. That calm was hard to come by when what she wanted to do was yell. Or cry. "I try not to hide things from my daughter and it seems to work well for us.''

Mary Jane had only been in this San Diego public school since the January semester change, and after two months the writing was already on the wall. The child was too intelligent for her own good, a free spirit, too outspoken—all of which made it hard for her to fit in with other kids her age.

She also had a father who didn't know she existed.

''Yes, well, then.'' The principal turned from Juliet to the fine-boned child sitting in a vinyl chair next to her mother, her skinny legs, mostly covered by an ankle-length denim skirt, sticking straight out in front of her. Mary Jane, her hands folded across her stomach and her short dark hair a riot of curls framing her cherub cheeks, looked the epitome of innocence. And in Juliet's opinion, that was exactly what she was.

''The thing is, Ms. McNeil,'' the woman started again a full thirty seconds later, ''I'm not so sure these talks you have with your child are doing much good. Nor do I think a simple apology will do it this time.''

''Spitting was wrong, I agree,'' Juliet said in a conciliatory tone. As a private defense attorney, she'd had a lot of experience reading jurors' faces. Mrs. Cummings had already made up her mind on this one. Juliet brushed an auburn curl over her shoulder and continued anyway. ''It's also not something Mary Jane has ever done before. I wonder, has anyone asked *her* about the incident?''

The older woman, her forehead creased in a clear expression of impatience, said, ''Yes, I have the complete report from Mrs. Thacker.''

"What reason did Mary Jane give for spitting at her teacher?"

A heavy sigh came from the seat next to Juliet. Her daughter's ankle-length black boots bobbed. Juliet didn't dare look over. She couldn't afford the distraction.

She also didn't have time to find another school right now.

But even without that look of confirmation from her daughter earlier, Juliet couldn't believe Mary Jane would really do such a thing. Drop something and break it, spill something, trip over something, probably. But spit at her teacher? The child was never deliberately mean.

"She spit on her teacher!" Mrs. Cummings said. "I really think the reason is irrelevant."

"Maybe."

Mary Jane could take the truth, but she was still a child. Her feelings could be hurt by thoughtless adults passing judgment without knowledge or understanding.

"Do you mind if we just ask her?" The whisper brush of hose against hose as Juliet crossed one ankle over the other sounded loud. "The first amendment to the Constitution of this country states that everyone has a right to a trial."

Her hands locked on the top of her desk, Mrs. Cummings didn't move. Though her smile was rather ghostly, it remained in place as she studied Juliet. Then, slowly, she turned her gaze to the little girl whose wide-eyed look almost lost her mother the ground she'd just won.

"Okay, Mary Jane, can you tell me why you spit on Mrs. Thacker?"

"I didn't actually spit on her." Mary Jane's voice, though somewhat subdued as she stared her principal in the eye, was her usual peculiar combination of childhood lisp and adultlike delivery.

Mrs. Cummings sat up straighter, her lips pinched with disapproval. "We have witnesses, several of them."

"I did spit and it did get on her," Mary Jane explained, eyes sincere. "I just didn't *mean* it to get on her. She walked around the corner and I couldn't make it stop coming out."

God, Juliet loved this child. "Why did you spit at all?" she asked.

Mary Jane glanced down, moving her boots back and forth against each other. "Jeff Turner said that I was backward because there were lots of things I don't know how to do 'cause I don't have a dad to teach me."

She and Mary Jane were happy together. Why couldn't the world just let them be?

"Things like spitting?" Juliet asked.

Mary Jane nodded. "So I told him I could too spit, as good as anyone with a dad. And he told me to prove it, so that's what I was doing when Mrs. Thacker came to call us in from recess."

Trying not to smile at that image, or to think about the hurtful things kids did to each other, Juliet looked back at the principal. And waited. This was her call.

"The point is—" Mrs. Cummings, hands together, leaned toward Juliet "—that your daughter, whether she meant to or not, spit on her teacher in front of all the other children. We can't just ignore that fact. Maintaining the discipline required to prevent mayhem with six hundred students all in one building for six hours every day takes diligence and carefully protected boundaries."

"I understand, but—"

"I was quite willing to sign the necessary forms to allow Mary Jane to attend this institution even though she lives outside our boundaries, but she has not lived up to her side of the agreement. I'm going to—"

She couldn't bear to see Mary Jane become the outsider again as a new kid in yet another school. "Please, Mrs. Cummings." Juliet sat forward. She'd beg if she had to. She was just beginning jury selection on the biggest trial of her career—opposing Paul Schuster, a prosecutor who put far much more value on winning than on truth.

"She's explained that the spitting wasn't intentional," Juliet said quietly.

The frown on the principal's plain face was not encouraging. Even if Juliet won this one, they lost. She couldn't feel good about sending Mary Jane to a school that didn't want her.

The child was uncharacteristically still beside her as Mrs. Cummings sat back, eyes lowered. Silent.

There was a time to speak, and a time to let the facts speak for themselves. Watching her imp of a daughter sitting so solemnly beside her, chin sliding lower on her chest as the seconds passed, Juliet willed the facts to speak quickly.

"I don't know how I could explain this to a classroom full of third-graders." The principal finally looked up, her gaze pinned on Juliet. "If I let Mary

Jane back into class, they're going to think that what she did was okay.''

"I don't work with kids all day long like you do," Juliet said, "but it seems to me that they'll think what you tell them to think. Couldn't this be a lesson in how things are not always what they seem? Or an example of how telling the truth can get you *out* of trouble?"

"Spitting at all is against school rules."

Filling with desperation, Juliet spoke urgently. "I know, ma'am, and I'm sure no one's sorrier than Mary Jane. But spitting on the playground can't be a reason for expulsion, can it?"

"No," Mrs. Cummings said, eyebrows raised. "Not by itself. But this isn't Mary Jane's first infraction." She looked over at the girl. "And I'm sorry Jeff Turner was bothering you. I'll have another talk with his father, but I just don't see how I can overlook the fact that you're in this office more frequently than anyone else in your class."

Juliet leaned forward. "The other incidents are in the past," she said, finding it difficult to breathe around the tightness in her chest. "Mary Jane accepted her punishment and made all necessary reparations. All we have on the table today is spitting and, judging by your own words, that's not punishable by expulsion."

The principal sat for a long time, and then her face softened slightly. "All right, I'll give her one more chance. But if there's a next time…"

Thank you, God. Juliet didn't hear the rest of the warning. The bottom line was that Mary Jane couldn't make any more mistakes.

"But you're going to have to stay after school for a week, young lady, and clean Mrs. Thacker's blackboards for her as punishment."

"Yes, ma'am."

"And apologize to her in front of your classmates."

"Yes, ma'am."

With that, Mrs. Cummings nodded.

Juliet gave her daughter a hug and a whispered "I love you," and hurried back to her office at Truman and Associates, one of the city's leading law firms. They'd had a narrow escape.

"MR. RAMSDEN, I'm Paul Schuster. Thank you for seeing me."

Blake took the older man's hand, was surprised by his weak grip, and indicated one of the two lush navy leather chairs in front of his desk.

"It's not often I get a call from an assistant attorney general," he said, curious. He'd read about Schuster; the man was one of the state's "winningest" prosecutors, according to the papers.

There were some who said innocent people were rotting away in prison because of that.

"As a matter of fact," Blake added, taking the man's business card, "this is a first."

"It's the first time I've been in the Ramsden Building, too," Schuster said, lifting the back of his black-and-white tweed jacket as he set down his soft-sided leather briefcase and sat. "Like everyone else in San Diego, I've driven by it countless times."

Blake nodded. The building was one of the first things he'd done after his return to the States—and the family business—five years before. One thing he'd learned during his four-year sojourn abroad was that image was everything. Show them you're big and impressive, and you will be. He'd also gained an almost spiritual appreciation for the artistry of the architecture he'd spent five years in college analyzing.

"It's as interesting inside as it is out. The spirals and columns are fascinating," the prosecutor added.

"You've never been to Barcelona, I take it?"

Schuster's frown held more question than anything. "No, why?"

"They're based on the Sagrada Familia, a famous Gaudi church." He could bore the man with all the other architectural details represented in the new home of Ramsden Enterprises, one of the state's oldest and most elite custom-home builders—and now its leading commercial builder as well—but he wouldn't. "Gaudi was an innovator, part of the art nouveau movement. He created fairy tales out of rubbish. And this particular project is one he never finished."

To his credit, Schuster appeared interested.

Rocking back in his chair, Blake placed his hands on his thighs. After five years, he still wasn't used to the creased dress slacks he wore.

"You're a busy man, Schuster. I'm sure you didn't come here to discuss architecture. Unless you're in the market for a new one-of-a-kind home?"

"What do you know about the Terracotta Foundation?"

"Only what I've read in the papers. It's a privately owned and administered foundation whose alleged purpose is to raise funds, through investments and donations, and disperse them to third-world countries.''

"How about Semaphor?"

Resisting the urge to adopt a less relaxed position, Blake said, "It's a nonprofit organization that raises public awareness of charitable foundations."

"Your father was on the board."

Blake knew that. The open position had been offered to Blake five years before, when he'd flown home in shock to take up the reins of the family business.

"Is there a problem here?" he asked as he leaned forward, putting his feet firmly on the floor and resting his forearms on the edge of his desk. The glass was cool on the skin left bare by the rolled-up sleeves of his dress shirt.

Schuster shook his graying head. "Not with you, no." The pockmarks on the man's face gave a hint of fierceness to his serious expression.

"And not with my father, either." Of that Blake was certain. Walter Ramsden might have been obsessive, inflexible, and impossible to live with, but he had been as honest as they came. In all his dealings.

"How well do you know Eaton James?"

CEO of Terracotta Industries, which owned the Terracotta Foundation. "Well enough."

Schuster raised one eyebrow. Blake looked away and stared out the twelfth-floor wall of windows that flanked the west side of his office, giving him a view that—if all civilization were wiped away—would take him straight to the ocean. Having it so close, that vast place of mystery and life, somehow calmed him.

"The man tried to swindle my father." Blake gave Schuster dates. Times. Quotes from an investment agreement. Accounts. "That's what I mean by well enough."

"Are you willing to testify to this?"

Of course. If he had to. The one thing that held steady in his life was his compulsion to tell the truth. To tell it and to live it. But he didn't relish showing his late father for the fool he'd apparently been in that incident, particularly since it was the only time in the man's entire life that he'd been led by sentiment rather than logic.

"I have a paper trail outlining a series of invest-ment frauds that, with your validation, could nail James to the wall," Schuster said. "Without your tes-timony—the explanation that will tie all the paper ev-idence together—he could walk."

"When do you need me in court?"

"YOU SURE LOOK gloomy."

Leaning her head against the back of the seat, Mary Jane nodded.

"Was it rough, apologizing in front of everyone?"

"Nah." She hadn't cared. She *was* sorry she'd spit on Mrs. Thacker.

"Then what?"

"I just wish I didn't have to go to any dumb school."

What she wished was that she could stay home where Mom always knew what she meant, knew that she wouldn't do bad things on purpose, and didn't think it was weird that she didn't know her dad.

She wished she'd never told that to dumb Jeff

Turner anyway. But he'd made her really mad when he'd said her dad didn't want her because her hair was so curly and she said weird stuff.

At least she hadn't told Jeff that her dad didn't know her, either—didn't even know *about* her.

"School's not dumb, Mary Jane. You're a very smart little girl, but if you don't learn facts and information, that intelligence isn't going to do you a lot of good."

"You could teach me at home."

"Honey, you know I have to work."

"Well, I can stay home alone and teach myself."

"Did someone say something mean to you after I left?"

Thank goodness it had been yesterday when Jeff had said her dad didn't want her. Because she couldn't lie to her mom, and she didn't want to tell her what he'd said.

"No."

What if the thing Jeff said was true? What if her father didn't want her?

"You sure?" Mom's face was all soft and kind of smiling when she looked over at Mary Jane.

She nodded. And looked out the window for a while, thinking about her dad. Mom had told her a long time ago who he was. Her mom didn't keep it a secret, because her grandma had kept secrets from Mom and Aunt Marcie that had turned out to hurt them a lot.

That big building downtown was her dad's. And she was glad he didn't know about her. If a man came to live with them, it would just mess up the best life she'd ever had. Still…

"Do you think Blake Ramsden woulda wanted me if you'd told him I was born?"

"He wasn't anywhere where I could have told him," Mom said. "You know that."

"But when he did get somewhere, do you think he woulda wanted me?"

Mom was quiet for a while and that scared Mary Jane. If Jeff Turner was right about this, was he right about the other dumb stuff he said, too? Did everyone really hate Mary Jane and laugh at her behind her back because she mostly got all the answers?

Did they say they didn't want to be her friend?

"I believe that if he knew you, he'd love you as much as I do," Mom finally said.

That was good. "But would he *want* me?"

"I can't speak for him, sweetie," Mom said. "But I don't see how he couldn't want you. I've told you before that I would contact him for you if you wanted me to," she added. "Would that help?"

"No!"

The trees were going by really fast and it made her a little dizzy, staring out at them. She liked them though. They were too big to be hurt by just about anything, 'cept lightning, and they helped you breathe.

"Did you want me?" She'd hadn't planned to ask that.

Mom pulled into their street and into their carport and stopped the car, but she didn't open her door. Mary Jane didn't either.

"Why all the questions about being wanted?" Mom asked, frowning a little.

She shrugged. A shrug wasn't a lie.

"When I first found out I was pregnant with you, I was scared to death." That was something Mary Jane had never heard before. She stared at her mom.

"You were?" She'd never seen Mom scared of anything. Usually she made the scary stuff better.

"Uh-huh."

"Scared of me, a little baby? How come?"

Mom's fingers pushed curls off Mary Jane's forehead. She liked it when Mom did that.

"I wasn't afraid of *you*. I was afraid that I wouldn't be able to take care of you. I was alone and not even a real lawyer yet because I hadn't taken the bar exam. I had no idea how I'd support us."

Oh. That kind of stuff. "But you did."

Mom smiled. "Yes, I did."

"So *then* did you want me?"

"Very much."

That was enough. But Mary Jane liked talking about this. It made her feel good. Like she really was special and not a loser like Jeff Turner said.

"When did you first know you wanted me?" she asked, still sitting with her seat belt on even though she was getting pretty hungry.

Mom had kind of a faraway look, and Mary Jane knew she was remembering. She wished she could remember, too.

"I always wanted you," she said, her voice soft like she was telling a dream. "But the first time I knew you were going to be more important to me than anything else in my life was the first time I felt you move."

"In your stomach?"

"Yep."

Mary Jane grinned. "What did it feel like?"

"Like a tiny little butterfly fluttering its wings."

That wasn't so bad. She wasn't ever going to have babies herself. That would be too gross.

But she was sure glad Mom had.

CHAPTER TWO

"My pawn to your king," Blake muttered to himself. Still in the gray suit and coordinating gray, black-and-white tie he'd worn to the office that day, he stood at the computer in his glass-walled home office the last Wednesday night in March. He pushed a couple of keys, hit Enter, took one final look at the game on the screen, and left the room. His opponent, a man he'd met in Kashmir, India, several years before, would be at least an hour figuring his way out of that one.

He had guests coming for dinner, Donkor and Jamila Rahman. A Christian father and daughter he'd lived with for a while in Egypt—before his marriage to Jamila's closest friend.

After checking the last-minute details on the dinner his housekeeper had prepared for him that afternoon, Blake moved from the kitchen, with its shiny black appliances, granite countertops and double oven, to the side of his house that didn't overlook the ocean. In contrast to the western side, these rooms didn't have windows. The house was built into the side of a cliff in the quaint village of La Jolla.

The east side was where he'd put his treasure room—a museum with track lighting, built-in shelves and marble tables that housed all the artifacts and souvenirs of his travels. It was also where he housed his wine cellar.

The cellar—more of a wall-size wine closet—had been his wife's idea.

A woman who'd been orphaned young, Amunet had grown up half Egyptian, half French and later, a New Yorker. She'd been visiting Egypt when Blake was there helping to rebuild a small village that had been hit hard by weather and poverty. Donkor, a man of means and a charitable heart, had been the largest donor and overseer of the project.

Blake chose the wine, checking the year, although he knew there was not one bottle in the house that wasn't worthy of a fine restaurant.

Donkor and Jamila had been the only "family" present at the urban Egyptian wedding Amunet had wanted. From the car parade with all the flowers and ribbons and honking of horns, through the ancient tradition of the Zaffa, a human parade of belly dancers and drummers singing to them, to the Kosha, two bedecked seats in front of the waiting guests where he and Amunet had exchanged rings, his lovely bride had been in her element. Surrounded by noise, excitement, beauty, dancing and activity, and enough people to distract her from anything that might have been missing.

Of course, Blake hadn't seen it that way then. He'd just been crazy in love with the unusual woman who loved him so intensely. And she'd been completely open to whatever path his heart directed him to take.

Or so he'd thought.

Putting the wine on ice, Blake carried it through

the kitchen to the dining room, which also sported a wall of windows that overlooked the ocean. He lit the candles, dimmed the lights, and flipped a switch that turned on the CD of soft flute and guitar music that would play throughout the evening.

He hadn't seen either of the Rahmans since his divorce four years earlier.

He was ready for their arrival with a good twenty minutes to spare. Not at all like him. Moving back through the kitchen and Amunet's garden room to his office, Blake looked in on his chess game.

It was exactly as he'd left it.

Then he picked up the newspaper he'd been avoiding since he'd come home. On the front page, in the very center and large enough for him to see the dimple at the corner of her cheek, was a photograph of Juliet McNeil, one of the partners at Truman and Eaton James's defense attorney.

He hadn't known, when he'd agreed to be Paul Schuster's witness, that Juliet would be opposing. Not that it would've mattered. Eaton James had broken the law. He had to be held accountable.

He hadn't seen her in almost a decade, except for a cursory conversation when they'd passed each other on the sidewalk a few years ago.

Still, if Blake was going to meet the lady again, he'd rather it be in more agreeable circumstances— or at least on the same side of the fence. On the other hand, it would be interesting to see her at work, against a man like Paul Schuster.

She didn't have a chance in hell of winning. And,

as he remembered it, Juliet wasn't a woman who easily accepted defeat.

He grinned, dropping the paper as the doorbell chimed.

"WE DIDN'T COME JUST to have dinner with you," Donkor, dressed in his usual garb of sedate suit and tie, announced as he pushed back his empty dinner plate. He'd had second helpings of the chicken cordon bleu and spinach salad Pru Duncan had prepared.

Jamila glanced up and then away. Blake had known, since she'd failed to meet his eyes when they'd kissed and hugged hello, that something was wrong. He'd also known that he'd have to wait to find out what it was until Donkor felt the time was right for talking.

"Is there something I can help you with? You need a place to stay while you're here in the States? You're always welcome to stay with me as long as you like. You know that. I have more bedrooms than I need." More solitude than he needed, too.

Donkor shook his head.

"We have to fly out tomorrow." Jamila's normally effusive voice was subdued. Dabbing at her lips with the cloth napkin, she gave him a brief smile.

"I thought you just arrived last night." He'd sent a car to the Los Angeles airport to pick them up. They'd stayed in the city due to the late hour.

"We did." She looked as beautiful as ever with her long dark hair up in a twist that left ringlets escaping down the sides of her face. Her olive skin was smooth and made up to perfection, her slim figure outlined but not openly displayed in her silk pantsuit.

"We have some news." Donkor's deep voice was as solemn as his daughter's had been.

And that was when it hit him. "You've heard from Amunet."

"Yes."

No one sipped wine. Or moved. Blake glanced from one to the other. They'd been completely sympathetic to both him and Amunet during the divorce. They'd understood that needs neither he nor Amunet had been able to alter had driven them apart. Certainly that wasn't about to change.

"You're here to tell me she's remarrying?" Donkor had been the only person, other than Amunet herself, who'd known quite how hard Blake had fallen. "Because it's really okay. She was a part of a dream—an unreal life that was destined to end. I think, at least in part, I must have known that all along."

"You would never have married her if you'd known that." Donkor's tone brooked no argument. "That's not your way."

Blake would never have taken vows he didn't intend to uphold. He'd forgotten, for a moment, that Donkor knew a lot more about him than how much he'd loved his wife.

Jamila wiped her mouth again. This time missing, and dabbing her eye instead. Her eye?

Blake looked over at her. She was crying.

Donkor spoke.

"Amunet is dead, son. Her funeral is on Saturday. In New York. We wanted to tell you in person."

SHE'D COMMITTED SUICIDE. His ex-wife, a woman who'd raised him to levels of emotion—both good and bad—that he'd never really understood, was dead. And while neither Donkor nor Jamila would ever have said so, the implication was that her death was partly because of him.

While she hadn't been able to bear the humdrum life of an executive's wife, trapped in one city, hosting cocktail parties and doing lunch, neither had she been happy as a divorcée. She'd been so contradictory, such a strange blend of modern and ancient, forward thinking and traditional. She'd traveled the world, first by herself and later with Blake—unmarried, uncaring what people thought. Going wherever the mood took her, to the grotto in Paris, a fishermen's bar in Ireland, the wilds of Africa. Nannying. Doing temporary office work. Dancing for food. But she'd been a virgin on their wedding night.

God, what a night that had been.

Sipping warm whiskey from a highball glass, Blake sat alone in his living room on a chair of the softest fabric, looking out over the shadows to the dim lights of ships on the ocean. Waiting for Paul Schuster's call. He'd told Schuster he'd be available to testify on Friday morning.

And he was going to be in New York.

Shaking his head, Blake took another sip. And stared. A light had been bobbing out in the distance for half an hour. The boat was headed in the direction of Alaska. A chilly place.

This was a night for chilled hearts.

He'd been prepared to receive an invitation to Amunet's third wedding. He'd missed the second, a Las Vegas quickie that had ended almost as soon as it had begun. And he'd already decided to attend the third, whenever it came along. He was over her—or he understood, at least, that they were never meant to be forever. They were from very different worlds, finding happiness in completely opposite things. He wished her well. Wanted her happy.

He'd never expected to be attending her funeral.

"I APPRECIATE the phone call," Paul Schuster said when he and Blake finally connected. He was as agreeable and friendly as he'd been the two other times Blake had spoken with him in the past weeks.

"Obviously I've been following the trial," Blake told the other man, still sitting in the dark, sipping whiskey—his third—and watching the ships. Sliding down, head against the back of the chair, he lifted an ankle to the opposite knee. "You're doing a great job. I'm sorry to be putting a damper on things."

"Don't worry about it," Paul said, with as much energy at ten o'clock at night as he'd probably had at ten in the morning. "Actually, I haven't even declared you as a witness yet."

"Juliet McNeil doesn't know I'm testifying?" He'd been wondering what she would think about seeing him again.

They'd had one incredible night together once.

A long time ago.

"No one knows you're testifying, including my staff," Schuster said, surprising him.

Blake sipped and nodded, his eyes half closed as he watched another ship approach. "I thought you had to declare as soon as you turned up new evidence. Give the defense a chance to review the information."

"I haven't seen the evidence yet, so technically I don't have any. I'd been hoping to get the paperwork today, which is why I had you on hold for Friday.

The way it's looking now, it's probably going to be Monday.''

"What are the chances of the records not turning up?''

"Slim to none.''

"But there's a chance.''

"Not one I'm willing to acknowledge.''

If Blake had been a little more clearheaded, he might have continued to push for percentages. He liked things on the table, in black and white or not at all.

"I'm glad I don't have your job,'' he said instead.

Schuster laughed. "Just call when you're back in town.''

Blake said he would.

He dropped the phone. Took another sip—a small one. It was going to be a long night and he needed to be up at the crack of dawn to get his business affairs in order before he left for New York.

But for now, there was nothing to do but sit. And wait. And think.

"JULES?''

Instantly awake as she recognized the voice on the other end of the line, Juliet sat up. It was late Thursday night, the first of April.

"Marce? What's up?''

"Nothing.''

"It doesn't sound like nothing. You've been crying.'' It wasn't something Juliet could ignore in the nonidentical twin sister she'd been watching out for all their lives.

Marcie laughed, sniffed, laughed again. "It really

is nothing, Jules, I promise. I don't know what's wrong with me. I'm just lying here having a hard time falling asleep and suddenly I start thinking about you, missing you and before I know it, I'm blubbering like an idiot.''

''You need to get out of that town.'' Unlike Juliet, who'd left Maple Valley behind the second she'd graduated from high school, Marcie at thirty-four was still living in the small, mostly trailer-populated northern California town.

That fact scared Juliet every time she thought about it. She'd seen what being cooped up in Maple Valley had done to their mother.

Marcie, in contrast to their destitute mother, was one of the more well-to-do inhabitants in town, having made a success of the local beauty shop. But still...

''I know,'' her sister said. ''I do need to get away.''

Where Marcie lived was Marcie's decision. They both knew that and had acknowledged it many times. But that didn't stop Juliet from caring, or worrying, or helping where she could help.

It would be different if Marcie was happy in Maple Valley. But with her proclamations of dissatisfaction, she constantly reaffirmed Juliet's fears. If she didn't get out of that town with its limited possibilities, she would wither and prematurely age as their mother had.

''So come to San Diego for the weekend.''

While Marcie didn't visit as often as Juliet and Mary Jane would like, she was a fairly frequent occupant of their Mission Beach cottage.

"I don't know. Hank has a big sale going at the hardware."

Juliet started counting. She had to at least get to ten before she'd be able to rein in the frustration that she had no right to unleash on her sister. She made it to four. And a half.

"So?"

"Well, it's hard on him. He'll be exhausted. I should be here."

"Why in hell should you be there?" She sat up in bed, pulling a pillow over her as the covers fell to reveal the spaghetti-strap shirt and bikini briefs she slept in. Their mother's life had been ruined by her choice to sacrifice herself, her needs and desires, for a man. Why couldn't Marcie see that she was doing exactly the same thing?

"Do you have clients on Saturday?" Juliet asked.

"Not that I can't reschedule."

"So come."

"Hank will be disappointed."

"Marcie! For God's sake! You aren't married to the guy!"

Last Juliet had heard, Hank still hadn't asked, after more than fifteen years of dating.

"I know."

"You don't even live with him."

"I know."

In the dark, Juliet stared out her bedroom window to the beach beyond. When the weather was warm enough, she loved to sit in her room late at night with the window up, listening to the waves as they crashed along the distant shore.

"He's not there, is he?"

"No."

"So come."

"Okay."

Blinking, Juliet pushed the pillow aside. "Really?"

"Yeah."

"Great! Mary Jane will be thrilled! We'll go to Seaport Village." It might be considered touristy by most San Diegans, but Juliet, Mary Jane and most especially Marcie loved walking through the shops and restaurants along the waterfront. "Bring your in-line skates. Mary Jane's been practicing and I think she's ready to go out with us."

More than anything, Juliet was ready to spend some time with her sister.

"Okay," Marcie said, her voice losing the weak thread of tears. "And how about I throw in a nice dress, too, and treat us all to a decadent dinner in Beverly Hills?"

"Throw in the dress. You don't need to treat."

"I know," Marcie said, her voice soft. "But I want to, Jules. Thanks."

"For what?"

"Being you."

"Thanks for being you, too," she said, the reply never growing old, no matter how many times it was repeated.

"Love you."

"You, too."

Juliet hung up the phone, a weight she hadn't even known she was carrying lifted from her shoulders. A weekend with Marce and Mary Jane, playing, having a late-night glass of wine or two with her sister, was just what she needed.

And after once again discussing the possibility of a life change for Marcie, perhaps she'd have a chance to talk to her sister about Mary Jane. The child had been a model student since the spitting incident the previous month. But the episode had brought back a fear to Juliet's heart that, this time, would not be so easily eradicated.

She thanked God for Mary Jane's ability to see all kinds of truths, to be aware of truth in different lights. And she was worrying herself sick about whether her daughter could fit into a society that preferred conformity to originality.

Sliding down in bed, she punched the pillow, leaned back and watched the shadows and occasional bobbing light on the ocean. She knew exactly what Marcie would say. Mary Jane was well adjusted, more secure than any kid either of them had ever known— certainly more secure than either of them had been, in spite of the fact that they'd always had each other—and there was no mistaking that the kid was genuinely happy. Hell, perfect strangers would glance at Mary Jane on the street and smile.

Marcie was going to tell Juliet she was raising her daughter well.

Juliet closed her eyes and willed sleep to come. She had another long day in court to get through before Marcie arrived. She was probably just tired from so many days of sitting through the prosecution's portion of the Terracotta case. Waiting for her turn had always been the hardest part of her job.

Yeah, that was it. She was just tired.

So why, then, was she finding it so impossible to get to sleep?

BLAKE LEFT NEW YORK as soon as the funeral ended. A small affair, hosted by the adoptive parents Amunet hadn't seen in ten years prior to this last trip home, it lasted less than half an hour. Jamila gave the eulogy. There were a couple of songs. An Egyptian poem was read. And then it was over.

That quickly, a life that had been too vibrant for this world was gone. Forever. It was the third time in five years that he'd buried those closest to him. First his parents, after the car accident, and now Amunet.

He called Paul Schuster from the airport to let him know he'd be back in plenty of time to appear in court on Monday, then boarded his plane.

With only one glass of cheap whiskey to deaden the uneasiness in his heart, he sat back in the blue leather first-class seat and tried not to think about life, or death, or the past couple of days.

In spite of everything, it had been good to see Donkor and Jamila. It was such a shame their lives kept them so far apart from him, in spite of how much they missed each other.

The whiskey didn't help much, nor did the movie they were showing on the six-hour flight. He'd already seen it. Twice. And there sure as hell wasn't a lot to look at through the window. Not when you were flying above the clouds at thirty-two thousand feet.

He would have picked a brighter color than the royal blue Amunet's parents had chosen for the inside of her casket. And dressed her in something long, white and flowing.

For the first time since he'd known him, Donkor had looked tired. Old.

The flight attendant came by and Blake asked for a bottle of water to make his whiskey last a little longer. He talked to her about the flight, and asked if she had to turn around and go right back to New York or if she'd be flying somewhere else first.

He didn't hear her answer.

He went to the rest room.

And he remembered the last time he'd flown with his ex-wife. They'd been on the way to California to bury his parents.

That led him along a painful road of memories, mostly of his father. The dictator. The honorable husband and father. The honest businessman. He thought about Eaton James, and his father's heart attack.

Finally, in desperation, head lying against the padded rest, he turned his thoughts to the upcoming trial. Testifying was something he could actually *do*.

And from there, with the hum of the airplane cocooning him in his own little world, he thought about Juliet McNeil and the night they'd met.

Though he'd never known her well, since they'd talked far more about their separate futures than any past experiences that would have defined them, he'd felt a particular affinity with her, borne of their one incredible night together. He'd been a very young twenty-three to her much more mature and focused twenty-five. She'd been preparing to sit for the bar exam, after winning enough scholarship money to put herself through the elite University of Virginia School of Law, and had made it very clear that she was not going to be swayed from her goals by entangling herself in a relationship that could only distract her. Having just completed his MBA, after earning a degree in architecture, Blake had been in the final stages of preparing for what was supposed to have been a year of world travel, a prerequisite his father had set for Blake's employment with the family business.

For Blake, the journey had been much more. It had been a time to finally achieve the freedom that had consumed his thoughts for years. A time to get out from under his father's expectations—and his own—that he live up to the old man. When he was growing up, he'd constantly had to prove his intelligence and worth. The trip had been a time to find out what he really wanted to do with his life…or slowly die without ever having been alive.

During his last weekend at home, he'd met Juliet at a bar on the beach.

"Would you like some wine with your steak?" Blake was a bit surprised by the disappointment that shot through him as the flight attendant he'd practically clung to for diversion earlier interrupted his reminiscing with a dinner that smelled delicious.

"Thanks." He nodded, holding up his arms as she placed dishes, silverware and a full wineglass before him.

The steak was good. And the other passengers were more talkative as they all shared dinner in their own little world. That was just as well, he thought, listening to the woman on the other side of the aisle as she told him about the grandson she'd just left behind in New York.

There was no point in making anything significant out of an encounter that had happened nine years before. Because if he was honest with himself, he'd have to admit that his memories of that night—the fabulous sex he and Juliet had shared, the conversation and laughter—were more a result of the amount of alcohol they'd consumed than anything else.

And Blake Ramsden was always honest with himself.

CHAPTER THREE

THEY'D JUST COME IN from a bike ride along the beach on Sunday, planning to have a quick lunch before Marcie had to leave for the airport, when the phone rang.

"I'll get it!" Mary Jane ran off to the study.

"I'd hope it was one of her school friends calling except that she doesn't have any," Juliet mumbled.

"It's probably Hank, forgetting what time my flight gets in. He offered to come pick me up so I didn't have to pay to park my car." With her long blond hair up on top of her head in a claw clip, her face clear of makeup and her slim leggy figure dressed in Juliet's white terry-cloth sweat suit, Marcie looked beautiful, healthy and vibrant. She barely resembled the worn-looking woman who'd met Juliet and an exuberant Mary Jane at the San Diego airport two nights before.

"Oh come on," Juliet teased her sister. "You kidding? A trip all the way to San Francisco? An adventure in the big city? He's probably been up since dawn."

Marcie chuckled and punched Juliet on the arm. "Hank's not that bad. He's taken me to dinner in San Francisco twice since Christmas!"

"Mom! It's for you!" Mary Jane called.

The sisters, as identical in size and shape as they were opposite in coloring, shrugged and grinned.

"I'll be right back." Leaving her sister to start lunch, Juliet took the call.

"WHAT'S UP?"

Marcie's question was immediate when Juliet, still wearing her black Lycra pants, sweatshirt and tennis shoes, returned to the kitchen five minutes later. The side trip to her room to breathe probably would have worked if she'd been facing anyone but the other two McNeil women.

"You've got that weird look on your face," Mary Jane piped up, her mouth full of peanut butter and jelly as she watched her mother come into the kitchen and take her seat. "The one where something might be wrong but you're going to pretend it isn't."

"Eat," Marcie said.

"I am eating."

With her short dark curls, Mary Jane might bear no resemblance to her blond aunt, but there was no doubting the adoration the two had for each other. When Mary Jane had found out her aunt was borrowing the white sweatsuit, she'd immediately run in and changed into her identical—if slightly more stained— one.

"Eat your chicken salad," Marcie turned to Juliet, indicating the plate waiting in front of her. "The protein will do you good."

It wasn't a large portion, about as much as Marcie had given herself. Juliet stared out the bay window of the kitchen alcove, telling herself that she was nervous for nothing.

She'd made some very difficult choices in her life. And while she'd also adopted the very annoying habit of second-guessing herself about one or two of them, she knew, deep inside, that she'd done the best that she could. She'd seen him a few years ago and the encounter had run exactly as she'd have scripted it, had she known ahead of time it was going to happen: quick, impersonal and uneventful.

He'd been married. And thankful that he didn't have children.

"You know that case I told you I was working on?"

Marcie watched her closely. "Eaton James." She stabbed a piece of chicken with her fork. "He's so big he's your only client right now."

Juliet nodded. Her sister always kept track.

"Blake Ramsden is going to be in court tomorrow, as a witness for the prosecution."

Mary Jane took another bite of her sandwich, adding a potato chip to the wad in her mouth. She chewed and swung her feet while she watched her mother, and listened.

Fork midmouth, Marcie stared. "How do you feel about that?"

"Obviously uneasy." Juliet focused on calm. Normalcy. She took a bite of chicken. "Surprise evidence is never welcome, particularly in a case as convoluted as this one is. True to form, Paul Schuster is attempting to confuse the jury with a paper trail that probably took years to accumulate, only half of which is really relevant."

"Can't you object?"

"She does." Picking up her glass of milk, Mary

Jane rolled her eyes. "The prosecution talks pseudo-logic, huh, Mom?"

"Yeah." Juliet smiled. The milk mustache only slightly detracted from the maturity of her daughter's contribution to the conversation.

"Doesn't it present a conflict of interest having him as a witness for the other side?"

"No." Juliet shook her head. "I certainly have no personal relationship with him!"

"Still…"

"I'll explain to Eaton James that I met Blake Ramsden in a bar years ago, but that there's been nothing between us since. He's not going to care."

"So what's Ramsden got to do with the Terracotta Foundation?"

"I have no idea. Schuster's faxing me a copy of the evidence he plans to present. I know that Ramsden's father donated a substantial sum of money to Terracotta several years ago to be put in some land investment that didn't pay off. Terracotta, and those particular investors, lost everything they put into the project. But no one has ever suggested any evidence of fraud. Eaton James was up front with everyone about the risk involved."

"Mr. Ramsden died when I was a little kid," Mary Jane reminded them all. "And Blake was still gone then, right, Mom?"

Juliet nodded.

"But he's been back a long time," Mary Jane added.

Marcie looked from one to the other of them, pushed the chicken salad around on her plate with a fork and took a small bite. Then she put down her fork.

"Okay," she said, crossing her arms. "Nice try, but we both know the court case isn't what I was asking about. Are you going to tell me how you feel about seeing him again?"

"You don't care, do you, Mom?"

Juliet looked at her sister. "You have a plane to catch."

"We don't have to leave for another half hour. At least."

If not for the somewhat questioning look in her daughter's eyes, Juliet might still not have answered. Truth was, she didn't have an answer.

"I guess I'm a little uneasy," she said. "I mean, I did know him briefly. It could be kind of awkward."

"Know him briefly? He's the father of your child!"

"Biological, only." Mary Jane was chewing again. She'd finished one-half of her sandwich, leaving the crusts, and had started on the other.

"A child whom, I might add, he knows nothing about."

Pulling her hair down out of its ponytail, Juliet shook her head. "That's a decision I made a long time ago."

"I know. And I understand why. But that doesn't mean it can't be changed."

"I don't want it changed!" There was nothing childlike in the small body at the opposite end of the small table from her mother. "It's always just been the two of us and I like it that way. Besides, it's not like he wanted to marry my mom."

With a quick frown in Juliet's direction, Marcie leaned toward Mary Jane. "I know he didn't, honey, and I know you like it with just you and your mom, but maybe you only feel that way because you don't know what you're missing."

"Missing?" The look the girl gave her aunt was similar to one that Mrs. Cummings had bestowed on Mary Jane in her office the previous month. "You think I want to be like Tommy Benson at school? Or Sarah Carmichael? Or Tanya Buddinsky?"

"Buddinsky?" Marcie asked Juliet.

"Her last name is Buehla." Juliet lowered her head a notch as she looked at Mary Jane. Her daughter knew better than to demean herself with name-calling. She couldn't quite keep the twitch of a grin from her lips, however. Tanya had had a field day with Mary Jane's possible expulsion from school the month before. She had spread some fairly inventive stories about Juliet and their little cottage on the beach as well.

Picking up her silverware, Marcie reached for Juliet's plate and put it on top of her own. "So why don't you want to be like these other kids?"

"They're splits!"

"Splits?"

"Their parents are divorced," Juliet translated.

"Yeah and they have to go part of the time to one house and part of the time to the other and their stuff is always getting left in the wrong place. And there's the holidays." Mary Jane's forceful tone made it sound as though those would explain themselves.

"The holidays?"

"One at one house and one at another and everyone's constantly fighting about it."

"Oh, honey, it's not always that way," Marcie said.

"Mostly it is, and anyway, how would you like to open your Christmas presents and then have to leave them right away and go someplace else?"

"To get more presents? That might be cool."

"Who needs more presents if you don't get to play with them?"

With one raised eyebrow, Juliet asked her sister if she'd had enough.

"How about needing more love?" Marcie asked softly, sending a stab to Juliet's stomach.

"You guys love me." Mary Jane didn't miss a beat. "More than most kids in my class are loved, I'll bet, even those with two parents married. Some houses are good with dads. This one is good without one."

"You sure about that, honey?" Juliet didn't know where the question came from. She'd been very open with Mary Jane from the beginning, telling the child that she would contact her father anytime she wanted her to.

Getting up, Mary Jane dropped her plate on top of her aunt's. "Positive." She picked up all three plates and carried them over to the sink. "Now, would you two just go on talking about Mom and quit worrying about me?"

Juliet loved her daughter, but how in the hell she'd ever produced such a precocious and outspoken one was beyond her.

With her chin on her hand and her elbow on the table, Marcie looked at her. ''So?''

''So what?'' Juliet fingered the edge of her tweed place mat.

''How does Mom feel about seeing Blake Ramsden again?''

Shrugging, she looked at her daughter getting water all over the counter and floor as she sprayed the three plates and put them in the open dishwasher beside her.

''He never contacted me after that one time together. Never followed up on the event to find out if there'd been any consequences. You know, hurt feelings, disease, and—even though we'd started out taking precautions—a baby…''

''I know.''

''He should have.''

''I agree.''

Marcie always had. Juliet would never be able to repay her sister for all the support she'd offered, then and now. She remembered the nights Marcie had sat on the bathroom floor with her, helping her study for her bar exam. Juliet had fought an almost constant battle between mind and body in those days. She'd often thought she could have made it into the *Guinness Book of World Records* for the length of time she'd suffered from a morning sickness that had never been limited to mornings.

''Besides, he was out of reach,'' she added, sitting back to give Mary Jane access to the table she was attempting to wipe down with a sopping-wet cloth. The place mats would soak up the extra moisture when the child put them back. ''For years. He'd mentioned that he was leaving for one, but it was closer to four.''

''I know.''

Of course Marcie knew. Her sister's patience was unending when she was listening to Juliet agonize over a decision made so many years before. Would she ever be completely free from guilt?

''I might've been able to reach him through his father,'' she continued, watching the little girl whose face was so serious as she folded the dishcloth and hung it on the rack inside the cupboard door. Mary Jane had a lot of energy, yet she concentrated fiercely on even the smallest tasks. ''But he'd been so adamant about the fact that he had to have that time away from his father. I respected that.''

''And you didn't want him to know you were pregnant,'' Marcie added.

With a quick kiss to her mother's cheek, Mary Jane ran off toward the bedrooms in the back of the house.

''I didn't want the entanglement of a relationship with him,'' Juliet agreed, only slightly defensive. ''Do you think I was wrong?''

''No.'' That opinion had never changed.

''I just couldn't do it.'' The words were torn from her as she remembered back, felt the crushing weight that had been a constant burden during those months of tormenting herself with a decision she hadn't been prepared to make. ''The only thing I knew about life back then was that I couldn't, at any cost, repeat Mom's mistakes. Because, really, who did she help, Marce? Us? Dad? Herself? Dad never wanted us. We'd have been better off not knowing that. He never wanted her, either. She lost every dream she'd ever had. And we paid for that, too. I couldn't do that. Not to me, or to my baby.''

Marcie's hand, as it covered Juliet's, was warm and soft. Grounding. ''It's okay, Jules, you don't have to tell me. I get it. We both saw what Mom went through marrying Daddy just because she was pregnant with us, everything she gave up. And Lord knows, we learned from everything that came after that. Why do you think I'm thirty-four years old and still living alone?''

''Because Hank hasn't asked you to marry him.''

''Well,'' Marcie looked away—and then back. ''There is that.''

''Move to San Diego, Marce. You've said so many times that you want to. Mary Jane and I have room here.''

''I'm half-owner of...a salon that—''

''Can be sold,'' Juliet interrupted. She turned her hand over, grabbing her sister's. ''That place has been running for fifty years and just like you bought it when Miss Molly had her stroke, so will someone else when you leave. If you loved it, that would be one thing, but you talk about it like it's a lead ball around your neck.''

''Maybe...''

''We hated what the divorce did to Mom, having no money, no way to support us. We hated that town, the way life just stopped there. The way Mom slowly gave up. And sometimes it seems like, instead of doing the opposite of what she did, you're letting the lure of security snag you, too. It scares me to death when I think of you there in Maple Grove, living in a trailer—albeit much nicer than Mom's—watching television every night. I can't bear the thought of seeing the same thing that happened to her happen to you…''

Marcie met her gaze head-on, eyes moist with emotion. "That's not going to happen, Jules. I'm not Mom."

She'd love to be convinced. But what if Marcie was just too close to the situation to see the similarities? Their mother certainly hadn't seemed to be aware that she'd needed help.

"You're more of an artist than a hairdresser, Marce. You've already had an offer from a Hollywood studio at that hair show, who knows what else could turn up if you looked. And you'd probably make three times the money you're making."

"Maybe."

For the first time, as she watched the thoughts play across her sister's face, Juliet allowed herself to hope. "Will you at least think about it?"

"Yeah." A couple of tears slid down Marcie's face. And then she smiled. "Yeah, I'll think about it."

"Okay."

Standing, Juliet felt better, a little bit in control of her life again.

"And you, sis—" Marcie stood as well, eye to eye with Juliet "—you going to tell Blake Ramsden he has a child?"

She opened her mouth to say no. Adamantly.

"How many more schools you going to go through before you realize you have to do something different?" Marcie pressed, her face close enough for Juliet to see the white flecks in her twin's blue eyes.

"Different doesn't have to mean telling Ramsden he fathered a kid nine years ago. Telling him won't make any difference at all if he doesn't want her. Mom pretended Dad wanted us and look how horrible it was when we found out the truth. I'm not going to risk putting Mary Jane through that."

"But you're considering telling him."

As they'd been doing since they were babies sharing the same crib, Juliet and her sister locked gazes, speaking on a level more intense than words. A conversation that permitted nothing but the deepest truth.

"I don't know."

SHE WASN'T DOING anything more than sitting with her back to him behind a table at the front of the room, but Blake could still feel the energy pulsing around Juliet McNeil as he walked into the courtroom Monday morning. It had been that way in the bar on the beach all those years ago, too.

He didn't know what it was about her, but the woman did not allow herself to be ignored.

Taking a seat in the last row of the courtroom, he leaned back, making his six-foot-two-inch body as inconspicuous as possible. Schuster had thought he'd be calling Blake to the stand about an hour into the one o'clock session. He'd waited until one-fifty to show up, hoping to be in and out in half an hour, forty-five minutes tops.

Having left for New York so unexpectedly, without an opportunity to prepare anyone to stand in for him, he still had catching up to do.

Two-thirty rolled around and still Blake sat. Schuster was better in person than the papers had ever painted him. Intelligent. Methodical. Bringing out every intricate detail that the jurors might otherwise have missed.

Details that meant nothing to Blake. The paper trail of mock companies, false invoices and nonexistent vendors that Schuster was laying was far too convoluted to follow without having started at the beginning.

That fact left Blake with far too much time and too little diversion to avoid the thoughts that continued to plague him in spite of his ordering himself to stop.

If he'd been here in San Diego five years ago, could he have prevented the events that followed? The deaths of his parents? If he'd come home when he'd originally said he would, could he have saved the life of the very beautiful and very lost free spirit he'd seen buried just two days before?

"I object! A personal land purchase made before my client was appointed director of the Terracotta Foundation is irrelevant to this case."

The judge, an older, slightly overweight man who looked to be in his mid-fifties, looked atop his reading glasses toward Paul Schuster. "Counsel?"

"If it pleases the court, Your Honor, I am attempting to establish a pattern of business dealings that has followed the defendant through most of his adult life—a pattern that is directly related to the case at hand."

Blake wasn't sure that Schuster had said anything relevant at all, but figured he had when the judge nodded. "You may continue."

Those were pretty much the same words Blake's father had said to him the first time he'd called home—a year to the date from when he'd left—to tell his father he wasn't through with traveling. The old man had taught Blake well and he'd presented his case so logically that there was no room for argument. He could feel his father's displeasure from halfway around the world, and knew that the elder Ramsden's acquiescence had been offered in a way meant to manipulate Blake right back to the fold.

He'd taken it at face value instead, thus successfully meeting one of the challenges he knew his time away had been meant to help him to master—standing up for what was right, even in the face of conflict.

Growing up under the thumb of Walter Ramsden had taught him to avoid conflict at any cost. It had taken Blake a long time to break the hold his father had over him. And more, to see that it wasn't himself who was so lacking.

The time away, while much longer than originally intended, had been fraught with painful introspection, introspection that had taken him many places, taught him what mattered and what did not.

"Ms. McNeil, do you have any questions?"

Schuster had finished with his second witness of the afternoon.

Juliet stood, her long body as gorgeous as he remembered, even in the sedate brownish skirt and matching jacket. Her arms were long and slender and she moved with such conviction.

"Not at this time, Your Honor."

Juliet sat, leaned over to whisper something to a suited man on her right. A member of her team?

Eaton James, the man Blake considered an accomplice with himself in his father's death, was seated on her left.

The judge turned to the elderly man on the stand. "You may step down." He asked Schuster to call his next witness.

Blake sat up, ready to go.

He leaned back with a deliberately deep inhalation as a name other than his was called. Lifting the sleeve of his jacket where it rested against his leg, he had to stifle the groan of frustration. It was three o'clock. If he didn't get out of here soon, he wasn't going to make it to the McGaffey site before work shut down for the day. The site check had been scheduled for the previous Friday.

He wondered what Juliet McNeil was thinking as she sat there watching the proceedings. What she'd whispered to her colleague. While Blake didn't know her well, he'd bet a year's income that her relaxed, almost bored, stance disguised a mind that was racing as fast as Schuster's.

Amunet had had a mind that was unable to slow down. Always thinking, planning, wondering, she'd had a hard time staying in one place for long without growing bored. With a trust fund left by her long-deceased French father, and a wanderlust in her soul to match his, she'd quickly become travel companion to him, playmate, and then wife.

That tug at his stomach was back. It happened every time he thought of the irrevocable step he'd taken, so sure, in his youth and arrogance, that he was absolutely doing the right thing. He'd been honest with her; he was a man who was looking for meaning in the sometimes meaningless acts he saw, trying to understand violence, starving children, death. And love. A man looking for answers with no way to predict where they might lead.... So why did he feel guilty about being led back home?

This time when the judge asked Juliet if she had any questions, she shook her head. Then she began gathering up her papers, sliding them into a leather briefcase.

"Then this court is adjourned until tomorrow morning, 8:30 sharp." The gavel came down hard, resounding around the courtroom, as if to emphasize the fact that Blake had just wasted an entire afternoon he couldn't afford to waste.

As people rose around him and shuffled out, Blake felt impatient to be with them. Juliet McNeil was busy speaking with the men at her table. Blake looked for Paul Schuster.

"I'll need you here first thing in the morning," the man said after coming down the side of the courtroom and joining Blake.

Blake nodded.

"You're next," Schuster added, "so it should go fairly fast."

With one last glance at the woman to whom he did not want to speak, Blake nodded again and, as a reporter approached Schuster, quietly left.

CHAPTER FOUR

"WHY ARE YOU CHANGING?"

With her arm half in and half out of one of her favorite navy silk-lined suit jackets, Juliet turned to see a fully dressed Mary Jane standing in the doorway of her closet Tuesday morning. She finished removing the jacket.

"You look cute," she told the child. Today Mary Jane had on a short denim skirt, an orange long-sleeved sweater, orange socks and tennis shoes. The kid had her own sense of style. Even in this, she stood out from the crowd.

"Thanks," she said, coming in to hold Juliet's jacket while she stepped out of the navy skirt. It had to go on the hanger first.

The child stood, unusually silent, watching while Juliet stepped into one of her most expensive suits—black skirt and tailored red jacket with black silk piping.

"What was wrong with the first one?"

"Nothing."

Pulling her favorite black pumps from their slot, Juliet did a mental run-through of the questions she had for Eaton James that morning in light of the new evidence the prosecution would be introducing. And of the first witnesses she'd be calling when the prosecution finally rested.

Mary Jane was looking in her jewelry box, pulling out the eighteen-karat gold-and-diamond heart necklace, bracelet and earrings she usually wore with this suit.

"Are you going to see my father this morning?" She handed them to her mother.

"Yes." Schuster was winding up and so far, he hadn't given them anything she couldn't rebut. They weren't arguing about the facts, but about whether or not Eaton James's intentions were fraudulent. There was no personal gain to give truth to that claim. The man might have been desperate and stupid, but he hadn't done anything with the intent to steal from his investors.

"Is that why you're wearing the red power suit?"

"No!"

With her head slightly lowered, Mary Jane peered up at Juliet, her full lips puckered disapprovingly.

"Okay, okay, yes, *maybe* that's why. I'm really trying not to think about it." She held out her bracelet and her wrist. "He's just a guy."

"Don't tell him about me, okay?" The girl's forehead creased as her little fingers fumbled with the clasp.

"Of course not, imp. I'd never do something like that without telling you."

"Promise?" Wide green eyes stared up at her.

"Yes." Unequivocally.

Pulling the little girl into her arms, Juliet knew there was at least one thing in her life she'd gotten completely right.

And that she'd give her life for it.

For her.

JULIET WAS LETTING THE prosecution lay everything out on the table, waiting for Schuster to show all his cards so that, when her turn came to explain those cards, she could do so without confusing the jury. The tactic didn't always work, but in a case as convoluted with paper trails as this one, it was an almost sure win.

That was why she'd let every single witness pass unquestioned by the defense. Those she needed, if any, she'd call back.

It was also why Judge Lockhard didn't have much patience with her. Judges didn't like it when defense attorneys refused to cross-examine.

And then Schuster called his last witness that Tuesday morning in early April. As she'd been doing for a couple of weeks, she waited while Schuster questioned Blake Ramsden, revealing to the twelve-member jury that until his death, Walter Ramsden had held a seat on the board of Semaphor—along with Eaton James. Semaphor served as a clearinghouse of sorts, collecting and providing data to potential contributors all over the world. Schuster maintained that James used this connection to find his prey.

"Objection!" Juliet stood, her gaze solidly on the judge. "Your Honor, the prosecution is leading the witness."

Judge Henry Lockhard sighed, frowned and said, "Objection sustained. Jury, please disregard the last remark and it will be stricken from the record. Counsel, you may continue."

Juliet sat. She reminded Eaton not to show any emotion other than respect, or perhaps any distress he might be feeling at the tarnishing of his good name. She waited for his nod and returned her attention to the notepad on the table in front of her.

She had no reason to size up this witness. She already knew his size.

Eaton James, when she'd disclosed her very brief association with the witness, had seemed more pleased than distressed.

"Mr. Ramsden, what do you know about Eaton Estates?" Schuster continued.

"It was a land development project in the Cayman Islands. Eaton James approached my father with an investment plan that projected at least a double return on any monies spent. In addition, three percent of all profits were to go to the Terracotta Foundation, specifically to feed orphans in Honduras. The Foundation made much of its money through such investments."

His voice hadn't changed.

"And did your father invest?"

"Yes."

"How much?"

"Half a million dollars."

"What happened?"

He was wearing a gray suit, white shirt and maroon-white-and-gray striped tie. His shoes were Italian leather—or something that appeared just as expensive. She'd noticed them when he'd approached the witness stand. Other than that, Juliet didn't look at Blake Ramsden. There was no point in studying the father of her child for evidence of genetic similarities.

"I was in the Cayman Islands at the time. My

mother called, telling me she was concerned because my father had been getting the runaround from James, and she asked me to check out Eaton Estates."

"And did the development exist?"

Schuster's shoes brushed the floor softly as he walked back and forth from the jurors' box to the witness stand a few feet away.

"Yes. It was a plot of land that was sinking into the sea."

The footsteps stopped.

"So, completely useless."

"Yes."

"Then what happened?"

Schuster began to pace again. Juliet knew by heart the expressions the man was wearing for the jurors' benefit. But hers would be the ones they took with them into deliberation.

"I called my mother and she relayed the information to my father, who confronted James. She called the next day to tell me James had admitted the land was worthless, but claimed that he'd only just discovered that himself. He'd been swindled with the rest of his investors."

"Mr. Ramsden, would you say your father was a savvy businessman?"

"Absolutely."

"As a matter of fact, he'd never made a bad investment in his life, had he?"

"This was a first."

"Why do you think he was so successful in that area? Luck?"

Blake gave a humorless chuckle and Juliet glanced up instinctively. And then quickly away. He wasn't smiling, his lips were twisted into an "I know better" quirk that Juliet recognized all too well. She'd seen it directed at her just that morning, from a pair of eight-year-old lips in her closet at home.

"Walter Ramsden would never have given up control of his life, or his money, to something as capricious as luck. He was successful because he had an uncanny talent for evaluating people—as though he had a second ear that heard what a person *wasn't* saying as clearly as what he was."

"And what did your father have to say about the Eaton Estates deal?"

"When I spoke to my mother after my father's meeting with Eaton, she said he was certain James was lying. That the man had known before he bought the property that it was wasteland. And that he'd paid a fraction of the cost claimed on the notes he'd passed on to my father. He also said there was no way of proving his suspicion, that Eaton had his bases all very well covered, including the fact that no extra money had turned up anywhere else."

"So, how do you explain, if your father was this talented…" Schuster paused and approached the jurors.

Juliet gave the man full marks for the little bit of emphasis he put on that word, leading the jury right to the thought they were already going to have, that perhaps Walter Ramsden wasn't as gifted as his son claimed, thus voiding the value of Blake's testimony. She knew, too, that whatever was coming next would plant in their minds something that would discount that suspicion. In a detached, analytical way, she waited to see how he pulled it off.

"...if Walter Ramsden did indeed have the ability to sense the potential legitimacy of his business associates, why did he invest in Eaton Estates?"

Surprised when Blake didn't immediately answer, Juliet looked up and saw the hesitation in his eyes, eyes that stared out but weren't focused. Pen to tablet, she scribbled.

"I know why. I'd been abroad at the time, studying architecture—and volunteering on various development projects. According to my mother, my father followed my progress from country to country."

He paused. Juliet was staring. This was nothing like the man she'd known that night so long ago. That Blake Ramsden had come close to hating his father— or at least the tyranny with which the old man had ruled his son.

"At the time the Eaton offer was first made, I was in Honduras, helping modernize a village whose population was three children to every adult. They were all hungry, poverty stricken. Eaton offered to feed those kids."

Damn. The jurors were swimming right toward Schuster. He was good. Almost as good as she'd heard.

And she knew what was coming next.

"If it pleases the court, I'd like to submit Exhibit double Z into the records." Schuster pulled out the document he had faxed to Juliet's home Sunday night. "This is a record of a land assessment inspection showing that the property was sinking.

"Please note, further," Schuster said softly, "the date of the investment is the month before the sale date." He walked the document over to Blake Ramsden. "Can you confirm this is the same document you saw?"

A long pause followed. Juliet shifted in her seat. Glanced at the judge. The jurors. Tapped her pen against the back of her left hand.

Eaton moved beside her, breathing heavily. Reaching over, Blake handed back the document. "Yes."

Juliet put her hand on Eaton's knee. "It's okay. Sit still. We get the ball last."

He sat back, but he wasn't calm. No one was. It was another five minutes before Judge Lockhard offered her the witness for cross-examination.

This time, Juliet accepted the offer. She had no desire to spend a second day in court with Blake Ramsden.

Picking up her black leather-bound tablet, Juliet rose. She didn't need the notes. She could recite them—and everything in between the lines—by rote. But she needed something to look at.

It felt good to stand. To move around after so many hours of sitting.

She was going to have to connect with the witness if she wanted the jury to connect to the response she drew from him.

With a long slow breath, she approached the witness stand. Looked up. Smiled.

And had to swallow when he smiled back.

Mary Jane's smile.

"Mr. Ramsden, I'm sure you understand, as does the jury, that the point in question here is not whether Eaton James had various business interests that showed no profit or loss, or even any movement. Anyone can establish a business and then not do anything with it. It is, as the prosecutor has so adeptly shown, just a matter of paperwork. The question is one of intent. Did Eaton James *intend* to rob people of their money? Or was he just an honest businessman who didn't have the luck of one as talented as, say, your father?''

She paused. Stood right in front of him and didn't look away. His tie was slightly lopsided, made to appear more so by the way the wider maroon stripe came around the left side, while the right was flanked by a skinnier gray one.

''According to your testimony, you believe that the former was the case, is this correct?''

''It is.''

His eyes were different. Older. And though she wouldn't have thought it possible, more compelling.

Not that it mattered. She was older, too. Different things caught her attention these days.

Things like the conversation she'd be having with Mary Jane that night at the dinner table. Her daughter was going to grill her. And Juliet had to be able to give straight answers.

''Tell me, Mr. Ramsden, how long did your father expect you to stay abroad?''

His eyes narrowed. ''A year.''

''And how long, in fact, were you away?''

''Almost four years.''

''Four years.''

She stood there, palms on the stand, nodding. ''Did you ever come home for a visit during that time?''

''No.'' Blake's face was impassive.

''But you spoke with your father often? Holidays,

Sundays, and so on. You were, after all, his only child.''

"I was, yes.''

Bingo. He hadn't answered the first question. Her interpretation of the expression she'd read earlier had been right on. It was a talent she'd come to rely on and breathed a sigh of relief every time it came through for her.

"And *did* you speak with him often?''

"No.''

"You didn't?'' She sounded shocked. "Well, how often then? Once a month? Twice, maybe?''

"I spoke to him once.''

"Once a year?''

"Once. Period.''

"In four years you spoke to your father only once?''

"Objection, Your Honor!''

It had taken him long enough.

"Your Honor—'' Juliet stepped up to the bench ''—Mr. Schuster's line of questioning was based on Mr. Ramsden's opinion of his father. I'm only clarifying the relationship upon which that opinion was based.''

"Sustained.''

In the early days, Juliet would have turned around to see Schuster's reaction. Such things didn't matter anymore.

"Just out of curiosity, would you mind telling the court when that one phone call took place?''

"A year after I'd left.''

"When you were due to come home.''

"That is correct.'' He nodded once, his gaze steady

on hers. The challenge only spurred a rush of adren-
aline that had given her the edge up most of her life.

"So...if your father's business acumen had
changed, say, due to old age, or perhaps a growing
forgetfulness or loneliness for his only son, maybe
you wouldn't have known."

The room was silent. Juliet could feel the jurors'
eyes, but even more, the force of their attention.

"I was in touch with my mother. She never indicated that was the case."

Had she been playing a game of mock court, as
she'd done with members of her study group in law
school, she'd have issued a polite and grinning *thank
you very much* for the opening he'd just given her.

"Ah, your mother. How did she take your absence?"

"Naturally, she missed me."

"Naturally. As, I assume, did your father."

Blake didn't answer. She didn't push.

"Would you think it possible, knowing your
mother as well as you did, realizing the difficult position she must have been in, that she could have colored the truth just a bit? Perhaps she focused on the
Honduran children as your father's reason for the purchase just to play on your sympathies, to bridge the
gap between the two of you. To make you feel you
still had his support?"

"My mother did not lie."

"I didn't say she did, Mr. Ramsden. I asked if it
was possible that certain aspects of the Eaton deal
took on more significance for her than others?"

He stared straight at her. And there was anger in
his eyes.

"Please answer the question."

"It's possible."

"That said, it's also possible that she misinterpreted the other things she relayed about this particular business transaction. Perhaps even to use it as leverage to bring you home."

"No."

"Did you know, Mr. Ramsden, that a letter was sent from Eaton James to all the Eaton Estates investors, telling them of their loss?"

"Yes, it arrived a couple of days after my mother called to ask me to visit the property."

"It was postmarked two days before."

"It arrived two days after."

"Or not." Juliet stepped back. "It's possible, Mr. Ramsden, that your mother already knew the land was worthless when she called to have you check it out, isn't it?"

"It's highly unlikely."

"But possible."

His chin dropped again, more slowly this time. And then rose again. "Yes."

Juliet turned, as though going back to her seat. And then, three-quarters of the way there, she turned back.

"One other thing." She saved lives by playing the barracuda. And right now, the future of an admittedly stupid but innocent businessman was on the line. "Your father died of a heart attack the next year, did he not?"

"He did."

"He was driving at the time."

"Yes."

"And your mother was in the car."

"Yes."

"You lost them both. I'm so sorry." She looked down. Thought about Eaton's wife—and teenage children—sitting behind them. The lives she was attempting to save.

Blake said nothing.

"Did you realize your mother knew about your father's bad heart?"

"Not until I got home."

"But she knew. Had known for almost two years."

"Yes."

"Wouldn't you think that knowing her husband could go at any moment might be motivation enough to do whatever it took to get her only son home?"

She'd done what she'd been hired to do. She'd discredited his testimony. And lost his respect.

For the first time in her life, Juliet hated her job.

"No more questions, Your Honor."

CHAPTER FIVE

JULIET MCNEIL HUNG around for a long time. Schuster had gone. The press had gone. Even Eaton James and his family had ridden down the elevator to the first floor of the California Superior Court. Still, though he had no real logical reason for doing so, Blake stood there at the bank of elevators and waited.

He was done here. Unless called for further testimony, he'd been dismissed and wouldn't be back. He'd lived in the same town with Juliet McNeil for five years and found no reason to be in touch with her. Had had nothing to say to her.

Voices came from down the hall. Male. And one very distinctive female. The men came around the corner from the courtroom. Nodded at Blake, pushed the down button. Juliet must have stopped off in the women's room at the juncture of the two hallways.

An elevator came. The two men, apparently attorneys on Juliet's staff, held the door, looking at him. Blake shook his head. And they were gone.

It was better this way, with no one around. Just a quick acknowledgment, for old times' sake. Something he might not have bothered with if not for the funeral he'd attended over the weekend—and all the memories aroused by the past week.

Hearing the swish of a door, Blake stood upright,

hands in the pockets of his gray slacks, facing the hall. Her head pulled back a bit when she saw him, but her step didn't falter. She had to be the most confident woman he'd ever met.

That confidence had attracted Blake nine years ago. And attracted him now.

"I thought you'd be long gone." That was another thing he remembered quite clearly about that foggy night so long ago. The woman had a habit of saying what was on her mind rather than couching her thoughts in platitudes. Disconcerting.

And yet, delightfully refreshing in that he'd known where he stood with her. There'd been no game playing. No social dishonesty.

"I never had the chance to say hello." He pushed the down button. "And didn't want to go without at least saying goodbye."

"Oh." Her hair was still long—the gold-streaked auburn color striking—and curled past her shoulders. "Well, I wish it could have been under different circumstances, but it was nice seeing you," she said. She didn't avoid looking at him, but gave equal attention to the lighted bar atop the elevator, indicating the car's current floor.

"You look good."

"You, too." Except that she wasn't really looking. And then she did. "I watched your office building go up. Impressive. You're doing very well."

Blake nodded. "I had good teachers." Including his father, the man he'd spoken of so harshly that night just before he'd left the country. Was that what this was about? A need to correct any misconceptions? He'd been a kid then. Too concerned with his own rights and far too insensitive to those of others.

"I'm…uh…sorry." She tilted her head in the direction of the courtroom from which they'd come. "For back there."

"We were on opposite sides of the fence," he told her—as though neither of them could have expected anything different.

The elevator came. Blake held open the door while she stepped inside, then joined her. Standing against the side wall, her briefcase held with both hands down in front, she'd already pushed the first-floor button.

"Still," she said, glancing over at him, "I wouldn't blame you if there were some hard feelings."

"Oh, there are definitely those," he admitted, thinking of James. "Just not directed at you."

The quick tilt of her chin, more even than the light in her eyes, gave away her surprise. "Well, thank you." She smiled.

And he knew he wasn't done yet.

"How would you feel about getting a bite to eat?"

The elevator stopped and she got out, frowning. "Tonight?"

"Doesn't have to be." He followed her over to a decorative column off to the side of the building's entryway and leaned against it.

"I…"

Blake could sense a refusal coming. "Or just a drink sometime," he offered. "For old times' sake."

"You've been home five years. Old times have taken quite a while to come calling." The easy grin on her face took any sting out of the words.

She was right.

"I...my ex-wife died last week." Blake was uncomfortable with the personal admission. "I hadn't seen her in years, but that, plus the whole Eaton James thing, has brought up a lot of old memories. I feel like I have some things to set straight. Unfinished business, maybe."

"We finished our business." Her head tilted up at him, those green eyes with their mysterious brown flecks, had him thinking otherwise.

"I'm not arguing with that," he offered. "I guess I'm just looking for some closure on that whole phase of my life. Think you could humor me long enough for a conversation?"

"I guess."

He wondered at her hesitancy. "You have a significant other out there who might not understand?"

"No." She shook her head. "I'm not married or otherwise significantly, uh, connected."

"Because you're still afraid that a relationship would take away your freedom?"

When he'd married Amunet, he hadn't thought he'd robbed his wife of her liberty, but he couldn't have been more wrong. Their marriage had certainly trapped her. Or changed her, anyway. Enough so that she'd eventually been driven to suicide?

"Not really," Juliet said, her gaze clear. "Anyway, it wasn't my freedom I was protecting back then. I just needed to know that I could provide for myself before I relied on anyone else. I needed to believe in me."

He nodded. That he understood. It had taken four years away and more time back home before he'd discovered that.

"Are you dating someone?"

She shook her head, lower lip protruding slightly. "No. You?"

"No." He couldn't tell if his reply had any effect on her. Not that it mattered.

"So what about that drink?"

"If you can make it early, say, four o'clock or so, I can do Thursday this week. Just once. For old times' sake."

Right after court.

Blake nodded. "Thursday it is."

HAVING BUILT a successful career on finding different ways to present the truth, Juliet failed miserably, over the next two days, to come up with a truth that would suffice as a plausible excuse to cancel her drink date with Blake Ramsden.

She just couldn't find a way to say, "I don't want to see you ever again because you're the father of my daughter and I don't want you to know that."

"You're wearing red again." Mary Jane was sitting at the kitchen table Thursday morning, chewing her favorite marshmallow-and-oat cereal, her legs bouncing beneath her.

"It's my third day on the hot seat."

"That's green day."

The kid knew her too well. She was too predictable. Had life really become so obsessively the same that someone could predict her day based on the colors she chose? Or was it just Mary Jane who'd always been too perceptive?

"I'm having a drink with Blake Ramsden after court this afternoon."

"While I'm at Brownies," Mary Jane said, nodding, her attention still on her cereal. "Good thinking."

Juliet dropped into the chair closest to her daughter, reaching over to push curls back from the girl's cheek, knowing they were going to spring right back.

"Don't you want to know why I'm meeting him?"

Wide eyes, such a strange contrast of all-knowing adult and unsure little girl, stared up at her. "I don't think so."

"Are you worried?"

"How can I be? I just found out about it."

"Are you mad?"

"No."

"But?"

"I don't want a dad. I like us just the way we are."

Life just never quit getting harder. No matter how many hurdles she maneuvered through successfully. "I like us just the way we are, too."

Frowning, Mary Jane pushed away her not-quite-empty bowl. "You promised you wouldn't tell him about me."

"I'm not going to tell him." She paused to assess the doubts that had been plaguing her for almost a week. Everything happened for a reason and the timing of Blake Ramsden's return to her life had occurred just as she was struggling to help Mary Jane find her place in the world.

Every day, when she dropped the child off at school, she waited for a phone call. And every afternoon, when she picked her up, she breathed a sigh of relief.

It wasn't normal.

Picking up the bowl, she took it to the sink, rinsed it, put it in the dishwasher. "Here's your lunch," she said, taking the brown bag out of the refrigerator.

Mary Jane reached for the bag, looking up, her expression not quite as open as usual.

"Hey, remember our deal," Juliet said, holding her daughter's free hand.

"What?"

"If ever there comes a time that you want to meet Blake, you let me know."

"I won't—"

"And," Juliet interrupted, "if ever there is a time when I think I have to tell him about you, I'll discuss it with you first. I promised, Mary Jane, and I've never broken a promise to you."

It took a moment for the clouds to disappear, but after a little bit of thought the little girl smiled up at her.

"I know," she said.

Juliet just hoped she didn't live to regret having made that promise.

WALKING INTO the upscale downtown bar on Thursday, Juliet took a cursory glance around, hoping Blake would be late. She could say she'd been there and leave before he showed up.

It would be the truth—and the best version of it she'd managed to concoct.

Her second best idea had been to look, but not very hard, only enough to say she'd been there and hadn't seen him, and then get the hell out before he saw her.

Her third and final hope had been that he wouldn't show.

She saw him as soon as her eyes adjusted from the day's bright sunshine to the bar's interior. Sitting in a rather secluded booth for two, he should have been easy to miss. But no, her eyes were drawn right to him.

"Hi." Juliet slid in across from him, trying not to notice how broad his shoulders looked minus the suit coat he'd been wearing the other day.

"Red, again," he greeted her with a curious smile. "A brave move for a redhead."

"My hair's not—"

"I know, I was teasing," he admitted. "Your hair is auburn."

They'd had that conversation nine years before. When she'd been wearing nothing at all and he'd been playing with her hair against her breasts, telling her he'd never seen anything quite like it.

It had been right after they'd made love the second time with the first condom—the time, she'd long ago decided, that she had conceived Mary Jane.

"And the suit looks great," he said when she didn't respond. "Beautiful in fact."

She wished he'd stop catching her off guard. "Thank you." It had been a long time since she'd felt desirable, and life was much more under control that way.

They ordered drinks, the bar's specialty, a mixture of rum, vodka and a couple of exotic fruits. Blake added an order of chips and salsa.

"We're driving," he explained as the waiter left. "It's not good to drink on an empty stomach."

She appreciated the forethought.

"Fine by me," she told him. "I missed lunch today

and I'm starving.'' She'd been busy calming Kelly
James, who was beginning to panic. That was the
worst thing Eaton's wife could do. This trial was all
about character—and proving that neither James nor
his family or associates had any doubts about his.

Blake asked about the trial while they waited for
their drinks. She felt like a Democrat talking to a
Republican. Or a Republican talking to a Democrat.
They both wanted justice to be done, wanted what
was best for society at large and saw the way to get
there on opposite ends of the spectrum.

"It's obvious the man is guilty," Blake told her
fifteen minutes into the conversation. "If you really
want to serve the Constitution, you'd see that and help
him get the fairest punishment.''

"He's not guilty until proven so beyond a shadow
of a doubt,'' Juliet reminded him. "And until that
happens, he deserves to be treated that way. As
though he's not guilty. Meaning, I believe what he
tells me and my job is to try to persuade those sitting
in judgment to do the same.''

"Regardless of what you think personally.''

"Personally, I know it's possible that he's a good
man and a rotten businessman who didn't knowingly
defraud anyone.''

"Establishing bogus companies is against the law.
Ignorance is no excuse for criminal action.''

"He claims they weren't bogus but, rather, ventures that never got off the ground.''

"So why are there invoices for goods purchased
from vendors that don't exist?''

"He was told the vendors did exist. He established
the companies with the belief that his associates were

on the up-and-up and he was helping them all get started.''

''With that theory, you could free up just about anyone for a white-collar crime.''

''The jury has to be convinced,'' Juliet told him. ''Ultimately, the truth must speak for itself.''

''The truth?'' he asked, munching on the chips that she had hardly noticed appear. ''Or some twisted bits of fact and fiction that pose as the truth?''

A topic close to her heart. ''How do you define fact and fiction?'' she asked. ''Some people believe in angels. They'd pass a lie detector test claiming that angels exist. That they've actually seen an angel. For others, reality is completely devoid of such possibilities. Who's right?''

''If someone can prove that angels exist, show a picture of ones they've seen—'' He stopped, smiled. ''I'm digging myself in deeper than I care to be at the moment.''

She didn't know if it was the drink or if there really was something about this man's presence that affected her, but that strange mixture of anticipation and appeal she'd felt nine years ago was settling over her again.

All these years she'd blamed it on the drinks. She'd had several back then.

Today she'd had three sips. So far.

''Okay, well, think about this,'' she said. ''You don't have to buy into it, just try it on long enough to see how it feels.'' She helped herself to a chip.

''I'm game.''

''Truth is the means by which human beings try to define reality, wouldn't you agree?''

"Yes." His nod was accompanied by a slow smile. "Most of us anyway."

"So the issue is defining reality."

"Maybe." He took another chip, his eyes narrowed.

"But any psychiatrist will tell you that for every single human being there is a different version of reality. Our realities are shaped by the belief systems we were raised with." She took another sip. "Say, for instance, from the time I'm a little girl, my mother punishes me for saying the word *ain't*. So I end up thinking it's a bad word. Just like *damn*. Or worse."

"Okay." His enjoyment of the conversation was obvious. His eyes lit up, just as his daughter's did when Juliet debated with her. Much the way they had that long-ago night, when Juliet and Blake had talked until the bar closed and they had to go somewhere else.

Juliet wasn't sure there'd been another man in her life who'd risen to the challenge without feeling challenged, without feeling a need to assert male superiority or authority, without ego being involved.

"So then I meet a friend whose mother uses the word *ain't* regularly. My friend uses the word. I'm absolutely convinced that she swears."

"A little feeble, but I get where you're going with that. I still don't see the application to Eaton James. In his case, reality is clearly defined by irrefutable documents."

"The documents aren't on trial. A man's intentions are on trial. You look at those documents and attach your meaning to them. But just because it's *your* version doesn't mean it's the *real* version. How can he be guilty of defrauding people if he didn't deliberately mislead them?''

"He invoiced mock companies for goods that were never produced. Those invoices were paid.''

"And he was under the understanding that the goods had been shipped.''

"There was no proof of that. No confirmation of sales. No receipts.''

"So he was too trusting. That's not a crime.''

Blake shook his head. "I didn't ask you here to debate Eaton James.''

Neither had she accepted for that reason, though she was content to do so if it kept her out of more dangerous territory. "Here's the thing,'' she said, returning to what she'd started to say earlier. "We all have different views of reality—which, as long as we follow society's rules, is just fine. And when it's perceived that someone breaks one of those rules, society's reality is determined by a vote from the majority. That's justice. In this case, the majority comprises the twelve people sitting in that jury box. Schuster presented the state's reality, I present James's, and it's up to those twelve individuals to determine which version is true.''

"I'll say this for you,'' Blake said, shaking his head. "You sure have a colorful way of looking at it all.''

"As opposed to you, who sees everything in black and white?'' She couldn't stop herself from issuing the challenge, probably because she somehow knew it would be taken in the manner intended—without defensiveness.

"I do like things to be clearly defined.''

"I remember that about you." She took a chip, dipped it in salsa, brought it slowly to her mouth.

"What?" The corner of Blake's mouth twisted slightly.

"That morning, after...you know." What in the hell was she doing? She paused before continuing. "You were quite serious about making sure that we both clearly agreed about what had and hadn't happened. And about what couldn't happen again. You wanted it all spelled out. We wouldn't exchange information because we weren't going to contact each other."

"I was leaving the country!"

"And I would've shot myself before I'd have become entangled with a man."

With both hands around his glass on the table in front of him, he looked over at her, a smile in his eyes, but his mouth was serious. "It was damn good for what it was, though."

She floundered. Wished she'd downed her drink the moment it came. Where was a safe version of the truth when she needed it?

"Yeah."

"YOU MENTIONED your ex-wife," Juliet ventured at the beginning of her second drink. They'd ordered a platter of ribs and chicken appetizers with veggies.

Mary Jane's Brownie troop was going to Sea World that afternoon, and she wouldn't be dropped off until bedtime. Juliet had no reason to hurry home. And it wasn't as though she'd ever have cause to see this man again.

"I didn't realize you were divorced."

The one time she'd run into him, he'd just returned to the States five years before—with a wife. Mary Jane had been about three at the time. Marcie had been visiting and Juliet had just run out to pick up some wine for the two of them to have with dinner. Blake had been over in her part of town looking at a prospective building site and had stopped for a six-pack of beer.

He loosened his tie. "She didn't like San Diego."

"How can anyone not like San Diego?"

He tried to smile, but failed rather miserably, in her opinion. "Guess that proves your point about individual reality, huh?"

There was more he wasn't saying. A lot more.

"So I guess you were right back then when you said it was a blessing you didn't have kids." Some dormant form of masochism had made her ask him about children that night.

"Until that point Amunet and I had lived a rather unconventional life. And neither of us was completely sure we wanted that to change. We were both fairly disoriented when we first settled in San Diego. Adjusting to a life of routine and stability is rougher than it sounds."

"Especially after living without it for so long."

There was gratitude in the blue eyes looking back at her.

"In the long run, I adjusted. Amunet did not."

There was more to that story, too. But Blake Ramsden's heartache was not any of Juliet McNeil's business or concern.

It couldn't be. It didn't fit into her version of their reality.

CHAPTER SIX

AT SIX, two hours after she'd arrived at the bar, Blake ordered a third drink. Juliet didn't appear to be in any hurry to leave, still nibbling on the half-eaten ribs and chicken.

And Lord knew he had nothing to go home to that night but more of the same mental battles he'd been fighting for several days. Amunet's death had nothing to do with him. In his head he knew that. Just as he wasn't in any real way responsible for his father's heart attack or the car accident that had robbed him of all his living family, before he'd grown up enough to realize how much he'd loved them. Needed them.

"I can't say that I remember parts of that night on the beach all that clearly," he dropped into the silence that had finally fallen between them. Picking up a piece of celery, he bit into it. "But I seem to remember being pretty down on my father."

Juliet's smile was soft. "Young people have a way of doing that."

The tenderness in her words reminded him of a moment that night nine years ago, just before they'd made love. He'd been about to tell her he couldn't, that he had nothing to offer beyond the moment and that it wasn't fair to her. She'd silenced him with a finger to his lips, said the words for him, and told him that even if he offered, she wouldn't accept anything. Couldn't accept anything. Rather than judging him and finding him wanting, she'd understood him.

"It's only when we've lived long enough that we begin to see that our parents really aren't stupid at all," she continued.

"Unfortunately, I lived long enough. My parents didn't."

"You had no way of knowing your father was ill."

Blake sipped, turned in his seat, lifting an ankle across his knee. "Logically, I realize that," he admitted. In five years' time, he hadn't been able to say that to anyone else. It was only recently he'd acknowledged it to himself. "And then I think about the fact that if I'd made one different choice in my life, come home after that year instead of making the phone call that turned out to be the last time I ever spoke with the old man, lives might have been saved."

It was a thought that wouldn't let go.

"Lives?"

A middle-aged couple was being seated in the booth behind them. They were the third party to have that table since he and Juliet had arrived.

"My father's, my mother's, Amunet's."

"You think you're that powerful?" Her words were soft, but her eyes gave him no mercy.

"I don't *feel* powerful at all."

She took a sip of a drink that must have been very watered down. She was still on her second and it was more than an hour old. She picked up a chicken wing, bit off a piece, chewed.

"Your father had a bad heart," she went on. "You didn't cause that. Nor could you have cured it."

He appreciated hearing the words. "I say that to myself every night, about two in the morning or so."

"You think your leaving him to deal with the business all alone shortened his life?"

He shrugged, studied the condensation forming on the outside of his glass. A couple of men at the bar were feeling no pain, their laughter growing louder with each beer they downed.

"It's also possible that his heart was going to go whether he was puttering around the yard at home or sitting in a high-rise office."

"Likely not as soon."

"Maybe not for a lot of men, but the man you described your father to be would never have been content slowing down. The stress of having to sit back and watch someone else run things would surely have killed him."

Blake raised his head and stared at her. "All the hours I've spent going around and around with myself about this, I never came up with that one. Not that I'm going to let myself off the hook that easily, but at least now I have a solid argument to make the mental war more interesting."

"You wouldn't be the man you obviously are if you let yourself off the hook easily," she said. "Perhaps it took someone who didn't know your father personally to see that less responsibility might not have been the answer."

His smile was slow in coming, but sincere. "I was actually feeling bad about having spoken so poorly of him to you. I hated that the only view you had of him was as a tyrant. And that I was responsible for that."

"Being an only son—an only child—to a successful, demanding parent is difficult, isn't it?"

He frowned. "What do you mean?"

"Not only did you have to deal with all the expectations that were strangling you nine years ago, but you had—and have—the responsibility of being the only one to carry on."

Shaking his head, Blake took a long, cold sip. "You're in the wrong profession."

She raised an eyebrow in question, finishing off the chicken wing and licking her fingers.

"You should have been a damn psychologist."

Juliet, breaking a chip into several pieces on her plate, looked down. "It's easy to see other people's problems," she said. "It's your own that bog you down."

"Not you." Blake grinned. "The formidable Ms. McNeil getting bogged down? It'll never happen."

He expected her to smile, to shoot off some sassy remark. She didn't.

"It's happened."

"When?" He'd meant the word to be playful. It came out honestly interested instead.

She shrugged, and with one hand broke another chip, slowly, methodically, into small triangular pieces. "Various times."

"Any examples?"

"Not tonight."

Another time then?

"Does it have anything to do with your being single?"

"Not really." She paused as the waiter stopped by and dropped off their check, and Blake half expected her to say she had to go. "Unless I'm so bogged down I don't see it, there's no particular issue that's responsible for my single state." He was surprised when she continued. "I just haven't met a man I want to spend the rest of my life looking at."

"Oh." He switched to the glass of water in front of him. Sipping. "So it's all in the looks, huh?"

"Damn right it is." Juliet grinned and then her eyes grew serious. "I haven't ever been with a man I thought I wanted to look at first thing in the morning, or across the dinner table at night, until the day I die."

He was a little surprised at the instant disappointment her words aroused.

"So maybe you just aren't the marrying kind."

"Maybe." Her smile was sad. "I don't think so, though. Looking at an empty pillow, an empty chair, instead, is a pretty lonely prospect."

"You're a beautiful woman, Juliet McNeil. If you want to find someone, you will." A beautiful woman. A passionate, smart, funny, strong woman. What man wouldn't want her if he were in a position to want anybody?

"I'm opinionated and willful and far too outspoken sometimes. And I expect a man to give as good as I hand out. I'm not sure such a man exists."

Grinning, Blake nodded. "I see what you mean about getting bogged down until you can't see straight. Because you sure have that one wrong."

"You think so?" She peered at him, head cocked to one side.

"I do."

"Well, I'll take your word for it. And hope that if I run into you again in another nine years, I won't have to call you a liar."

"A liar is one thing I'll never be. At least not consciously."

SHE HAD TO GO. Mary Jane was going to be home in another hour or so. "You said your ex-wife died.

What happened? Cancer?'' She had no idea why she asked. She'd already decided his heartache wasn't her concern.

That didn't mean she couldn't offer comfort, especially since she had the idea he needed some. And he didn't seem to be in any hurry to leave.

He glanced down, then back up, focusing just beyond her. If at all. ''Suicide.''

''Oh.'' She hadn't expected that at all. When was she ever going to learn to keep her big mouth shut?

''Apparently she'd decided that because of the choices she'd already made, her life was never going to be what she wanted. She'd blown her chance and didn't want to settle for anything less.''

For Juliet it was almost an instant replay of another time in her life. And the second time around was no less sad. Or wrong. ''You never know what might be waiting around the corner,'' she murmured, mostly to herself.

She'd learned that one firsthand.

If she'd had any idea what dimensions Mary Jane would bring to her life, she sure as hell wouldn't have spent the nine months of her pregnancy afraid that life, as she wanted it to be, was over.

''For all her wild ideas, her free spirit, Amunet held a pretty strong belief that marriage was forever. And that a woman should only marry once.''

''So once you divorced she couldn't marry again?'' Pretty outdated, but Juliet certainly understood that different things mattered to different people. Look at her own twin.

''She did marry again. Quickly. I think to try to escape the state of being divorced.''

"So she was married when she died?"

He shook his head, still focused someplace else—someplace inside. "It didn't last. And then, to her way of thinking, she had two strikes against her."

Juliet's breath caught as he finally glanced at her.

"You blame yourself for this, too."

"Not completely."

"Yes, you do."

He finished his drink. Pushed the glass to the end of the table for their waiter to pick up on his way past. "I hadn't seen or spoken to her in a couple of years. I certainly had nothing to do with the bottle of pills she got hold of. Or the fact that she took them."

"Of course you didn't. But you blame yourself anyway."

His gaze was certain. "I made some choices in my life that were selfish, thoughtless. I married a woman I barely knew at a time I didn't even know myself. I promised her forever when I had no idea where I was going to be, who I was going to be, the next week. Sometimes I think the only thing I did right back then was refuse to have children when she asked me. I'd hate to think what the kid's life would've been like being raised by a mother who felt trapped by his or her presence."

"I guess it would depend on the role you played in the child's life." Her stomach knotted. She had to go.

His slow grin surprised her. It wasn't effusive, or filled with humor, but it was genuine. "It's been good seeing you again," he said.

"Yeah, you, too." She really had to go.

"You wouldn't want to do it again sometime, would you?"

Probably. And no, never.

"How do you go from that night nine years ago to settling for an occasional drink?"

They couldn't. That night was there. Between them. Incredible. Time out of time. They'd be driven to do it again. And then...

"You probably don't," he admitted.

"That's what I thought."

"Anything more than an occasional drink wouldn't be right. We hardly know each other."

"Too much too soon." Too much, period. She had a life. One that didn't—couldn't—include him. A life that, if he knew about it, could make him hate her. And what kind of effect would it have on him? He was already bearing an unrealistic responsibility for three deaths due to his youthful quest for self-discovery. He'd told her that night on the beach that he didn't want children, didn't want to be in a position to have such control over another individual that he might affect another person as his father had affected him. If he knew that, in his zeal to run, he'd run from his own daughter, he might never fully recover. And always, most important, was Mary Jane. What if Blake knew the truth and still didn't want kids? His abandonment would devastate Mary Jane.

"It's probably best that we just leave it as a great memory," he said.

God, she hated how that sounded. So final. "I think so."

He was quiet for a moment, then paid the check that the waiter brought. "For now, I think so, too."

Relief caused her stomach to go weak. The disappointment she'd deal with later, when she was alone that night.

They stood. Walked to the door. Juliet was very careful not to let any part of her touch any part of him.

He held the door. She walked by, feeling his heat, but absolutely determined not to touch him.

She turned to the left. He stood by the door.

"I'm parked over this way."

She nodded. "I'm back there."

"This is it, then." He didn't come closer. If he'd come closer, maybe...

"Thanks for dinner. And the drinks." She walked backward slowly as she talked.

Hands in his pockets, he stood there, watching. "You're welcome."

"Be happy."

"You, too."

There was nothing more to say.

"If you ever find yourself in need of a good attorney, don't hesitate to call."

People on the street were glancing oddly as they passed. A teenage couple stopped to watch.

"And if you ever need a home built..."

"I know where to find you." She was at the corner. "See ya."

If he replied she didn't hear him. As soon as she rounded the corner, Juliet ran.

SHE HADN'T BEEN HOME half an hour when the front door slammed. She waited to hear her daughter's robust voice but was met with silence.

"Mary Jane?" Pulling over her head a T-shirt that

matched the black-and-white drawstring bottoms she'd changed into, Juliet came out of her room.

There was no answer. Other than a cupboard slamming in the kitchen. The sound of a glass on the counter. The refrigerator being swung open hard enough to rattle the bottles stored inside the door.

"What's up?"

The child, dressed in jeans with a matching jacket over a purple lace shirt, spilled the milk she was pouring. "I quit Brownies."

"You can't quit Brownies. Only I can do that. I paid for it."

"Then I haven't quit, I'm just not going back." Leaving a puddle of milk on the counter, Mary Jane brought her glass to the table and sat down, her chin at her chest. Her cheeks were puffed out with indignation, her lower lip protruding as though she was about to cry.

"Can we talk about it first?"

"Yeah," she said with more challenge than acquiescence in her voice. "But I'm not going back."

Juliet ignored the milk on the counter. Pulling out the chair closest to Mary Jane's, she sat. "Why don't you tell me what happened."

"It's not what happened, it's what's going to happen."

She was having trouble following Mary Jane's line of thought. "What's that?"

"Mrs. Byron said we have to do a father-daughter banquet." Mary Jane looked over at her accusingly, as though she'd planned the whole thing. Juliet didn't even *know* Mrs. Byron. The woman, whose daughter was brand new to the troop, had just been made activities director. "I don't have a father. I don't want a father.'' The little girl stood with such force her curls bounced against her cheeks. ''And I don't want to go to Brownies anymore.''

''No one's going to force you to go to Brownies,'' she said to the retreating back.

When it rained, it poured.

LATE AFTERNOON, a full two weeks since he'd seen Juliet McNeil, Blake was in his office looking over a library bid to be submitted to city council the next morning, when his secretary buzzed him.

''Paul Schuster to see you, sir.''

''I thought you'd gone home.''

''Just leaving.''

''Drive carefully and I'll see you tomorrow,'' Blake told Lee Anne Boulder, the mother of three who'd lost her husband in a construction injury two years before. ''And please, send Schuster in.''

Slipping his arms back into the navy suit coat he'd dropped on the chair in front of his desk when he'd come in from a lunch with the mayor several hours before, Blake met the attorney at the door. Why hadn't the other man called to let him know he was coming?

Schuster got right to the point.

''Eaton James was on the stand today.''

''That must've been entertaining.'' He motioned to a leather couch on the other side of his office. ''Can I get you something to drink?''

''Thanks, I could use a stiff one.''

''Whiskey?'' Blake walked over to the wet bar along the far wall. It was there strictly for business meetings. He'd never once used it alone.

A habit his father had taught him very early in life.

A man who drinks alone at work has a problem with drinking.

"Whatever you've got."

Pouring a couple of shots of twelve-year-old scotch, Blake handed one to the older man and took a healthy sip of his own. If Schuster was here to tell him they were going to lose, he was going to need more than one.

"When you were in court, answering Juliet McNeil's questions, you testified that you were in the Cayman Islands five years ago."

"I was. On and off. I was working on a project in Honduras and used to fly over for a week every now and then. Why?"

"Did you ever do any business there?"

Something in Schuster's voice, his low-key demeanor, set Blake on edge. Putting his glass on the coffee table, he took a seat across from the prosecutor.

"Never." Where the hell was this going?

"What did you do there?"

"Lay on the beach. Kayaked. Snorkeled. Ate. Made love with my wife."

Schuster's gaze was guarded as he looked up. "Where did you stay?"

"Various places, hotels, a bed-and-breakfast. Once we even camped on the beach. Why? What does any of this have to do with James's testimony?"

Was the man trying to claim that Blake had something to do with the Eaton Estates deal, other than checking to see if it was legitimate at the request of his mother?

"James launched a bombshell in the courtroom today. I'd bet my career on the fact that no one was as surprised as his counsel."

Chills slid through Blake. Ignoring the drink he'd left on the table, he watched as the other man swirled his whiskey. Drained the glass. Set it down.

"He claims there's a bank account in the Cayman Islands that holds every dime of all monies unaccounted for in his books. Those paid invoices for shipments that never seemed to happen? Well, that money was being squirreled away in some bank in the Cayman Islands."

"He admitted it," Blake said, elated and sickened at the same time. "We won." And then, observing the other man's bowed head, he added, "You won."

"Not so fast." Schuster shook his head, looking old and tired in a jacket wrinkled from hours of sitting in court. The energy that seemed to pulse through him twenty-four hours a day was eerily absent.

"James didn't admit to anything but being black-mailed."

Frowning, Blake sat back, a curious numbness spreading through him. "What? By whom?"

"Your father."

CHAPTER SEVEN

SITTING BACK with his arms resting on the sides of his chair, Blake hoped he looked relaxed. He was working hard to maintain the facade.

"My father." They were the only two words spinning around in his mind. There should be more. Would be more. He knew that. For now, focusing on remaining calm was keeping him detached.

Or a sense of survival was.

Schuster, forearms on his knees as he leaned forward, nodded. His hands were clasped as though he didn't quite know what to do with them.

"My father had no reason to blackmail Eaton James."

The man's pockmarked face thinned as he continued to watch Blake. "Apparently he did."

No, he didn't. James was a liar, on trial for fraud. "Why?" If Blake was going to clear his father's name, he had to have the facts.

"After James claimed that he lost the money your father had invested with him, your father hired a private audit firm to inspect James's books. His right to do so was in the contract he'd had his lawyers write up at the time of the investment."

Blake recognized his father's hand in that. Walter

Ramsden had been at times almost maniacal in his need for control.

He'd been equally so in walking the straight and narrow.

"The firm found everything in order, according to the document James received. Your father, allegedly, was not satisfied with the record."

None of which seemed at all unusual to Blake.

"According to James, your father threatened to call someone he knew at the IRS unless James turned over his records to him, so that he could see for himself what was and wasn't there, with the understanding that if he found anything that even hinted at tampering, he'd call the IRS anyway."

With a hand to his chin, Blake nodded. Sitting still was excruciating. Almost as painful as listening to what should be a fantastic story, but was, in fact, quite believable, about his deceased father. He could too easily see Walter Ramsden giving James a fair chance to prove himself before turning him in, and then considering himself judge and jury of that proof. After all, Walter Ramsden firmly believed that he always knew what was best.

The damnable thing was, he pretty much always had.

Except, of course, in his decision to invest with Eaton James.

"Threatening to call the IRS on a firm whose bad investment has just lost you a huge chunk of money is hardly a crime, and nowhere near the vicinity of blackmail."

Unless someone like Juliet McNeil, who colored the truth to match any decor, was painting the picture?

Running a hand through his graying hair, Schuster picked up his glass. "Mind if I have another?"

"Help yourself." Blake motioned to the bar. He should get up and do it, and get one for himself, as well. Except that he hadn't finished the one he had.

The back of the man's slacks looked as though he'd slept in them more than once. Apparently sometime during the afternoon, the prosecutor—whose attention to his appearance was normally obsessive enough to be noticeable—had lost track of the crease in his pants.

With a glass that was twice as full as the one Blake had poured originally, Schuster took his seat.

"James testified that after your father looked over his books, Walter claimed the legitimate start-up companies under Terracotta's umbrella were fraudulent. Apparently a couple of the new ventures had well-known San Diego businessmen at the helm as the principal signers. Because the auditors knew the reputations of the businessmen in question, they didn't audit their books, but rather accepted as fact the invoices and receipts going to and coming from them."

Just like the well-known national firm that had been in the news at least twice in the past two years. Blake frowned. "My father thought the companies were nonexistent fronts to hide Terracotta Foundation losses or gains."

"Apparently."

"And these principal signers, how would James have convinced them to act as principals for businesses that were not legitimate?"

"McNeil asked James that very question," Schuster said, shaking his head. "I swear, the woman had no idea what her client had up his sleeve, but she sure rolled with the punches.''

Blake couldn't tell if the older man was repulsed, or reluctantly in awe. He suspected a combination of both.

''And what was James's reply?''

''That your father was obsessed and, he suspected, not quite as mentally alert as he'd once been…''

Blake burned. His old man had had many faults, but a lack of mental sharpness had not been one of them. That was something his mother absolutely would have told him about.

''He said that your father found the fact that all of the principals held seats on the Semaphor board suspect. He accused James of playing on the trust of his philanthropic associates—''

''Something my father had fallen prey to.''

''Exactly.''

Sitting forward, Blake picked up his glass. Sipped slowly. This wasn't sounding so bad, after all.

''If my father had been wrong, if the companies weren't fraudulent, what did James have to be afraid of? I think that the fact that the state found the same evidence is pretty telling, don't you?''

Schuster swirled the liquid in his glass, took a drink, then frowned at Blake. ''Not so fast,'' he said, his eyes deadly serious. ''In the first place, if your father didn't have something on James, the blackmail attempt would not have been successful.''

He'd actually forgotten, for a moment, that that was where they were headed. James's ridiculous attempt to buy his freedom.

"And secondly, your father is the one who turned evidence over to the state."

Goddammit. He hadn't been told that.

So Schuster's entire case was hinging on the validity of his father's claims?

"Obviously you found ample evidence to corroborate the charges." The case would never have grown to this magnitude, would never have attracted attorneys like Schuster and Juliet McNeil, if there wasn't substantial proof.

Schuster sighed, dropped his head. "Much of the paper trail I've spent the past five years unwinding was created at the direction of your father. In a private meeting, of which no one knows, he told me where to look. And what I'd find."

"And he was right."

"Of course he was right, or we wouldn't be here," Schuster said impatiently, looking up. "James maintains that your father planted the evidence."

Glass in hand, Blake sat back. Hard. The moment had gone from incredible to absurd.

"If my father turned everything over to you, what did he supposedly have to use to blackmail James?"

"I met with your father just days before he died. Twenty-four hours after James had met with him, giving him a particular piece of information that he believed would not only get him out from underneath your father's control, but would turn the tables on him. He had information with which he could blackmail your father, instead."

"He admitted to blackmailing my father?"

Schuster shook his head. "No, he claims he only

used the information to get your father to leave him alone. He had no intention of doing anything illegal.''

Taking another sip of whiskey, although he knew he needed his mind completely clear, Blake set the glass down.

''But he claims that, until he came up with whatever hold he had on my father, my father used the evidence of fraudulent companies to blackmail him.''

''Yes.''

''So again, I ask, if there was nothing fraudulent in those books, why give in to blackmail?''

Not that he believed, for one second, there'd ever *been* any blackmail. Blake might have gone three years without speaking with his father, but there were some things he just knew.

''James had made some very stupid mistakes. Namely some bad investments—not unlike the Eaton Estates deal—that, had they become known, would have lost the Terracotta Foundation all of its investors. Think of it, a nonprofit organization losing money instead of gaining it to benefit third world countries. He'd made other investments that were keeping him afloat, but who's going to give money to a man they can't trust? He'd have been bankrupt with no possible way of recouping his losses, his reputation ruined.''

''So why didn't the original audit of Terracotta show those losses?''

''Because James started up a couple of other small companies that he used to hide the losses.''

''The companies my father questioned.''

''Correct.''

''So were they legitimate, or weren't they?''

Shrugging, Schuster finished off his whiskey. "That's the six-million-dollar question that only the jury will be able to decide at this point. The companies themselves exist, such as they are. It's a matter of having a license. It's all paper. What James *is* guilty of, which your father discovered, is that he forged the names of the principals for both of the companies in question."

"Forged the names of men on the Semaphor board?"

Schuster nodded. "Reputable businessmen, both of them. He'd gambled on the fact that, were he to be audited, the firm would take the names at face value and not look at those books. A chance that paid off." The prosecutor dropped his head a second time.

"Chances are I'm going to lose this one because I went for a charge of fraudulent schemes and the man is guilty of forgery," he said. "I haven't done a forgery case since my first year out of law school."

He might lose a case. But what about justice?

"If this is true—" which Blake was certain it was not "—why wouldn't James have come clean with his attorney from the beginning?"

"Who knows?" Schuster said, standing to pour himself another drink. Blake was going to have to call the man a cab. "McNeil has one hell of a reputation. Maybe he was hoping she'd get him off altogether. Save his reputation, his business, his lifestyle. And when he got scared, he figured facing the much lesser charge of forgery was better than spending the next fourteen years in jail. Ego and fear. Two of the three things that most often get a man."

"And the third is?" Blake didn't give a damn. He

was stalling. Avoiding the rest of what Schuster had to tell him.

"Sex," the man said, his lips pursed with disgust.

"So what motivation did James give for my father blackmailing him? How did he explain the fact that Walter Ramsden, a man everyone in the business community knows to be honest to the point of self-righteousness, didn't go immediately to the authorities with the things he'd found?"

The prosecutor's eyes were surprisingly clear as he stared at Blake. "You."

"What?" He hadn't meant to raise his voice.

"You hadn't seen your father in four years, Blake. That's a long time when a man is in his seventies. Especially a man who is suffering from a bad heart. A lack of physical strength had taken its toll. Apparently Ramsden Enterprises wasn't doing as well as it once had."

"Nothing that couldn't easily be fixed." Blake tried to keep defensiveness and emotions out of his reply. He couldn't afford clouded judgment at this moment. "As with any company in today's market, we needed to diversify. To expand. The day of small family concerns had passed."

"Expansion takes time. Planning. And more energy than your father had. He needed the money to stay afloat until you came home."

Standing, Blake grabbed his glass from the table and took it to the small built-in dishwasher at the bar. "Well, there you go then," he said, his back to Schuster. "That will be easy enough to prove. Just look at our books. I did, thoroughly, when I came home. True to form, my father left not one dime unaccounted for—either incoming or outgoing. There was absolutely no influx of money other than what was invoiced and signed off with double signatures.''

''You actually think your father would have put the money someplace it could be found? Tracked?''

''No.'' Blake turned. ''I don't. Because my father would never have taken the money to begin with.''

''According to Eaton James, he put it in an account in the Cayman Islands.''

Blake's eyes narrowed. ''How convenient. James mentions a place that's well known in the business world for its ability to hide money as though it didn't exist. Without the Cayman Islands' cooperation, he knows there's no real way to prove his claim one way or the other. And he'd also know that the government is known for its blindness to such matters.''

Schuster's eyes were narrowed, too, although he remained seated. ''He has a bank account number. That was the information he presented to your father just before Walter came to me.''

There was more. Blake felt it coming. With both hands bracing his weight behind him, he leaned back against the counter. ''You're going to tell me the account has my father's name on it.''

''No.'' Schuster surprised him. ''According to James, it has yours.''

''NIGHT, MOM.''

''Good night, imp. Sleep well.'' Leaning over, Juliet kissed her daughter's cheek, pulling the covers up to Mary Jane's chin. No matter how hot the weather, she wouldn't sleep without being completely covered, at least by a sheet.

She forced herself to stand in the doorway until the child opened her eyes for one last blown kiss, a ritual they'd started when Mary Jane was a toddler. Never had bedtime taken so long.

More often than not, she let Mary Jane talk her into staying up past her bedtime. Mary Jane didn't seem to require as much sleep as most children. A characteristic of precocious children, her pediatrician had said when, at two, the little girl had played happily in her crib all through naptime.

She gave her daughter another fifteen minutes to settle into sleep before she could no longer stand the tension and called her twin. From a cell phone, sitting in her bedroom with the door closed, just in case Mary Jane got up.

"He's a criminal, Marce!" she blurted as soon as her sister picked up.

"Who's a criminal?"

She could hear voices in the background. The television. Again.

"Blake Ramsden." The father of her child. "What kind of defense attorney am I that I didn't even suspect?" The thoughts that had been torturing her all evening came tumbling out in no apparent order. "What kind of mother? I've been working on this case for months and not once did I have even an inkling that the road to Eaton's freedom was paved by Ramsden Enterprises. It's like I was blinded by a nine-year-old memory that might have cost a man several years of his life."

"So what bothers you more, Jules?" Marcie's voice was soft yet tough. "Your ego, because you might not be as infallible on the job as you think? Or your heart, because you might have made a bad choice for the father of your child?''

''I didn't choose the father of my child. The child chose me.''

''You used the same condom twice!''

''I was drunk!''

Marcie didn't say another word. It was a silence that drove Juliet insane every single time her sister used it on her.

''Why are you doing this?'' Juliet whispered a full thirty seconds later. ''You've never said anything like this before.''

''It didn't matter before. He had a life in another world.''

A laugh track exploded in the background.

''You think I got pregnant on purpose?'' Because if Marcie thought she'd ever consider something as cold-blooded as that—to go out looking for a man for the express purpose of having his kid—then her sister didn't know her at all.

''I don't think you consciously chose the course.'' Marcie's reply came quickly. ''But I've always suspected that somewhere, in the back of your mind, the thought was there.''

Juliet leaned her head against the wall, legs straight out, and studied the subtle texture of her nylons. She really shouldn't be sitting on the floor in her suit.

''You need family, Jules,'' Marcie said slowly. ''We both do. And there was no way you could possibly contemplate marriage—not until you'd proven to yourself that you had a full life on your own.''

''I made it through law school by the time I was

twenty-five. I had a life.'' The carpet was making her legs itch.

Marcie nodded. ''You had the beginning of a life. But not enough of one to take away your fear. I've wondered if maybe part of you needed to know that even if you were in Mother's position—pregnant and alone—you had what it took to make it. You couldn't live with the fear of thinking you might not be able to handle it,'' Marcie was saying. ''You were afraid of finding out that if it ever happened to you, you'd do exactly what Mom did.'' She was going to hang up now. ''I don't think you got pregnant on purpose, no.'' Marcie's words went a little way toward calming the panic in Juliet's heart. ''But I don't think it was completely a mistake that you didn't insist on a new condom the second time around. We make little subconscious choices all the time and then act on them without even knowing that's what we're doing.''

It was Juliet's turn to use the silent treatment. Mostly because she was speechless.

''You know,'' Marcie continued, ''like when you pull into the parking lot of an ice-cream shop without even realizing that you were hungry for ice cream.''

''I hardly think craving a hot-fudge sundae can be in any way likened to having a baby.'' She pulled off her pumps, one by one.

''The brain's ability to see to the needs of the subconscious can be the same in both cases.''

None of this was making sense. And it wasn't anything she'd needed, or expected, when she'd dialed her twin's number. ''Is Hank there?''

''No.'' Of course not. It was Thursday and Hank worked late at the hardware store on Thursdays doing inventory.

With one hand, and leaning from side to side where she sat, Juliet pulled off her panty hose, wadded them and tossed them in the wire-framed designer laundry basket in a corner of the closet.

"So you're accusing me of going out that night with some thought in the back of my mind that it was time to get pregnant?"

"No! Of course not, Jules." Marcie's voice gentled. "I know you better than that. I'm only saying that when the proper circumstances presented themselves, you acted on them. You were with a man who attracted you. He was intelligent and confident enough to argue with you, he was gorgeous, he was from a stable family well known for honest dealings, and—the crème de la crème—he was leaving the country for an indefinite period of time! There'd be no one to get in touch with, to answer questions from, to avoid, or to call. No one to turn to in case you got cold feet about going it alone."

"You actually think I thought all that through?"

"No. But I think the sense of freedom spoke to you." Juliet's heart sank when it became obvious that Marcie wasn't going to budge on this one. Usually when that happened she was at least partially correct.

The laugh track sounded again.

Except for her insistence on staying in Maple Grove.

Juliet started unfastening the buttons on her blouse. "Can I have some time to think about this?"

"In other words, you want me to shut up and never mention it again?"

"Yeah."

"Only if you promise to…no, forget that. Yeah, I'll let it go."

"Only if I promise to what?"

"Nothing."

"What?" Her blouse hung half-open.

"I was just going to say that I promise to leave this alone if you'd quit worrying about Hank and Maple Grove."

That wasn't fair. Marcie's happiness was at stake. "I—"

"Don't say it," Marcie interrupted. "You don't need to. I know you can't stop."

"I just—"

"I know, Jules," she said, her voice low. "Truth is, I'm not even sure I want you to stop."

Juliet froze, afraid to hope. "You mean it, Marce? You're actually thinking about moving here?" Her heart rate sped up as she ran through the possibilities.

"Not really," Marcie's reply wasn't as disappointing as it might have seemed. It wasn't the adamant no that was all she'd ever issued in the past. "I just don't want you to quit asking. It's good to know I have a place to go."

"Always, sis."

"Yeah. Still, it's good to hear, you know?"

Juliet did know. After losing everything they had to go live in squalor in a trailer the size of one of their bedrooms at home, security had gained a pretty high spot on the priority list of both girls. Right beneath the need to provide it for themselves.

In the space of a weekend, she and Marce had gone from living in a San Francisco mansion with every possible luxury and socially prominent parents to a rusty, skinny, two-bedroom trailer in Maple Grove with a broken woman who had no training, no marketable skills and not enough esteem to pull herself up. They'd left behind the man who'd lost his fortune and found himself a rich woman who was happy to keep him in the style to which he'd grown accustomed in exchange for his company. The man who'd come home one Friday afternoon to bid a cold adieu to the wife he'd grown to hate and to the children he'd never wanted and didn't intend to see again.

Juliet could still remember the moment when, thinking that she could solve everything by wrapping her skinny arms around the man she'd adored and telling him that she'd help him get his money back, her father had shoved her away so hard she'd landed on her butt on the ground.

"You going to tell me what kind of criminal Mary Jane's father is?" Marcie asked when the line hung silent.

"He's been harboring illegally gained money in a bank account in the Cayman Islands."

"No way."

"I know," Juliet said, shrugging out of her blouse and leaving it on the floor beside her. "I couldn't believe it, either. I'm still not sure I do, but the evidence is pretty conclusive. Eaton James gave me the account number today just before lunch along with paperwork showing who opened the account. It's in Blake's name."

"Oh, God."

"Yeah, and it was opened during a period of time he already admitted to being in the islands."

"Damn."

That was exactly what Juliet thought.

CHAPTER EIGHT

"HAVE YOU CALLED HIM?" Marcie's question started the butterflies fluttering around inside her again. She'd spent the past hour telling her twin about the day's events, the shocking developments in a trial of which she'd thought herself in complete control.

Juliet lay in her bed, pillows propped up behind her, the comforter pulled to her hips. Darkness, broken by a moonlit glow from the open shutters, gave the room a sleepy feel.

"I have no reason to call him," she said aloud, something she'd been repeating to herself since Eaton James had delivered his startling testimony that afternoon. "I hardly know the man."

"You had dinner with him two weeks ago."

She wished she'd never told her sister that.

"And very clearly said a permanent goodbye," she muttered.

"But you were there in the courtroom. You heard the whole thing. And, even if you haven't spent many hours with him, you did fill those hours with some…fairly intimate communication."

"We had sex." They'd also had a baby. But since he didn't know that, it didn't count. Did it?

"Do you want to call him?"

"Dammit, Marce, can't you just leave me in blissful self-deception for a while?"

"If that's what you wanted, you wouldn't have called me." Her sister said. And then added, "Would you?" with a little less confidence.

"No, I wouldn't have. I rely on the absolute honesty between us," she admitted. "I always have."

"Okay. So…why do you want to call him?"

Juliet sighed, ran a hand through hair that was loose and falling free around her face. "I don't know. I just feel uneasy, you know? I mean, I've been working with Eaton James for months and he never breathed a word about any of this."

"But I'll bet you assured him, when he first came to you, that you could get him off, didn't you?"

"I think I would have."

"And would you have been able to do that if he'd told you about the forgery?"

The Monet lithograph on her wall was a square shadow with little glowing pinpricks where the light hit bright color. "No." It could be said that she presented different forms of truth, and left out incriminating evidence when it suited her client's case to do so, but Juliet McNeil never knowingly lied. "It's his first offense. I'd have gotten him off with nothing more serious than a light probation term."

"And a damaged reputation that would've been hard to recover, at least professionally. Not many people trust their charitable contributions to a crook."

James had said something similar when she'd come unglued on him late that afternoon. Just what she wanted, a client who tried to outmaneuver her. When would she ever fully grasp the fact that in her world, it was always each man for himself?

"What happens now?" Marcie asked a couple of minutes later.

"I expect the D.A. to drop the charges. He'll never get a class-two felony out of this. James'll be charged with numerous counts of forgery and get his hands slapped."

"And what about Blake Ramsden?"

Glancing out the window at an ocean she couldn't see in the dark, Juliet held tight to the phone with a sweat-slick palm. "I suspect he'll be charged with a class-two felony."

"You think Schuster will do it?"

"Yeah. That's one thing you can count on Paul Schuster for—he'll take up any case he thinks he can win. Even more so because he's going to be driven to get a win out of all the months he's spent on this. Hell—" she chuckled without humor "—knowing Schuster, he'll probably figure out a way to make it look like he knew that Blake was guilty all along."

"Except for the little matter of having wasted the state's money to press the charges against Eaton in the first place."

"Who knows." Juliet couldn't remember a time when she'd been so tired. At least not since she'd been eight and a half months pregnant and hauling herself out of bed before dawn to get to work.

"Is he guilty?"

"How do I know?"

"You're usually pretty tuned in to these things."

"As I proved with my adept handling of the Eaton James defense," she mumbled.

"No one's right all the time."

She sighed, fiddling with the bottom hem of the almost threadbare T-shirt she was wearing. "I don't know if he's guilty or not." She finally gave in and let herself think about the situation head-on. "My heart tells me he's not, but logic tells me he probably is."

"I sure wish I'd met this guy!"

"Why?"

"He's the only man who's even got close enough for your heart to hear."

Juliet took the next three minutes listing several men in her life who'd been closer to her than Mary Jane's father had ever been.

Marcie mostly let her get away with this small refusal to face the truth as she saw it. Juliet hoped that meant her twin wasn't really sure about the state of Juliet's heart. Because she couldn't afford, in any way, shape or form, to have her sister right on this one.

"Do you think there's a chance Blake Ramsden will call you?"

Marcie's question was another one she'd been trying—without success—to avoid. "I don't know," she said.

"Do you want him to?"

"I don't know the answer to that, either." Part of her did. If he was charged, as she knew he would be, he'd need her—if she could convince Eaton James to sign a waiver allowing her to represent Blake. Not only was she one of the most successful defense attorneys in the state, she had an intimate grasp of the details of this particular case.

And she *wanted* to be there for him.

He'd given her the most precious gift of her life. Just because he didn't know that didn't mean she didn't owe him something in return.

Maybe even, because of that secret, she owed him.

And another part of her, the frightened, lonely part, wanted him to stay as far away from her and her happy little life as humanly possible.

MARY JANE DIDN'T GET scared that often. Which was why when she did get scared, it really scared her.

Something was up that was worse than anything at school or stupid people who didn't like her. All weekend her mother had done normal stuff with her. She hadn't cried, or asked for time alone, or forgotten that she'd promised to take Mary Jane for ice cream after they cleaned the bathrooms this week. She just hadn't *argued.* Even when Mary Jane had brought up some of the craziest things she could think of, just to get her mother talking.

What if Mom was sick? The thought made her feel as if she was going to throw up. What would happen to her if something ever happened to Mom? She could go live with Aunt Marcie in Maple Grove, of course, which wouldn't be all that great, but it wouldn't be horrible like going to an orphanage. But no one would love her like Mom did. No one.

No one would think she was the most special thing on earth. Or tell her about important things even though she was just a kid. No one else, not even Aunt Marcie, would argue with her about things that had no answers like whether or not a chicken came first or an egg.

They'd all say she was just a kid and wait for her to grow up.

Turning over in her bed, Mary Jane bunched up the pillow and squeezed her eyes shut. Tomorrow was Monday, and school was even worse when she was sleepy.

She was being dumb. Mom wasn't sick. If she was, she'd tell Mary Jane for sure. Besides, she'd had lots of energy and made Mary Jane clean the bathrooms twice while she scrubbed the kitchen floor, even though they hadn't spilled anything.

Feeling a little better, Mary Jane was almost asleep when she remembered that still didn't tell her what *was* wrong.

It must be really horrible.

It had to be or they would've talked about it. The only other time Mom hadn't talked to her at all was when her grandma had died. Mary Jane had been really little, only about three, but she could still remember. Mostly she remembered that summer when she was going into first grade and had asked her mother what Grandma had died of and her mother had talked a lot but never really told her. Only, Mary Jane hadn't figured that out until later.

Someday she was going to ask again. Maybe. When she was bigger.

So who died? It couldn't be Aunt Marcie. They'd just talked to her on the phone that afternoon. And there wasn't anyone else who mattered that much. Was there?

Her stomach hurt and Mary Jane turned over, but that didn't help. She thought about the book she'd been reading, about the horse and the race and how

Bonnie was going to win the race and get to keep her very own horse. But then she remembered that Bonnie didn't have a mom and that made her scared all over again.

One time, on a night before the first day of school, Mom had told her to count sheep when she couldn't sleep. Mary Jane hadn't wanted to tell her she didn't see any sheep when she closed her eyes.

Maybe they were having trouble paying their bills and they'd have to leave the cottage on the beach and Mom didn't want to tell her because she knew how much Mary Jane loved living on the beach. But at school once, when she'd told a couple of the kids where she lived, the one girl, Corinne, who was mostly nice to her, had said that it cost a lot of money to live on the beach.

She wasn't really worried about staying in this house on the beach. As long as she and Mom were together, she didn't care if they were like the homeless people she saw on the benches along the road to the airport. But did they let kids live like that? She didn't think so.

So did that mean if they couldn't pay their bills someone would say that Mom couldn't keep her? Surely then Mom would be willing to go back to Maple Grove and stay with Aunt Marcie, even though Mom hated Maple Grove so much.

Her head hurt and Mary Jane rolled onto her back, staring at the ceiling though mostly she couldn't really see it. Just shadows.

She was being dumb again. They had lots of money. Mom was almost famous and got paid a lot for her job. But maybe she was losing a big case and then people wouldn't come to her anymore.

Mary Jane tried hard to sleep. As hard as she could. But it just didn't come. The more she couldn't go to sleep, the more scared she got.

Finally, when she couldn't stand staying in her room all alone, she climbed out of bed, tiptoed down the hall to Mom's room, lifted the covers quietly and slid in so gently the mattress hardly moved. She'd just lie there on the side of the bed, without even a pillow, so Mom wouldn't know she was there.

Even if her neck hurt, she figured this was better than being in her own room. But then Mom's arm came around her and pulled her close. Mom didn't say anything. Just kissed her lightly by the eye and went back to sleep.

And finally, snug and warm and right where she wanted to be, so did Mary Jane.

EVERY TIME BLAKE'S PHONE buzzed, he jumped. That wasn't like him at all. He'd lived through a hurricane and a near bombing, seen poverty worse than anything he could have imagined, slept in places where bugs were more abundant than pillows or sheets, and even been thrown in jail once in a godforsaken place he never had found on a map. And the one thing he'd learned about himself during those years of challenges was that he faced adversity with calm.

He'd just never been on the verge of being charged with a crime he hadn't committed. He'd thought a hundred times over the weekend about calling Juliet McNeil. Had even gone so far as to spend several hours on the Internet finding out what her legal standing would have to be in case he asked her to represent him, given the fact that she was counsel for another man up for the same charges in the same case.

As far as he could tell, there was no statute that prevented her from doing it, as long as she had a waiver from the previous client.

Blake had no idea what the chances were of Eaton James agreeing to that. But surely, once Schuster dropped the charges—as he'd told Blake he was going to do—James would be feeling charitable.

Charity was, after all, his business.

His intercom buzzed. Blake's pen went flying. "Yes?" he asked after inhaling deeply in an attempt to control his response.

"I'm going to lunch, sir. Would you like me to bring you back something?"

Thanking Lee Anne for asking, Blake declined. The only thing that sounded good at the moment was a visit to the little bar across the room. He retrieved his pen.

And moved over to stare out the wall of windows down at the bustling city he hadn't realized he loved—or missed—until he'd come home.

He'd done a bit of research on other legal matters that weekend. Namely, how a person was actually charged for a class-two felony. After finding out that fraud of the type in which he and his father had allegedly engaged *was* a class-two felony.

There were people he could have called. Ramsden had a team of attorneys. Construction attorneys. But certainly they could recommend a good criminal attorney in the space of seconds. He just hadn't been able to bring himself to admit to anyone that he was actually facing the possibility of being in so much trouble. He didn't want to give the idea any validity by discussing it.

Neither could he remain completely ignorant. Ignorance had never been the Ramsden way.

Most of the close friends he'd had before leaving the country, friends from college, had moved on, married, settled into careers all over the country. He'd reacquainted himself with a few of them, but being so wrapped up in expanding Ramsden into commercial construction, he hadn't developed any relationships close enough to call on in a time like this.

As he understood his situation, Schuster—who would be filing charges on behalf of the state—would have to take along an investigator who'd questioned key witnesses to appear before a grand jury.

Once the investigator corroborated Schuster's claim about how witnesses would probably respond in court, a charge would be entered and either a warrant issued for his arrest or he'd be subpoenaed to appear in court for arraignment.

The whole process could be done in a day or two, which Schuster had already had. They could be coming for him at any moment.

A noise sounded in the outer office. A door closing? Glancing over his shoulder so quickly he pulled a muscle in his neck, Blake waited. After a couple of minutes had passed with no other activity, he strode over to yank open the door. He'd rather just face what was to come than—

The office was empty. But he could see where a calendar had fallen from its nail on the wall. Lee Anne had taken the calendar down earlier that morning, looking up a proposed completion date and had obviously not put it back securely. Slowly, calmly, he walked over and hung it up.

In his office again, Blake didn't hesitate. He picked up the phone, dialed the number he'd already memorized, and waited. The chances were pretty slim that a woman as busy as Juliet McNeil would just be sitting at her desk on a Monday. For all he knew, she spent most of her days in court. Certainly she'd have a staff to do most of the investigative and research work she needed.

Her skills were in the courtroom.

"Juliet McNeil..."

Traffic buzzed beneath his window. People who looked more like little bugs than human beings scurried down the sidewalk, collecting at street corners waiting for lights to change. A man stood, leaning against the side of a brick building across the street, smoking a cigarette.

The sky was a perfect cerulean blue. The sun bright.

"Hello?"

"Sorry." Blake finally decided to speak rather than quietly replace the receiver. "It's Blake Ramsden."

"Blake! Oh my God. You've heard."

"Heard what?"

"Oh, then I take it you haven't seen the noon news?"

He'd been too busy dreading being in the news himself. "No, what's up?"

"Are you in your office?"

"Yes."

"I'm actually not far from there," she said. "Mind if I come by?"

What the hell was going on? "Of course not. I'm on the twelfth floor. What did I miss on the noon news?"

Could they announce to the press that he'd been charged before they told him?

"As convoluted as everything is, I don't want to have this conversation with you over the phone. Do you mind?"

Yes. He was a little short on patience. "No."

"I'll be right there."

She'd clicked off before he'd pulled the phone away from his ear.

BLAKE WAS WAITING for her at the elevator outside Lee Anne's office. He'd tried to find some local news on his computer but hadn't had any luck.

She looked all business in her maroon linen suit and matching pumps. And still, in that first instant her eyes met his, Blake saw something else there. Some kind of knowing that had existed between them from the first moment they'd met—two strangers drowning fears and doubts and worries about their futures in a bar on a California beach.

A couple of his staff architects walked by and nodded, their interest in seeing their boss with a beautiful woman a little too obvious.

"Let's go inside," he said, indicating the brass placard that identified his suite of offices.

"President and CEO," Juliet read aloud. "Impressive."

"It would be if I hadn't simply inherited the job."

She glanced back at him, her forehead creased. "From what I hear, you've done miraculous things. In just five short years, you've turned this company into the leader in a very competitive industry."

"You've done your homework." It made him uneasy. She'd come armed.

She nodded. But didn't explain. Nor did she meet his eyes, focusing instead on his inner sanctum.

"Nice. I like all the windows. The view is magnificent."

He stood beside her as she stared down at the city. "Nothing quite beats the ocean, in my opinion, but this is nice, too. I just imagine that all those buildings are gone and then there it is."

What kind of sappy idiot was he turning into? So he might go to jail. He'd handle it just as he'd handled everything else that had come his way.

"What did I miss on the noon news?" It was time to get on with it.

"Oh, Blake…" She turned, her eyes wide as she looked up at him. "Eaton James killed himself this morning."

"What?" His stomach dropped. Another suicide? The brightness in the room diminished, as though the sun had gone behind a cloud. A cloud that was following him, would continue to follow him, for the rest of his life?

He had nothing to do with this one. Nothing.

"What happened?"

"Apparently he said goodbye to his wife and kids as usual when she left to take them to school. This was her morning to volunteer at a food bank. Then he went out to the garage, ran a vacuum cleaner hose from the exhaust to the back window of his antique Model T, turned on the car and climbed inside. When his wife came home a couple of hours later, he was dead, slumped over the steering wheel.''

''God.'' What was it with people taking the easy way out and leaving their loved ones behind to deal with the consequences?

Not that he really knew about that. It wasn't as though his father had killed himself. Or that he himself had still been among Amunet's loved ones. Still, the sting was so acutely felt, so real. ''Did he leave a note?''

Amunet had. And it had only brought about more questions with no answers.

''Just to tell his wife that his life insurance wouldn't pay her anything because of the circumstances of his death, but that the money in the Cayman Islands would be hers when it was freed up and should be enough to care for her and the kids for the rest of her life.''

Blake's skin was cold. ''That was it?'' No I love yous? Nothing to tell her children? His children?

''Except for the name of a man he recommended to handle her financial affairs, saying he was someone she could trust.''

Blake stood there, staring out at a day that looked exactly the same as it had mere moments before. And felt as dark as night.

Two weeks ago, he'd been a busy, if somewhat reclusive, builder with a moderately quiet life. Today, standing in that same office, he was living in a world gone mad.

CHAPTER NINE

NOW THAT SHE WAS THERE, Juliet wondered if she should have come. She'd heard Blake's voice on the phone and thrown all thoughts to the wind but one. She wanted to tell him about James herself and in person.

As though his calm presence could somehow dissipate the unease inside her.

They stood at the window of his office, staring out at all the people below. They'd been there yesterday. And would be tomorrow. But how often did anyone stop to think about what those people were feeling? Did anyone consider the suffering of those they passed on the street? Or even acknowledge that every single one of them had problems and sorrows and regrets?

"Why didn't you tell me this on the phone?"

Heat rose up Juliet's neck to her cheeks. "I'm not sure," she had to admit. She had no time to figure out another way to present the truth. "I overreacted."

He turned. She could see him in her peripheral vision, looking at her. "You're sure there's not more to it than that?"

"Schuster's meeting with the grand jury this morning. He'd subpoenaed Eaton James to testify." That was at least part of it.

Hands in the pockets of his tailored slacks, he rocked back and forth in his expensive leather shoes. "Is he going to get the indictment?"

"My professional opinion?" she asked, peering up at him.

He nodded, staring outside again. She could feel his tension, though whether it was because he stiffened beside her, or because her heart was in some way connected, she wasn't sure.

Wasn't sure she wanted to know.

"Yes."

He nodded then. That was all. Juliet needed more.

"What are you thinking?"

"I don't know if I'd call it thinking." He glanced down at her. "Right now I'm pretty close to a state of panic."

She wanted to help him. Needed to help him. To reassure him. And knew that, with Blake, only the cold hard facts would do.

"You have no criminal record and present no danger to the community. They aren't going to arrest you. You'll receive a subpoena for arraignment, appear before a judge and Schuster—they'll appoint an attorney to defend you if you don't already have your own— and you'll enter a plea of guilty or not guilty. A trial date will be set, probably about three months later, and then it's business as usual except that you'll most likely be told not to leave the country."

"What exactly should I expect to be charged with?"

She didn't want to answer that. "Since more than a hundred thousand dollars is involved, I would count on at least one count of theft, fraud due to misrepresentation, and because another individual was involved—your father—there'll probably also be a charge of conspiracy.''

He paled. ''*At least* one count?''

''If it's proven that James took investors' money to pay your father, there could be as many counts of fraud as there were investors.''

His jaw tight, Blake gazed out again, but no longer down at the people below. From something he'd said earlier, she suspected he was looking for the ocean beyond the buildings, hidden from view. Would there come a time when he wouldn't be free to go to the beach, listen to the waves, feel the sand beneath his feet, and the water lapping at his toes, see the great whitecaps jump up the sides of ships and crash against rocks that were slowly being worn by their force?

''So then what?''

''You go to trial,'' she said. ''If you're charged as I described, there will be a twelve-member jury, which will probably take a couple of days to select. Could be longer. The trial itself could last several weeks.''

She paused, hating to do this to him.

Blake's whole body was rigid, his expression unyielding, as though he was braced to hear it all at once. For some people, that was easiest.

''Remember, this will be a new jury and any evidence that's already been brought forth on the Eaton Estates deal or anything else pertinent to your father's association with Eaton James will have to be reintroduced.''

"What kind of effect is James's suicide going to have on the jury?"

She shrugged. "Depending on how it's presented, it could work in your favor. The man's future was looking brighter than it had in months. While he was going to have to face forgery charges, he was off the big hook. So—why now?"

"What do you think?"

"Perhaps there's more to the story, and he realized, after taking the stand, that the things he revealed could lead to other things being discovered that would point to some guilt of his own. Another benefit as far as your trial is concerned, James's former testimony would only be hearsay and as such inadmissible as evidence. In other words, it doesn't exist."

Juliet wrapped her arms around herself, her light-weight suit insufficient in the warmth department.

"On the other hand, he won't be here for your attorney to question, either. Which will make it more of a challenge to find whatever James might have hidden in his telling of the facts."

He nodded. Rocked slowly and then stopped. She had a pretty good idea what he was waiting for. She wished there was a way to minimize the truth.

"And if I'm found guilty?"

"Due to the amount of money in question, you could be facing up to fourteen years in prison, per count, which the judge could rule to be served con-currently or consecutively. However, a maximum sen-tence on a first offense isn't likely. It'll depend a lot on the intent and motivation the attorneys leave with the jury."

His shoulders sagged. "I could spend the rest of my life in prison."

Damn fine job she'd done of lightening that load.

"However, since this *is* a first offense," she added without validating the correctness of his math, "it's within the judge's power to sentence you to probation. Depending again on the facts that come out during the trial, which will indicate your potential risk of a repeat offense and consequent harm to the community."

"Repeat offense." His voice overflowed with disbelief. She couldn't tell whether that was because the idea of finding himself in this position was ludicrous, or because he was an innocent man in shock.

"I can't believe that anyone, seeing what you've done with this company in the last five years, will believe there's much risk of that."

She was going to remain neutral. It was the only smart, logical, safe choice. He was not a father to Mary Jane. He was only the biological contributor. A sweet memory from her youth. Whether or not he was being falsely accused was not her concern.

And if she told herself that often enough, she might eventually get the message.

"Ironic, isn't it?" He turned to glance down at her with a crooked, humorless smile. "Just weeks ago, you were joking about my ever finding myself in need of a good attorney."

She remembered. And she'd said it, at least in part, because he was the last person she'd ever expected to need a defense attorney.

"I told you to call."

"You were James's attorney. Does that preclude me from hiring you?"

His gaze was focused on the sidewalk again.

So was hers.

"There'd be confidentiality issues, but assuming his wife signed a waiver, they wouldn't prevent me from taking your case."

Her heart was pounding. He was going to ask her to represent him, and she felt she had to help him. And that she could. She also knew she was asking the impossible. Of herself. Of fate. And of an eight-year-old girl who did not deserve to have her life any more chaotic than it already was.

Whether or not she'd done right by this man in keeping her secret nine years before, there was some-one else, equally important, to consider here. Mary Jane McNeil. Juliet's nine-year-old choice had shaped Mary Jane's life—and she couldn't arbitrarily disrupt that life because of latent guilt.

But, God, she wished she knew what she *should* do.

"Would you be willing to take this case?"

She leaned forward, following the trail of a girl walking four various size dogs, all with leashes head-ing off in separate directions, alternately pulling her and tripping her. Either she was brand new to the job, or needed to find herself another career.

"It depends."

"On what?" He sounded more curious than con-cerned at that point. Juliet supposed his senses, his emotions, were on overload.

She turned to look at him. "Are you guilty?"

He stared right back with unblinking eyes. "Do you need to ask?"

"If I'm going to be your attorney, I do."

"I'm not guilty."

Blake offered to order them something to eat. Telling herself she wasn't agreeing to anything but an informal lunch, Juliet accepted. And joined him on the couch when the chicken-salad-on-wheat sandwiches arrived. Whether she took his case or not, whether she could get the waiver or not, there were some things she could advise him about, just as a friend. Things he would need to know to protect himself, rights most people never had reason to learn about.

Like the fact that he had a right to have copies of all documents the prosecutor was going to use against him, including the statements of all witnesses who would be called to testify.

He listened. Nodded. Ate slowly. Asked a couple of intelligent questions. He didn't take notes.

And as soon as there was a break in her explanation, he changed the subject.

"You said earlier that Schuster's meeting with the grand jury this morning was only part of the reason for your overreaction about speaking on the telephone. What was the rest?"

Juliet set her paper-wrapped, half-eaten sandwich on the table in front of her. "Had enough trial talk for now, huh?" she asked. There was more she could tell him to arm him for the fight ahead.

"I need to take this one step at a time," he told her, his gaze open, honest. "Let's see what the grand jury decides. Until then, there's no point in getting in any deeper.''

I can't handle any more right now, she translated. And understood.

Wadding up his empty paper, he took a long swig from the cola can he'd produced—one for each of them—from the small refrigerator. His throat was long, slender, as he tilted back his head. Slender yet strong. The muscles in his throat moved with each swallow.

Never, ever had Juliet been so intrigued by a throat.

''I imagine that it's not often the accomplished Ms. Juliet McNeil overreacts,'' he said, his expression less pinched as he leaned into the corner of the couch, one arm resting along the back, and raised an ankle to his knee. ''I'd like to know what caused it.''

It wasn't something she talked about. Not even with Marcie. They had spoken of it, of course. In the beginning, right after it had happened. And then Juliet had gone to counseling separate from the grief counseling they'd both had, and they'd never spoken of it again.

''The news about Eaton James really threw me.''

Putting her cola on the table, Juliet turned to face him.

''You've spent a lot of time with James lately. I imagine you got to know him well.''

Not that well. ''He was a client. Nothing more.'' She'd had so many she didn't even remember them all. Or at least, not the specifics of each case. Some of them she did, of course. But if she didn't stay detached she'd never be able to do her job.

''I just can't stop thinking about his wife. She's

left, not only with an uncertain and perhaps insecure future, but with a lifetime of what-ifs and if-onlys.''

And those could kill a person. If she let them.

Blake's eyes narrowed again, but with compassion rather than suspicion. "It sounds as though you know what you're talking about."

A memory surfaced. Briefly. She and Marcie, standing at the grave outside Maple Grove.

And then, nothing.

"You were talking about it at dinner last month," she reminded him with the surface confidence born of years of self-protection. Of the determination to survive. "Your ex-wife—and all the questions her passing raised."

"The doubts, you mean?" His fingers lay against the back of the sofa. "I hadn't seen in her in years. I know no logical reason to suspect that I'm partially to blame, that I might have done something differently, something that would have resulted in her making a different choice."

"But you wonder, anyway, don't you?"

He nodded. And he knew that she knew exactly what he was talking about. The look in his eyes told her he knew. And that he wasn't going to push further if she wanted to let it go.

"My mother..." she began.

She wanted to let it go.

He continued to watch her, while she attempted to force long-buried memories back into the darkness from which they'd come.

"I have a twin sister. Did I ever tell you that?" She knew she hadn't. Very few people in her San Diego life knew about Marcie. Or Maple Grove. And

Blake had never been in her life. Even during that time on the beach, conceiving a child with her, he hadn't been privy to her life. They'd talked about where they were going, not where they'd been.

His eyes widened. "A twin? There are two of you?"

Juliet chuckled. "I'm not sure if that tone in your voice means the idea of such a thing is good or bad."

"Completely startling!" he said, smiling at her.

"We're not identical," she told him. "We're the same size and pretty much the same shape, but she's got the most beautiful natural blond hair and blue eyes." California's dream.

Blake chuckled. "I can just imagine what the two of you must have done to all those pubescent boys in high school. An intimidating redhead and an innocent blonde. Side by side."

He thought her intimidating? He sure didn't act like it.

"How do you know she was the innocent one?"

Blake's eyes took on a glint that dared her to lie. "Am I wrong?"

"No." And then, when he said nothing more, "Why are you staring at me with that weird grin on your face?"

"It's not weird. I'm just getting over the shock of you as a twin. I always pictured you so independent."

Yeah, a lot of the world saw her that way. And that was her fault. "Nope, Marce and I are joined at the hip. Always have been."

"Her name's Marce?"

"Marcie." She grimaced. "Marcella, actually. Our mother named us after her two favorite heroines."

"Don't tell me, you're Juliet from *Romeo and Juliet?*"

Enjoying the laughter in his voice, Juliet turned a little more, lifted her arm to the back of the couch, her fingers within inches of his. "Don't laugh, Ramsden."

"So who's Marcella?"

"She's a magical little character who played with Raggedy Ann and Andy. It's an old book published back in 1929, but *Marcella* was my mother's favorite children's book, full of magic and whimsy and love. From what I can tell, the story embodied everything my mother was before she met my father. Blinded by that whimsy and love and her belief in magic, she ended up pregnant with Marce and me, got married and pretty much ruined the rest of her life."

Head tilted, he continued to study her in a way that left Juliet feeling strangely supported. "How so? She had two beautiful daughters."

"She had a self-centered philanderer for a husband. He'd only married her to avoid the scandal of leaving a young girl pregnant and alone—and therefore getting cut off from his father's fortune. Of course, he made her sign a prenup that denied her any rights to his wealth in the event of a divorce. Not that it mattered. After he squandered all the money, he ran off with a very wealthy older woman who supported him. As long as she was alive, he didn't have to work. So, since he had no actual income, my mother couldn't sue for child support." She tried to tell it as though it didn't matter because, if she tried hard enough, someday it wouldn't. "My mother's mother had been born and raised in Maple Grove, California, a little out-of-the-way migrant town. She'd gotten pregnant without being married, too, but hadn't fared nearly so well. The migrant worker she'd fallen for had moved on and she never heard from him again. With no other way to support herself and her daughter, no way to get out of that town and get some education, she spent her life doing laundry, cleaning houses, mending, picking fruit, anything she could do to afford a little trailer on a lot outside town.''

Juliet stopped, her throat dry and choked as she heard what she was saying. Things she didn't tell anyone. Things she tried never to think about. She had to leave now. Get back to her office. To real life.

Except Blake had taken hold of her fingers along the back of the couch. How could she not have known he was holding her hand?

"Go on."

"When our grandmother died, at the ripe old age of forty, my sister and I were still babies. She left my mom that little trailer in Maple Grove. When we were thirteen, Mom suddenly found herself an ex-rich socialite—humiliated, friendless, with no training, other than in how to dress nicely, spend money and sit on charity boards. So she ran home to the only other life she knew."

"And took you and Marcie with her."

"Yeah." To a town, a world, they'd never even heard of.

His fingers rubbed gently against the top of her hand. "That must've been rough."

She tried to smile. "It wasn't so bad for Marcie and me. We had each other."

"And your mom?" With eyebrows slightly raised,

his empathetic expression implied that he knew that part of the story wasn't easy.

"She cleaned houses, worked in the school cafeteria, took in laundry. And during my last year of law school, she swallowed a bottle of sleeping pills, ran a bubble bath, went to sleep and drowned."

Blake's exclamation wasn't anything she'd ever heard before. Or wanted to hear again. But she shared the sentiment. More than she wanted to.

"I'm over it now," she quickly assured him, sliding her hand from beneath his to wrap her arms around her middle. "It took a while, but once you work through all the guilt and misplaced responsibility, you move on."

"Do you?" The glance that had been so warm seconds before was piercing.

"Of course," she told him, nodding for emphasis. "What other choice do you have?"

"I'm not sure it's a matter of choice." He sat forward, head bent, elbows resting on his knees. "Do we choose to forget and move on? Or do we just push things away and refuse to deal with them?"

He wasn't just talking about her. She wished he had been. She'd have been able to defend herself against such an attack. But when she put herself in his shoes—wondering about his parents' deaths, and his ex-wife's—putting herself in Mrs. James's shoes, feelings arose that she wasn't prepared to face.

They'd been there, slowly attacking from the inside, since she'd first seen the news earlier that day, seen the press photo of Eaton James that had been shown on air during the trial, when there wasn't any bigger scandal to talk about.

"Can we *choose* to forget?"

"I think we can." She was a walking testimony to it.

"Really?" Turning his head, he glanced at her over his shoulder. "You've forgotten, then?"

Damn him.

"What do you suggest we do, Blake? Run around burdened down with all the problems and challenges life hands us—until they pile on so high they're too heavy and we die? Sounds suspiciously like what my mother did. And maybe your Amunet. And Eaton, too. There's got to be a better way."

He nodded. "Or maybe it's a question of the differences between people," he said. "Maybe some of us have a built-in defense mechanism that kicks in and protects us when life feels overwhelming, some sort of self-preservation. And the rest of us have other great characteristics but lack that core of self-preservation that will sustain us."

"Do you think so?"

He shook his head. "I honestly don't have any idea. It's just a theory I've come up with to try to understand."

But if he was right, if those types of people didn't have what it took to help themselves, wasn't it up to those around them to provide that help?

"In the end, we're each responsible for ourselves," Blake said, as though reading her thoughts.

It was something he'd done more than once on their long-ago night together.

What was it about this man that made him some-how...different?

They sat silently for several minutes, thoughts wan-

dering. She had to go, Juliet knew that. She just
wasn't ready to leave the peculiar sense of peace that
had settled around her.

Thinking about trying to explain the moment to
Marcie, she couldn't find a way. Blake's life was in
complete turmoil. Hers wasn't much better. And still,
in this room together, for these few minutes out of
time, they'd created a moment of calm.

It was a precious commodity.

"So how soon should I expect them?"

He hadn't moved, other than to turn his head on
the couch. Hadn't said who he was expecting, either,
but she knew. Them. The Law.

"Could be late this afternoon. Or tomorrow."

Licking his lips with the tip of his tongue, Blake
said nothing.

"It's always possible the grand jury will find that
Schuster doesn't have enough evidence." Possible,
but not likely. She just couldn't leave him sitting there
without hope.

"Schuster's as seasoned as they come," Blake
said, his voice a monotone. "How often do you think
he goes to the grand jury without sufficient evidence?"

"Never."

"That's what I thought."

"You'll call me?"

His gaze locked with hers. "You'll take the case?"

"If I can," she told him, wondering how the hell
she was going to get him off when the evidence so
clearly pointed to his guilt. And how she was going
to survive however many weeks it took to do the job,
becoming intimately acquainted with the father of her

child, torn to the roots of her soul about one solitary choice that had seemed so right at the time and now just seemed too huge to handle.

She couldn't tell Blake about Mary Jane now. That much was clear. The timing was all wrong. For everyone.

She could only hope that, by some miracle, she'd be able to hold things together for all three of them.

CHAPTER TEN

THERE WERE MANY REASONS Blake didn't sleep that night. Walking around the home he'd built upon his return to the States, he felt haunted.

By Amunet and the things he should have seen but didn't. The things he still didn't see. By Juliet and a night that had taken on surreal qualities in its perfection and therefore stood before him as a measure by which to judge every relationship he'd ever have—a measure by which every relationship could only fail. A measure that was pure fantasy.

Haunted. And hunted, too. By a judicial system he'd always taken for granted would offer him security and protection. Would they come with the light of dawn? To his home? His office? Would he soon no longer be free to wander his house in the dark? To hear the ocean as it crashed against the shore?

Was this all he'd ever be, what he was in this moment? Was there to be no chance for a family? A chance to have loved ones in his life again? People he could call his own?

And God in heaven—he knelt down at the window of his living room, fists and hands resting against the glass as he faced the ocean—he knew what they did to guys in prison.

When he couldn't stand the pain of viewing the

magnificent, moonlit ocean before him, he squeezed his eyes shut. And let the tears escape.

How the hell was he going to survive?

THEY CAME TO HIS HOME. Before Pru arrived for work Tuesday morning. Up and dressed in a blue suit, white pressed shirt and red tie, Blake was glad they'd spared him the discomfort of having his staff gathering around him. This particular moment he wanted to face alone.

"Mr. Blake Ramsden?" the uniformed man at the door asked.

"Yes."

The fifty-something peace officer held out his badge. "I'm Deputy Thomas from the sheriff's department, sir."

Blake read the badge because it seemed to be expected of him. He didn't doubt the credentials of his messenger.

"I need to give you this." The man held out a folded piece of paper, innocuous-looking for all the consequences implicit in its contents. "You've been charged with a crime, sir, and are required to appear at 8:30 a.m. Friday morning...." He named the branch of California Superior Court not far from Blake's office. "If you fail to appear there will be a warrant issued for your arrest."

Blake had a breakfast meeting with the mayor Friday morning. Not that he considered mentioning it. Guaranteed, neither Schuster nor the Superior Court of California gave a damn about Blake's breakfast. No matter whom it might be with.

Already his freedom was being curtailed. Whatever happened to innocent until proven guilty?

Blake took the document. Signed where he was told to sign. Thanked the man. And closed the door.

"I THANKED HIM!" were the first words out of his mouth ten minutes later when Juliet McNeil answered her phone.

"Thanked who?"

Somewhere in the back of his mind was the realization that she didn't ask who he was.

"It's only seven-thirty in the morning," was his reply. "I expected to get an answering machine. And you answered yesterday, too. I wouldn't have thought you'd spend much time in your office, answering phones. You hard up for cases, Counselor?"

Forearm leaning against the wall, Blake ran his other hand down his face. "I'm sorry, I don't even know what I'm saying," he continued. He held the hand clutching the folded paper above him.

"It's okay." Juliet's tone was soft, almost a whisper. "The number on my card is my cell phone. It takes messages just as effectively as an answering service would and cuts out the middleman."

Blake heard about half of what she said. He had her cell number. That was good.

"So you answer it at home?"

"Not usually," she said. "I saw your number come up on the screen."

He'd given it to her the previous day, just before she'd left his office. He hadn't expected her to memorize it.

"Who did you thank, Blake?"

"The deputy who served me."

He was standing in the kitchen, his back to the windows, avoiding the ocean. Today it didn't say anything to him but words he didn't want to hear.

"What's the charge?" Juliet asked.

"I don't know. I didn't read the document."

"Did you look at it?"

"No." He glanced up at the offending piece of paper. "It's still folded." Not that he held out any hope that not looking would change the result.

Right now, he needed more than hope. He needed strength, whatever he could muster. He needed this woman to represent him in court.

"You want to meet me at my office in an hour and we'll look at it together?"

"Sure, but don't you need to get that waiver?"

"It's done."

The muscles in Blake's stomach relaxed. She was reliable and quick and committed. She'd be able to take his case. He had the best on his side.

And he was going to be spending some of the darkest days he'd known with the best memory of his life.

"WAS THAT AUNT MARCIE? Why didn't she call our number?" Mary Jane asked as Juliet came into the kitchen Tuesday morning.

Mary Jane's skinny long longs swung back and forth beneath the table. In jeans, her white frilly blouse tucked in, the little girl was just finishing up the cereal Juliet had poured for her earlier.

"It wasn't Aunt Marcie."

"Who else calls us this early?"

Juliet checked the lunch she'd already packed for Mary Jane. Chips were there, on top, where they wouldn't be crushed. Juice box in the bottom. "It was work."

"Uncle Duane?"

Duane Wilson was one of the other partners in the criminal division at Truman and Associates, with whom Juliet often talked through her cases. He and his wife, Donna, had never been able to have children and, now in their mid-fifties, had "adopted" Mary Jane for their grandchild "fixes."

"No."

Mary Jane slid down, carried her bowl to the sink, turned on the water.

Juliet grabbed an orange for later. Looked in the freezer for dinner ideas and decided to just order pizza.

"Is it about that guy that died?" The little girl stood beside her at the freezer, her eyes full of that extraordinary mixture of empathy and childlike innocence.

God, how was she ever going to make this work?

Just as she didn't ever want her daughter to keep secrets from her, she didn't keep secrets from Mary Jane. But the little girl hadn't been herself lately, refusing to go to Brownies until the father-daughter banquet was over and she didn't have to hear about it anymore. And she'd brought home only an average grade on her math test the previous week.

Fine for many kids. A first for Mary Jane McNeil.

Any mention of her father—or any father—upset her. She was becoming obsessed with hanging on to the partnership she and Juliet had formed over the years.

She'd climbed into bed with Juliet twice in the past week.

"Yes," she finally said when her daughter's curl-framed face started to pucker with worry. "It absolutely does have to do with all of that." Completely true. If not complete.

The validation didn't seem to reassure the little girl. At least not immediately. Mary Jane continued to study her for several more seconds. Juliet's heart ached with the things she couldn't change, a world that was going to hurt her little girl no matter how diligently she tried to prevent it. There were just some things a mother couldn't do.

And she'd thought she'd already learned all the toughest lessons.

THERE WERE FOUR COUNTS of theft, four counts of fraud due to misrepresentation and one count of conspiracy—all class-two felonies. Maximum sentence fourteen years for each. And if the judge ruled that the sentences were to be served consecutively, that could mean one hundred and twenty-six years behind bars.

"I'm going to beat this." Blake sat on the edge of the upholstered chair in front of Juliet's desk in her office at Truman and Associates. Forearms on his knees, he looked down at his clasped hands. Looking for strength. He could do this. He just had to figure out how.

Juliet sat back opposite him, her olive green skirt and jacket a complement to the not-quite-pink chair.

Sliding the official notice into the back of a padded leather binder, she glanced over at him, pen poised above an empty legal pad. If not for her lipstick and skirt, she could have passed for the president of the United States, he thought, with that regal and confident bearing.

He was lucky to have her representing him.

"First things first," she told him, her voice even, all business. "The arraignment Friday morning. How much do you know about the process?"

Blake missed the warmth, but calmed in the wake of her professionalism.

"Absolutely nothing."

"Okay." She nodded, fire-lit curls falling over her shoulders. Blake would give almost anything to be back nine years, losing himself in those curls, instead of sitting there facing possible imprisonment. "It goes like this…"

Blake fought to remain calm and attentive as she spent the next ten minutes describing the actual procedure of the upcoming hearing. As each second passed, a sense of calm grew more elusive. More than anything, he needed to be out on the beach. Running. As fast and as far as he could.

"I'm assuming, from all you've said, that you intend to enter a not-guilty plea."

"Absolutely." There was a measure of peace in just saying the word. Of having even this minute bit of control—this one thing about which he was completely certain.

"And another thing." He could be cutting his own throat, but there was no room for compromise on this one. "We do this honestly."

Juliet's face hardened. "I always tell the truth."

Where were all the years' worth of people skills he'd acquired when he needed them most?

"Listen," he said, rubbing his hands together as he leaned forward. "I don't mean to offend you at all. I just know one thing about my life and particularly now, it's all I have to stand on. I am always honest. I don't play with the truth, or tell parts of it. I can lose my business, my health, my loved ones. In the end, all I have is my integrity and if I waver now when I'm facing the biggest challenge ever, then whether I beat the charges or not, I've lost everything."

The words renewed his strength. At least for the moment.

"I understand." Juliet crossed one leg over the other. "And I feel just as strongly about integrity as you do. I also happen to know that there are many levels of truth and sometimes you have to look beyond the obvious to get to the part that counts."

A logical justification for living life in shades of gray? Or one of those mysterious understandings that made life rich and full?

He had no idea. And a lot to think about.

Juliet spoke then about release conditions.

Blake's skin grew cold. Clammy. After his meeting with her in his office, he'd immersed himself in work. He hadn't given any more thought to what happened next. "What does that mean?" He'd assumed when they hadn't already arrested him that he was free, at least until after the trial.

"The judge will determine at the arraignment whether or not you should be held on bond and, if so, how much it will be. With these charges, it could be as much as a million dollars. You'll be taken into custody until the amount is paid.''

God in heaven, take me now. Even he couldn't scrape up that amount all at once. He'd be arrested. Sent to jail.

A pen tapping lightly on his knee brought his mind back from the abyss he'd been repeatedly falling into since Schuster's visit five days before. Juliet leaned down, bringing her face directly in front of his. ''We don't want that,'' she said, her glossy lips giving him something to concentrate on. ''The other option is to release you on your own recognizance. That's what we want.''

His own recognizance. Blake liked the sound of that. He could handle that.

Still bent over, he looked up at her. ''How does that happen?''

She sat back, her eyes steady as she watched him. ''Hopefully the prosecutor will recommend it.''

''Schuster?''

She nodded. ''I suspect that's what will happen. Considering the facts, it should. If for some reason it doesn't, then it's up to me to convince the judge that it would be appropriate for you to be released without bond.''

His gaze didn't waver. ''Can you do it?''

He'd feel a lot better if she'd smiled right then. ''I'll do my best, but we could be hurt by the fact that you left the country for four years without a single visit. To counteract that, I need to know everything there is to know about every single tie you have to this community. Your address, whether or not you

own your home, for how long, your exact job title
and where you stand with Ramsden Enterprises, any
other property you own, employees you have, local
family, friends.''

Blake sat up. Finally something to do. "I'll tell you
whatever you want to know."

And he did. He owned his home, had been in residence there—camping at first—since construction
began five years before. He was owner and CEO of
Ramsden, which was a nonstock company with an
impressive year-end bottom line. In addition to his
own home, he owned several properties that were being developed, he had more than one hundred employees, many more subcontractors he knew well and
trusted, many acquaintances, no living relatives anywhere, not many close friends. Except Donkor and
Jamila Rahman.

"They're here, locally?"

Blake shook his head. "Egypt."

Sighing, Juliet said, "The idea is to convince the
judge you're going to stay here, not flee to friends on
another continent," she told him. And then, looking
up with the familiar warmth in her eyes, asked,
"When was the last time you saw them?"

"A little over three weeks ago. At Amunet's funeral."

"And before that?"

"A few years. But we're in touch regularly."

"Once the trial gets going, would they be willing
to testify on your behalf?"

Fly across the world to come to his aid?

"Yes." Another certainty.

Blake hadn't even thought about Donkor finding

out about all of this. His employees, customers and business associates didn't even know yet. But they all would. Soon enough, too soon, everyone was going to know that Blake Ramsden was on trial for nine counts of felonious crimes. Even if he was able to prove his innocence, that stigma would never completely go away. There would be some who wouldn't forget.

Some who would always have doubts about him.

He'd done nothing but work hard, pay his bills and tell the truth. Yet, in the space of a few days, his image, his reputation and his life had been irrevocably changed.

"MY MOM ALWAYS tells the truth!"

Pumping as hard as she could, Mary Jane tried to get high enough not to hear what that stupid Jeff Turner was saying. She shoulda' picked the monkey bars for recess instead of the swings. No one was on the monkey bars.

"She does not." Jeff's face, almost as high as hers, whizzed past. "She says stuff…" He passed again.

"…in court that gets criminals…"

"…out of jail."

She was too high to let go of the chains to put her hands over her ears.

"Shut up, Jeff!" She hollered so loud it made her throat sting.

"It's the truth," Jeff yelled right back.

Mary Jane looked the other way when he passed. "I asked my dad," he said.

She heard his words anyway. The girls she wished were her friends were playing four square on the blacktop. She could hear them calling to each other. And laughing.

"Then your dad lies," Mary Jane screamed, just fed up with…everything. Human beings were just too hard to know. Putting her feet down in the dirt, she took the initial bump from fast to slow with only a small jerk at the back of her neck.

Jeff was slowing, too. Oh, no. If he was going to follow her around and say stuff that made her mad then she was going to go inside even if she wasn't allowed to at recess. Maybe she could go to the nurse and get her temperature taken.

Mary Jane's feet slid in the dirt, sending up a cloud of dust onto her favorite white jeans with the little blue butterflies stitched all over them. She wouldn't tell the nurse she was sick, because she wasn't. But she could ask to have her temperature taken.

And if that didn't work, maybe she'd have to skin her knee on the blacktop. That had gotten her out of recess once at her other school before this one.

"Mary Jane's mother is a liar!" the mean skinny freckle-faced boy said as they both came to a stop.

Mary Jane stood up, her face hot. "My mother does not lie!" She screamed even though she was stopped now.

"Does too!"

"Does not!"

"Does too!"

"You take that back, Jeff Turner."

"She lies and lets criminals go free and then they hurt people."

"Take that back!"

"No way," the boy said, grinning in a really mean

way that made Mary Jane want to hit him in the face. "Your mother lies!"

Stamping her foot, her tennis shoe kicking up more dust, Mary Jane gritted her teeth. "She does *not* lie." She had to get away from him. She was afraid she was going to cry.

Because she knew her mother didn't lie. Ever. But she was very scared there was something her mother wasn't telling her. Something big and important and bad. She'd been acting weird for days and then got that call the morning before, during breakfast, and then she was even weirder last night.

"She does, and so do you!" Jeff said, putting his face so close to hers, some of his spit landed on her chin.

"Gross! Get away from me," she hollered at him, pushing at his shoulder.

Jeff's hand flew out, pushing back. Hard. Mary Jane landed on her bottom, hands out behind her. Jeff walked past just leaving her there, and Mary Jane kicked him. She didn't mean to. But he was mean, and too close and he was just going to get away with saying all those horrible things.

When he turned around and kicked her back, she grabbed his foot and he fell.

And that was when Mrs. Thacker came out and saw them.

Mary Jane froze, her shin, where Jeff had kicked her, stinging. Waiting in fear, she watched her teacher approach. She was going to be sent to Mrs. Cummings again. Maybe even get kicked out of school. And all she'd wanted to do was swing and have recess be over so she didn't have to watch those girls play four square.

All she ever wanted to do was be good. So why was she always in so much trouble?

DRESSED IN HER red power suit, as Mary Jane had called it ever since hearing her mother say it one time on the phone to Marcie, Juliet showed up at the California Superior Court Building in San Diego at eight-twenty Friday morning. She'd hoped to be there sooner but had had another meeting with the intimidating Mrs. Cummings.

Surprisingly enough, this visit had not been so one-sided. Mr. Jeffrey Turner had been made to apologize not only to Mary Jane for pushing her down, but to Juliet for the slur on her good name.

And Juliet felt sick. Her once joyful, easygoing daughter had been in a fight at school with a boy. The fact that the boy had been slandering Juliet was no explanation. Mary Jane had always been gifted with an ability to let things slide off her too-skinny shoulders.

The child was holding far too much tension inside, if something as unimportant as an obviously inaccurate slur against her mother could trigger such uncontrollable behavior.

"Hi." Surprising how he could express such relief with one word. Or maybe it was the look in Blake's eyes as he approached her in the foyer outside their courtroom that told the story.

"Good. Brown suit, beige shirt, sedate tie, just like I asked," she said, looking him over from a purely professional standpoint. Brown was an earth color, and instilled feelings of dependability and solidity.

"I shined my shoes, too," he said, his attempt at a grin falling only a little short.

"And a fine job you did," she said, taking a breath deep enough to distance herself from the trouble with her daughter, as she stared down at the brown leather wingtips.

Blake sighed, shoved his hands in the pockets of his slacks. "I guess we should go in."

She squeezed his elbow. "Relax, we'll be fine. The most important thing is to appear cooperative while emanating confidence in your innocence."

"Yes, ma'am," he said. And then, with a look of quiet concern, "Is there a reason why, if you're so certain this will go well, you're so tense yourself? This has to be all in a day's work for you."

She was going to have to do better than this. The first day and already he was reading things she didn't want him to see. "Just came from arguing another case with another judge—so to speak."

He frowned. "You've already been in court this morning?"

"No," Juliet guided them toward the heavy wooden door of the courtroom. "I was in her office."

Blake held the door for her, allowing Juliet to enter before him. She passed beneath his arm, close enough to feel the heat from his body, and in that second, the worry of the morning settled into something more manageable.

Which worried Juliet. A lot.

CHAPTER ELEVEN

BLAKE TOOK IN the courtroom with one glance. It was smaller than he'd expected. Or perhaps just too close for him.

She'd told him there'd be anywhere from thirty to ninety people—defendants, prosecutors and defense attorneys. Arraignments were done all at once on certain mornings, ten to thirty at a time, and the court distributed a press release so at least there'd be no reporters. Each arraignment would take approximately two minutes. He was prepared.

Juliet motioned him to take a seat in one of the back rows and he gladly obliged. He preferred to have everything in front of him, where he could see it. And he appreciated that she'd somehow known that, or at least stumbled unknowingly on his first choice.

The judge's bench was empty. Too bad it couldn't remain that way. For a moment, Blake was back in fourth grade, maybe nine or ten, sitting in a chair in the waiting room of the dentist's office, waiting for his name to be called. He'd been there to have a cavity filled and the idea of having a needle poked into his mouth had been traumatizing him for days. He'd tried to speak with his father about his fears, about the risks of leaving the cavity unfilled. The old man had laughed at him. Told him it was merely a case of mind over matter and as a son of his, Blake would master that in no time.

Just think about baseball, his father had told him.

Blake hated baseball.

"They'll do any 'in custodys' first," Juliet leaned over to whisper. She smelled heavenly—an artistic cross between seductive and innocent. She'd obviously switched to a much more expensive perfume than the simple musk she'd worn nine years before.

Registering what she'd said, Blake looked over the thirty or so heads in front of them. "In custodys?" he repeated.

Paul Schuster walked in, pretended not to see them and took a seat on the opposite side of the room, one row up.

"The defendants who're locked up," Juliet said, pulling his attention back to her.

He looked around but didn't see any handcuffs. Or guards, either.

"If there are any, they'll be done via conference call. We'll just listen," she said. He nodded and wished she'd just keep talking to him. As horrible as the morning was, Blake was glad to have her there beside him. Her presence calmed him.

Some people at the front of the room stood. "All rise."

After being announced, the judge entered and sat. So did Blake. And he had the thought that he'd like to keep right on sitting there, feeling Juliet's warmth, until it was time to go home.

The ocean beckoned.

His LEGS STIFF, Blake sat straight as yet another twosome—attorney and client—filed out of the room.

This time the accused had been a woman in her mid-thirties, accused of drug and child abuse. He wasn't sure he believed her not-guilty plea. Judging by the impersonal look on her attorney's face, he wasn't sure that man did either.

He, Juliet and Schuster were the only ones left in the room. At least he'd been spared an audience to his humiliation.

Blake's nerves hummed. He itched to run. Never, in all the years living under his father's rule, had he felt this trapped.

"Blake Ramsden," the brown-haired judge called, looking over a pair of reading glasses to the almost-empty room.

Juliet was slightly in front of him as Blake approached the bench and stood. After obtaining a document of several pages from the court clerk, Juliet rejoined him. Schuster came up last, standing on the other side of Juliet.

Just as he had for every other defendant before Blake, Judge Henry Johnson read Blake his rights. The man looked friendly enough, not more than forty or forty-five, very few frown lines.

Pulling off his glasses, Judge Johnson looked straight at Blake, his expression serious. "How do you plead?"

Blake stood silently, as he'd been told to do.

"My client pleads not guilty, Your Honor."

Judge Johnson wrote something down, then lifted some papers and looked over at his clerk, who was glancing at the computer screen in front of her. She jotted something on a little piece of paper and handed it to the judge. Just as she had for every other case they'd watched that morning.

"Trial is set for July twenty-third, 8:30 a.m.," he said. Almost three months away, just as Juliet had predicted.

The judge glanced up again, his gaze skimming over Blake and Juliet to land on Schuster. "Let's talk about release conditions."

"Due to the fact that the defendant spent four years out of the country without so much as a visit to his elderly parents, added to the fact that he has no local family, the state recommends that the defendant be detained, Your Honor. And because there is at least one million dollars sitting in an account in the defendant's name in the Cayman Islands, we are asking that Blake Ramsden be held on a million-dollar bond."

A razor-sharp pain shot through Blake's chest. He'd been prepared, done what he could, but most of his money wasn't liquid. They were going to take him away from that room and lock him up. He'd been telling himself all morning that he just had to get through two minutes and then he'd be on his way to the beach. And back in his office, working, by noon. Juliet hadn't expected them to hold him.

Ignoring Blake, the judge turned to Juliet. "Ms. McNeil?"

She ignored Blake, too. Did that mean she wasn't going to be able to help him out of this one?

His first time up to bat and already he was striking out. He'd always struck out when his father had dragged him off to Little League practice, too.

Track had been his sport, not that his father had

ever noticed. It wasn't nearly as much of a spectator sport. Due to Blake's grandfather's requirement that Walter work after school from the eighth grade on, spectating was the only kind of athletics Walter Ramsden had been able to participate in.

Dad, if you're around anywhere, keeping that watchful eye on things, I could sure use some help, just this once.

"Your Honor, with all due respect, I believe that Mr. Schuster grossly underestimates my client's ties to this community," Juliet said. She moved one step closer to Blake and his breathing came just a bit easier. She might not be able to get him out of this, but she was here. Supporting him.

"He owns a home, sir, on a cliff overlooking the ocean in La Jolla. He's resided there for five years and it is his only residence." Juliet spoke as though her client owned a portion of heaven and could therefore be trusted.

The actual facts didn't sound like much to Blake, but it was all he'd given her to work with. She'd do everything she could. And she was the best.

"He is also the sole owner of a very successful company here in San Diego, with more than one hundred employees and subcontractors all over the state. And while he has no local family, sir, he has no family anywhere else, either, to whom he might be tempted to return." Her voice didn't rise or get dramatic, yet maintained a note of conviction.

"Mr. Ramsden has many, many acquaintances and friends in this city, sir, including the mayor, with whom he was scheduled to have breakfast this morning. San Diego is where he was born and raised. Other

than an educational stint abroad, encouraged and, in
part, funded by his father, he has never left this city
for more than the duration of a family vacation. His
life is here, sir. I believe that, in light of these ties to
his community, Mr. Ramsden should be released on
his own recognizance, sir. I can personally guarantee
that he will be present and ready to face charges at
eight-thirty in the morning on the twenty-third of
July.''

Blake stared.

She was a woman. Beautiful. Soft. Compassionate.
And she was a barracuda, daring anyone to disagree
with the obvious. Blake imagined she'd intimidated
many people over the years.

He didn't figure Thomas for one of them.

The judge looked him over. Put on his glasses
again. Read something in front of him.

''Very well, Counselor, I will take your word that
Mr. Ramsden will appear as ordered. Please advise
your client that he is not to leave the state. And Ms.
McNeil, if he does not appear back in this court on
the date and at the time designated, you'd better not
ask this court to take your word for anything—ever
again.''

''Thank you, Your Honor.'' Juliet didn't crack a
smile.

Blake did.

JULIET SET ASIDE the entire weekend to spend with
her daughter. From the time she picked her up from
school on Friday—as she did most afternoons unless
she had a late day in court, when Duane Wilson's
wife, Donna, did the honors—until she dropped the

child back at school on Monday morning, she was going to lavish every bit of attention she had on Mary Jane McNeil.

And sometime during that sixty-five-hour period, she was going to tell her daughter about her newest client.

She wasn't sure it was the right, the best or the fairest thing to do. She just knew she couldn't keep the appointment she had with Blake Ramsden on Monday morning to discuss his case and come up with a plan unless she'd come clean. Mary Jane had been willing to fight to protect her mother's honesty.

Juliet had no choice but to do the same.

She'd intended to tell her little girl on Friday night, but after dinner out at a local hamburger joint—Mary Jane's choice—the child had been taken with a fit of the giggles that had set the tone for the rest of the evening. They'd rented a silly movie, spilled popcorn in Juliet's bed while watching it and done each other's hair, and Juliet had painted Mary Jane's face.

It had been just what the doctor would've ordered, had he been asked, Juliet decided early Saturday morning, staring at the smooth and beautiful features of the child sleeping so peacefully beside her. Mary Jane's curls spiraled around her head like a dark halo. The little girl's rounded nose and full sweet lips almost brought tears to her eyes.

God, give me the words to tell her about Blake in a way that makes it okay for her.

She'd said this same prayer several times during the previous night, holding the child against her while she slept. She'd do anything for Mary Jane. It was just damn tough, sometimes, to know the best thing to do.

Give her a court of a law, an intimidating judge, a dishonest prosecutor, a wrongfully accused murderer, and she was fine. Give her a fifty-pound child with springy curls and eyes just like her own, and she had no idea what to do. There'd been no degree to get in motherhood. No Mary Jane manual.

And Juliet had never been comfortable with just winging it.

The phone rang and she panicked until she realized it was her home phone, not her cell. Blake Ramsden didn't have access to the unlisted number.

She reached over her still-sleeping daughter for the receiver on the nightstand.

"Hello?"

"Jules? Did I wake you?"

Juliet stretched. Grinned. "No, but I'm still in bed," she told her twin. "Mary Jane's here, too." The three McNeil women, together, at least in a sense. Her day was complete and it had only begun.

The little girl moaned, turned over.

"I need to talk to you."

Juliet's smile faded. With one last look to make sure that Mary Jane hadn't awakened, she slid out of bed.

"What's up?" she asked softly, tiptoeing out of the bedroom with the cordless phone and down the hall to the kitchen. Normally Mary Jane could sleep through an earthquake—except, of course, for those few times when Juliet needed the child to stay asleep. She seemed to have some kind of sensor that alerted her to those.

"I...I..." Marcie hiccuped.

"Marce? Talk to me." Juliet's voice was firm, but it hid a heart full of fear. If Hank had hurt her...

"You aren't sick, are you?" She held her breath until she knew. Anything else they could handle.

"No."

"You're sure?"

"Positive."

Okay. Her sister was talking. One-answer questions seemed to be the trick. "Is it Hank?"

"No." The word broke on another hiccup.

"If he did anything..."

"He didn't." Marcie's words were quick. Too quick?

"He doesn't know..."

"Know what?"

"Jules?" Marcie's generally controlled tone rose in a wail.

Juliet sank to a chair at the kitchen table, staring out at the ocean. There had been times in her life when that view had been the only thing that saved her. Its vastness and strength, its vitality, and its unwavering existence always helped put life in perspective. "Yeah, Marce, I'm right here."

"Are you busy?" At seven o'clock on a Saturday morning?

"No."

"Can I fly down?"

Juliet's stomach knotted. "Of course. You got a flight or you need me to call for one?"

"I've got one." She named a flight that left San Francisco in a little under three hours.

That was good then. If her sister was capable of

making flight plans, things couldn't be all that bad. Could they?

"You going to make me wait until you get here to tell me what's going on?"

"Nooo…" Marcie's hiccup strayed to a sob. "Oh, God, Jules, I can't believe, after everything…"

"What?"

"I can't believe I've been so stupid."

What could be so difficult to talk about? Juliet twisted a finger in her hair, something she hadn't done since she'd been a first-year lawyer and learned that the gesture was a sign of inner weakness.

"You've done something?"

"I…I…I can't seem to tell you, Jules. You're never going to believe I was this stupid."

"Just say it." Juliet fought the tension gripping her, so that she could give her sister the empathy she so clearly needed.

Something she'd be a lot better equipped to do if she knew what she was trying to be empathetic about.

"Is it about money?" She crossed her fingers. That would be an easy fix.

"No."

And then something a little more horrific occurred to her. "You aren't in trouble with the law, are you?"

"No." Marcie almost chuckled, but hiccuped instead. "Of course not."

Juliet laid her cheek on her hand. Her voice lowered, softened. "Tell me."

"I'm…pregnant."

Juliet's entire body stiffened. Her skin felt hot. And then cold. The phone started to slip from her hand.

"Say something."

She would. As soon as she could think.

"I love you."

Inane, maybe, but it was all she could come up with.

"I love you, too," Marcie said, and sniffled.

"Hey, Marce, don't cry." Her sister's tears brought Juliet's mind at least partially back to action. "We'll get through this. You know we will. We always do. Together."

The assurance was as much for herself as for her sister. "You're coming here. That's the right choice."

She had to get Marcie out of Maple Grove. Away from settling for life in a trailer, raising a child alone only to have the child go off and find a better life, a fuller life, leaving Marcie with nothing but a bottle of sleeping pills and a bathtub filled with bubbles....

"It's only for the weekend," Marcie said. "I have to open the shop on Monday."

"Who cares about the shop?" Juliet said, half-crazed with panic and half-determined to take control and make sure that they all lived happily ever after.

"I do."

Yes. She knew that. "I'm sorry, Marce. It's just a bit of a shock, you know?"

"Tell me about it." The droll tone didn't erase the tears in Marcie's voice, but it helped calm Juliet anyway.

"Okay, did I hear you say Hank doesn't know?"

"Yeah."

Good. That gave them time to figure things out before Marce was pulled in ways she might not want to go. As their mother had been.

"And you aren't planning to tell him? At least not this morning, before you fly out?"

"No. I don't know what I'm going to do."

What did that mean?

"You're having the baby, right?" She couldn't believe she was asking.

"Of course."

"And keeping it?" Neither of them would ever consider anything else. They'd been abandoned by a parent. Twice.

"Of course."

"Good, so go pack, get down here, and we'll figure out the rest."

"Okay." A loud sniffle sounded again.

Juliet watched waves roll onto the beach in the distance, wondering how many generations of babies had been born, how many generations of people had died, while that water just kept right on rolling in and out.

"How long have you known?"

"The time it took for you to answer your phone," Marcie said, speaking the entire sentence without a sob. "I knew I'd be in trouble if what I suspected was true, so I made the plane reservation, dialed your number on my cell phone and waited until I got the results before I hit send."

That sounded more like the Marcie she knew.

"I'm only about a month along. I bought the test four days ago," her twin continued, apparently needing to get things out now that she could speak. "Every night I told myself I'd do it, but I just kept thinking that ignorance was better than the truth. I guess I was probably just waiting until I was free to fly down."

The fact that Marcie had needed to come to San Diego during her time of crisis was not lost on Juliet. Her sister might be more aware, less like their mother, than Juliet had begun to fear these last couple of years. She just needed a loving boost to give her the courage to take those first frightening steps out of Maple Grove and the false sense of security she had found there.

"Does Hank know you're coming here?"

"Not yet. I planned to call him from the airport."

"You're driving yourself in?"

"Yeah." Marcie sighed, sounding exhausted, which she probably was. Remembering back to her own trip into this same hell, Juliet doubted that her sister had slept more than a few restless hours all week. "I know it's more expensive to park the car, but I want the time alone."

"I understand."

"I gotta go if I'm going to make my flight," Marcie said, her voice weakening again.

"Okay. Be safe, Marce. I'll be right here waiting for you. You aren't alone, you know? You aren't ever alone."

"I know."

"And while you're on that plane?"

"Yeah?"

"Think about nothing but what an incredible joy Mary Jane has been all these years."

"You'd do it all again, wouldn't you?"

"Absolutely," Juliet said.

It was about the only thing she knew for sure.

CHAPTER TWELVE

THE PAPERS ON THE DESK in front of him were just as he'd left them. Same issues. Same unanswered questions. Same requests.

There was security in that.

Filled with what felt like a healthy dose of determination, Blake sat behind his desk Saturday afternoon, feeling better equipped to face what was to come. It was the first time he'd been to the office since the arraignment. He'd intended to come the day before, to carry on as though it were business as usual—partially to convince himself it was. But in the end, he hadn't been able to make himself do it.

He'd called Lee Anne to let her know he'd be in on Saturday afternoon and to ask her to leave anything that needed his immediate attention on his desk. He'd spent Friday at the ocean instead. Running on the beach, strolling along the water's edge with the seagulls, letting the waves wash over his bare feet, sitting in the sand watching the tide roll in, skipping rocks. He'd even bought a ticket for one of the tourist cruises and had dinner with a boatful of strangers out on the water.

Mourning the family he'd never had, he'd never felt lonelier in his life.

Today, Blake was back, in jeans and a polo shirt

instead of a suit. Working on a weekend when most of his employees were off. It was a start.

There had been several messages for him at home the night before, from people who knew him well enough to have the unlisted number. They'd heard about the arraignment on the news and, he was certain, had questions.

He'd answer all of them. He owed them that. But he owed himself this time to toughen up first. Having those he trusted doubting his trustworthiness was one of the worst things he could imagine—other than going to prison.

There were more calls on his office line. He listened to them, but didn't return any. Just like the others, he'd deal with them later.

He went through the mail. Pretty much standard fare, as the postal service didn't move as quickly as telephone technology. There was a thank-you note from Amunet's adoptive parents for his help with her service. Apparently Amunet had spoken highly of him when she'd finally come home to New York.

Had that been before or after she'd decided to take her life?

There was an invitation to give an address at the 61st Annual International Builders' Convention and Exposition in Orlando the following January. It was easily the world's largest annual construction trade show, for home as well as commercial builders—and under normal circumstances, Blake would have accepted the honor proudly.

But could he? They needed a response by early next month.

He dropped the invitation in the teakwood box on

a corner of his desk to look at again in another week or two. Not that he'd have any better idea than he did now whether he'd be a free man in January of next year.

Blake's computer beckoned. While he had a staff of talented architects, there were some design jobs he still took himself. It was the part of the business he loved best.

And that library project had been calling to him all week. This afternoon, all distractions aside, he intended to lose himself in trusses and structure and yet-to-be developed aesthetics. If he could sustain the drive, if the work could keep the demons at bay, he'd work all night.

But first, there would be e-mail. Since he did far more communicating electronically than by phone or post these days, he expected there'd be a lot.

He pushed the power button and waited while the machine booted up. It never ceased to amaze him that no matter how much he invested in computers, how much faster each new version worked, it never seemed fast enough for long.

That, he supposed, was why the leaders in the computer industry were so rich.

A noise sounded in the outer office. Blake glanced over, on edge. Expecting to be there alone, he hadn't shut his door.

If it was a reporter, come to hound him...

"Sir?" He recognized Lee Anne's voice just outside his door.

"Yeah, Lee, come on in," he called, relieved and yet not. Lee Anne had a family to feed single-handedly. Could she afford to wait around to see whether or not she still had a job after July?

"I'm sorry to disturb you, Mr. Ramsden," she said, coming in a little hesitantly. He'd never seen her in jeans before. A sundress once, at a company picnic the previous summer. But never jeans. They made her look younger.

"I just wanted to bring you this."

She placed a decorated gift bag on his desk. "See you Monday, sir."

"Thank you," Blake called to her retreating back. And then he realized that he had no idea if there was anything to be thanking her for.

Still, in all his travels and studies and experience, he'd never heard of anyone quitting with a gift bag.

Curious, he pulled it closer, surprised by its weight. Underneath a wealth of white tissue paper, he found a triangular frosted glass paperweight. Inscribed in the center of it was his favorite quote from nineteenth-century author, songwriter and motivator M. H. McKee: *Integrity is one of several paths. It distinguishes itself from the others because it is the right path, and the only one upon which you will never get lost.*

Blake stared for a long time and then placed the paperweight in the center of his desk, where he would see it every time he looked up.

The ocean-scene screen saver he'd chosen was scrolling through scenes. Tapping an arrow key to stop it, Blake settled in to work. He opened his e-mail software but before it could download his messages, there was another sound from outside his door.

Stu Walters, his chief accountant, stood on the

threshold. "Just had to leave this," he said. Walking in, he set a small wooden box on Blake's desk, and left. Blake glanced down and inscribed on the lid he read, *The man who fears no truths has nothing to fear from lies.* Sir Frances Bacon.

Bailey Warren, a talented young architect who'd been with Blake since college, was next. He brought a glass letter opener inscribed with words from someone named Jim Stovall. *Integrity is doing the right thing, even if nobody is watching.*

Melinda Nelson arrived just as Bailey was leaving. She was from Contracts. She left a water globe of a boat on the ocean with an inscription on a gold plaque attached to the block of wood that held it. From Samuel Taylor Coleridge. *Our own heart and not other men's opinions form our true honor.*

His full-time construction attorney, Fred Manning, gave him a promise of full support and a plaque that read: *Virtue, morality, and religion. This is the armor, my friend, and this alone that renders us invincible.* Patrick Henry.

An hour later, Blake was sitting there completely bemused, speechless and dangerously close to blubbering like an idiot. He'd seen more than twenty of his hundred employees, many bringing gifts from groups of others. On the desk in front of him was seemingly every size, shape and design of plaque, wall hanging, paperweight, letter opener, caddy or other office gift, every single one of them inscribed with messages about integrity.

Character is the accumulated confidence that individual men and women acquire from years of doing the right thing, over and over again, even when they don't feel like it. Alan Keyes.

Blake had never heard of Alan Keyes, but he felt a great fondness for him.

As he sat there, taking it all in, a quote from Molière caught his eye. *If everyone were clothed with integrity, if every heart were just, frank, kindly, the other virtues would be well-nigh useless, since their chief purpose is to make us bear with patience the injustice of our fellows.*

And there was the one he came to again and again, given to him by the group in the mailroom. A Chinese proverb. *If you stand straight, do not fear a crooked shadow.*

They forgot just one.

I am a very lucky man. Blake Ramsden.

SUNDAY AFTERNOON, when Juliet and Mary Jane would ordinarily have been taking Marcie to the airport for her flight back to San Francisco and the drive to Maple Grove, Marcie and Juliet took Mary Jane, a blanket and a picnic outside to the beach, instead.

The day was deceptively perfect, a balmy seventy degrees, sun shining brightly.

"How come you don't have to go back today, Aunt Marcie?" the girl half called over her shoulder, skipping along in the sand in front of them. It was a private stretch of beach, open only to the home owners in the area. This afternoon, no one else was outside. Several of the cottages near them were summer and vacation getaways and frequently vacant.

"I called Tammy and asked her to take my clients tomorrow," Marcie said softly, sharing a worried glance with Juliet, a worry the pure blue sky overhead couldn't assuage.

Juliet wanted to tell her sister that everything would be just fine. She tried to convey that with her eyes and her smile. But she couldn't really. Because she was worried, too, about their futures—and, at the moment, about Mary Jane's reaction to the upcoming conversation.

At least one of the things they had to tell the little girl wasn't going to go well. Juliet was certain of that. Just as certain as she was that she had to tell her.

Wearing denim shorts with a long-sleeved pink T-shirt, Mary Jane bounced on ahead of them, their self-appointed spot picker.

Juliet was happy to let her go. She and Marcie had talked long into the night and both were pretty sure about what had to be done. For all of them. It just wasn't going to be easy.

"Right here," Mary Jane said, choosing a spot in the center of the private beach, some distance from their cottage. It was just like her, always wanting to be in the middle of things.

Seagulls hopped down by the water. The waves were calm, a steady flow back and forth, bringing in little treasures—and taking some with them.

"I'm going to look for shells," Mary Jane announced, kicking off her flip-flops.

"No, you're not," Juliet told her. She used Mary Jane's shoes to weigh down two corners of the blanket, kicking off her own sandals to get the other two corners. "Have a seat."

Marcie pulled bottles of water out of the canvas

bag they'd packed. There was fruit, bread, cheese and cookies as well, but it was still too early to eat.

With a pinched face, Mary Jane sat on top of one of her sandals. "What's wrong?" she asked, passing a frightened look between her mother and her aunt. "Is this about me?"

"No," Marcie said with a surface grin as she kicked off her backless tennis shoes, pulled up the legs of her navy running suit and joined her niece. "Not everything in the world is about you, Squirt."

"I know that."

Moving the bag to one edge of the blanket, Juliet finally had nothing left to do but join the other two. Sitting cross-legged, she formed the third point of the McNeil family triangle.

"Sweetie, your aunt Marcie and I have a couple of things to tell you."

Mary Jane's green eyes widened. "Two of them?" Though she was picking at a yarn tie on the quilt, her gaze met Juliet's.

"Yep."

"Big things?"

"Uh-huh." Juliet nodded. She was still wearing the black Lycra pants and white Hollywood T-shirt she'd put on to in-line skate that morning. She and Marcie had come down to the beach with coffee, instead, to keep talking.

"Am I in trouble?" Mary Jane's timid voice pulled at Juliet.

"No, you're not."

The eight-year-old's shoulders relaxed slightly as some of the tension eased out of her small frame. Before she'd had Mary Jane, Juliet had never guessed how much another person's happiness and peace could mean to her. How much she'd give to have every single pain Mary Jane would ever feel come to her instead.

"Should I go first?" Marcie asked, looking from one to the other.

Juliet nodded. It might be better if she told Mary Jane about Blake first, and then followed up with Marcie's less threatening news, but if Marcie was going to offer even this small reprieve, she was willing to take it. Maybe some magical way to present things would occur to her in the meantime. Because as it was, she had no idea what she was going to say to her daughter.

"What's wrong, Aunt Marcie?" Mary Jane asked, frowning at her aunt with concern. "Are you going to marry Hank?"

"Nooo!" Marcie half chuckled, half choked. "You know neither one of us wants to get married. But if I was, I'd hardly call that something being wrong!"

"Wellll." The child drew out the word. "It would mean that you're staying in Maple Grove forever and you always say you don't want to do that."

Marcie and Juliet exchanged another glance. *Out of the mouths of babes.*

"No, I'm not marrying Hank," Marcie said, knees up to her chin, holding her toes. "Actually, things are going to change a lot. I'd like to move in with you and your mom," she said, and then, before the girl could respond, continued. "Your mom already said it was fine with her, when I asked her, but it has to be okay with you, too, since it means you'd have to give up your playroom for good instead of just the times I visit.''

''I don't play in there anyway.'' Mary Jane's face was straight.

''But?''

The little girl shrugged. ''Just…sometimes…Mom and me…but when you're here…''

''You love having Aunt Marcie here,'' Juliet said, confused and feeling slightly protective of her twin, who looked as if she might cry again. Juliet hadn't expected any resistance at all from Mary Jane on this issue, which didn't bode well for what was to come. ''You can't wait for her to visit.''

''I know,'' Mary Jane said. ''But…''

''What?'' Juliet felt lost.

Mary Jane looked at her aunt, and then back at Juliet. ''It's just that, when you guys are together, you're the pair. And then I'm…''

Understanding hit. ''Oh, Mary Jane, come here,'' she said, dragging her daughter across the blanket and onto her lap. ''You and I will *always* be a pair. No matter who else is around or in our lives.''

Mary Jane stared up at her, the brown flecks in her eyes glistening.

''You're going to grow up someday and maybe get married, and have kids, and the special love you and I share will still be right there. Unchanging. Do you understand?''

The little girl nodded, her sweet dark curls jostling against her cheeks.

''You are my daughter, flesh of my flesh, heart of my heart. And nothing, not even death, will change that. Ever. Got it?''

"Yes." Mary Jane was still subdued.

"And we'll always have our time, just you and me," Juliet continued, finding words from someplace. "While Aunt Marcie lives with us, you can pick a night of the week, or a weekend day, or both, and it'll be just the two of us."

Looking over the child's head, Juliet caught an expression of longing—and fear—on her twin's face. Was Marcie imagining a similar moment, with her child in her lap needing assurance and love?

"And you and Aunt Marcie can have a day, too, if you'd like," she said, still watching her sister. Marcie smiled, nodded, and still appeared on the verge of tears.

"Okay," Mary Jane said. "Because, you know, Mom, Aunt Marcie likes to look for sand crabs *and* go to museums and you don't."

Juliet turned the child so she could look her straight in the face. "So, you're okay with her moving in with us?"

Mary Jane's nod was enthusiastic. "When are you coming?" she asked her aunt, sliding back down to the quilt. "Today? Does Hank know? And what about your shop and people?"

"I don't know how soon," Marcie said, her blond hair shadowing her face as she smiled down at the child. "Maybe next week if I can get the arrangements made. And no, Hank doesn't know yet and I'm going to ask Tammy if she wants to buy out my half of the business. She'll have to hire someone to take over my clients, or I can try to find someone for her."

Mary Jane nodded. "Hank'll sure be surprised."

"Yeah." Marcie frowned. "But if we really loved

each other, we would have wanted to get married a long time ago,'' she said. ''And since neither of us has ever wanted that, I think we probably don't.''

''So if he doesn't love you that much, Hank pro'bly'll get over it pretty quick,'' Mary Jane said, her forehead creased in a frown.

''Probably.''

''Man, he's dumb!'' the child said.

Marcie's answering smile faded quickly. And then the conversation faltered. Remembering back nine years, to her own feelings of panic and uncertainty, Juliet tapped her daughter on the knee.

''There's a reason Aunt Marcie is moving in with us, sweetie,'' Juliet said.

''Because she's going to work at a studio?''

''No. Because she's going to have a baby.''

The little girl's mouth dropped, her eyes wide. ''You *are?*'' She stared at her aunt.

With a tremulous smile, Marcie nodded.

The sound of waves lapping against the sand was comforting in its unchanging routine. Juliet concentrated on it.

Mary Jane glanced at Marcie's slim belly, and then back up. ''A boy or a girl?''

''I don't know yet,'' Marcie said. ''It's too soon to tell stuff like that.''

Looking down again, Mary Jane asked, ''But you're sure it's in there, right?''

''Positive.''

''Well, then, we're going to have to get the crib out of the attic.''

And that was that.

Juliet hoped the second topic of conversation would go even a quarter that well.

MARY JANE INSISTED the baby was going to be a girl—to make them two pairs. She spent the next twenty minutes, as they unwrapped the cheese and bread and fruit, trying out different names. So far she'd settled on six of them. She ate enough, steadily, so the food was disappearing, although her mother and aunt had done no more than eat a grape or two.

Juliet shifted her weight, the sand hard beneath her.

"So what was the second thing to talk about?" Mary Jane asked, chocolate-chip cookie crumbs on her lips as she chewed. Clearly, she thought she'd heard the worst of it.

"I…" Juliet started. Stopped. Looked out at the ocean. "I…"

"Your mother has a new client," Marcie said. "And you're not going to like who it is and you're probably going to think there's more to it than there is, but there isn't, and you're just going to have to trust us on that one."

"Huh?"

"Blake Ramsden's been charged with fraud and he's asked me to represent him." It wasn't how she'd wanted to break the news, but other words failed her.

Mary Jane's mouth froze. The cookie in her hand crumbled. And her eyes creased, their depth lit with sheer panic in the bright sunlight.

"And you told him no, right?" the child asked as though warding off a blow.

Juliet was aware of Marcie next to her, watching them, but she kept her gaze focused strictly on her daughter. "Is that what you'd want me to do, Mary Jane?"

"Yes."

On one hand, Juliet completely understood—had expected this, even—but another part of her was disappointed.

"She's only eight years old," Marcie's voice came softly beside her. Juliet listened for the waves—for reassurance—and for whatever voice inside was going to tell her what to do next.

"He's a man I once knew, Mary Jane. Someone who was kind to me, made me laugh, gave me the greatest gift I will ever receive…"

The little girl stared, the expression in her eyes a mixture of belligerence, fear and a small hint of that peculiarly mature blend of tolerance and innocence with which she normally approached life.

"And I think someone might be framing him for a crime he didn't commit," Juliet continued. She'd always told Mary Jane the truth. In the end, it was the one thing the child could count on and Juliet wasn't going to let her down. Their entire relationship was built on that trust. "If he doesn't find a way to prove that, he could spend the rest of his life in jail."

Juliet waited. Continued to watch her daughter's bent head. The child was hugging one upraised knee, the remains of her chocolate-chip cookie still clutched in one hand. Little bits of melted chocolate oozed through her fingers.

"Why does it have to be you?"

She could hardly make out the mumbled words.

"Because I'm familiar with the case. Because he

trusts me. And because I'm one of the best defense attorneys in the state.''

''I don't want you to.''

''I know, sweetie, and I thought about that,'' Juliet said, hurting, as she watched her daughter struggle. ''But there's no reason this can't work out just fine for all three of us.'' She'd worried about finding the right words, but in the end, they just started to flow.

''How many times, in the past eight years, have you met any of my clients?''

Mary Jane glanced up. ''None.''

''Okay, so percentages say you don't have a whole lot to worry about there. If you've never met one of my clients, and they've never met you, why should this time be any different?''

''I guess...''

''Now,'' she hurried on when Mary Jane took a breath as though preparing to argue. ''Second, there's me.'' The little girl looked scared again. ''For eight years, my life has been very, very blessed because of you. Sometimes I start to feel a little guilty about that.'' The admission wasn't easy. ''Because Blake Ramsden doesn't even know about you and has never had a chance to be happy knowing you.''

The girl's face paled. ''You said you weren't going to tell him about me unless I—''

''I'm not planning to tell him about you,'' Juliet interrupted. ''But right now, his life isn't happy or blessed at all, and if I can help him, if I can win him his freedom, then I've sort of paid him back. Do you see that?''

Mary Jane's nose crinkled. She ground her chin against her knee. Marcie reached over, ran her fingers through Mary Jane's curls. "You don't have anything to be afraid of, sweetie."

Mary Jane raised her head. "Kind of like a life for a life?" she asked Juliet, her tone a little less defensive.

"Kind of."

"I still don't like it."

"I know."

"You promise you won't tell him about me?"

"Not without telling you first."

Mary Jane didn't look satisfied, but after staring intently for a long moment, she didn't argue the point any further.

CHAPTER THIRTEEN

MARCIE STARTED loading empty sandwich wrappers into the canvas bag they'd brought with them. Mary Jane continued to sit, now hugging both knees.

Thinking about the man who was her father?

"Is there anything you'd like to know about him?" Juliet asked, just in case.

Did the child ever wonder what kind of person Blake was? Whether he was smart? Or liked dogs?

"So you're *sure* he didn't do it?"

Leave it up to Mary Jane to find the most difficult question. "I don't know, sweetie, but I don't think so."

The little girl nodded. "I don't think so, either."

She leaned over to the edge of the blanket, opened her hand and dropped the cookie she'd been holding. With a quick brush of her hand, she jumped up.

"Can I go look for shells now?"

Feeling there was more she should say, Juliet just nodded. And Mary Jane ran off.

"That went surprisingly well," Marcie said, lying back on the blanket and closing her eyes.

Outwardly, Juliet agreed with her sister. But as she watched her daughter strolling listlessly by the water, her heart told her differently. This wasn't over yet. Not by a long shot.

ON MONDAY, Blake went to the pound and picked out a puppy. A Labrador-greyhound mix—pitch-black with a long nose, pointed ears that stood upright and looked too large for its small head and a skinny tail that hung down almost to the floor. He'd toyed with the idea all weekend. It was a positive move, manifesting his belief that he'd be free to raise the pup. He'd accepted the January speaking engagement, too.

Buying a puppy was something he'd often thought about since returning to San Diego—he liked the idea of having something to come home to at the end of a long day. Or to spend time with on weekends that sometimes stretched too long.

But he couldn't quite escape a twinge of guilt at the thought of taking the pup home, making them a family, only to have to abandon the little guy to someone else three months later—three months older, three months less adaptable—as his master went to prison.

Still, getting up Tuesday morning after an almost sleepless night, Blake felt better than he had in weeks.

"Freedom, my boy, you win," he told the whining pup as he let him out of the crate he'd purchased the day before. "Tonight you sleep on the bed, so we can both sleep."

Freedom yawned, shook himself, wagged his tail and peed all over Blake's shoe.

JULIET CALLED early Tuesday afternoon. He thought about telling her about the pup, or the series of gifts taking up every bit of available space in his office, but she was all business.

"I've heard from Paul Schuster," she told him, her tone without inflection—not welcome, doom or even boredom. ''When would be a convenient time for us to meet?''

He offered to come to her office immediately. She preferred to come to his. Blake didn't argue.

''SCHUSTER'S OFFERED a plea agreement.''

She'd only just arrived, barely taken time to give him a somewhat unfocused smile of hello, before she'd taken the seat he'd indicated on the couch and opened her satchel.

Blake had been about to offer her something to drink. Instead he sat down. Hard.

''Meaning?''

She met his gaze for the first time since she'd arrived. ''He's offered to lessen the charge to two counts of fraud.''

Her suit was navy today, with a slim knee-length skirt, white blouse and short tailored jacket.

''If I plead guilty?'' he asked. Blake had been doing a lot of reading on a subject of which he'd been completely ignorant. The details of criminal proceedings had just never interested him.

Juliet nodded.

Slow down, he admonished himself when he might have bitten out an instant refusal. He had to take this calmly. One step at a time. Detaching from emotion so that he could think.

''Why would he be willing to do that?'' Because he wasn't so sure he could make the original charges stick? Then why press them in the first place? Unless something had happened between last week and this.

''Two reasons,'' Juliet said, leaning forward as she explained, her voice softening to the tone he'd grown to expect from her. "First, it's palatable to the prosecutor because it puts the onus on the judge. Second, it's easier—and less time-consuming—than going to trial."

"I hadn't read Paul Schuster as a man who takes the easy way out." Blake still wanted to believe that something had happened to make the prosecutor less confident that he could win.

Juliet smiled, almost as though she knew what he was thinking. "It's not the easy way out. He's spent a lot of time on this case, he thinks he's got his man, and now he's ready to move on to get the next one."

"He's bored," Blake translated.

"I wouldn't put it that way, but you're a first offender, Blake, and to Schuster, this isn't nearly as big as Eaton's alleged fake companies. He knows, no matter how good a case he builds, you aren't going to get a maximum sentence anyway."

If you stand straight, do not fear a crooked shadow.

Blake read the Chinese proverb. He'd hung the plaque by the door to his office so he saw it every time he glanced up from his desk—and again every time he left his domain.

"What happens if we accept the agreement?" He wasn't going to. He couldn't. Because to do that would be a lie. He wasn't guilty.

"You get a maximum of fifteen years."

"And realistically?"

"Seven to seven and a half."

Seven and a half years in prison didn't sound any different to Blake than a lifetime.

"Tell Schuster no thank you." As soon as he got

home tonight he was going to teach Freedom how to run on the beach.

"You're sure?" Juliet asked, though her expression was completely calm, as though she'd expected as much. "You don't want to think about it?"

"There's nothing to think about," Blake told her. "I didn't do it."

She didn't reply. At least not with words. Her gaze, as it held his for seconds longer than might have happened had they not been alone, seemed to gleam with support.

MARCIE CALLED on Wednesday night, just as Juliet was about to grab a can of Mace and a walkie-talkie that allowed her to hear if Mary Jane woke up, and head out to the beach.

"I told Hank I was leaving."

Her twin sister had been crying.

"Did you tell him why?" They'd discussed both sides of that particular issue. Juliet thought Marcie should tell him. Marcie had been afraid that if she did, and he pressured her to marry him, she'd give in.

"Yes."

"And?"

"He wants me to marry him."

Portable phone in hand, she stepped just outside the back door, to feel the sand beneath her bare feet and be closer to the waves that had a way of promising her that life would go on.

"We suspected that." In some ways, Hank was an old-fashioned guy.

"Yeah." Marcie sounded tired. Beaten.

Juliet held her breath, crossed her fingers and prayed that Marcie hadn't traded her soul for the false lure of safety and security their mother had. If Marcie was head over heels in love, that would be one thing, but... "And?"

"I said no."

Whew. Juliet's breathed hissed out on a long sigh. "How'd he take that?"

Marcie chuckled. As much as she could while choking back tears that had obviously been falling a lot already that evening. "He said he'd like to help me move, that he was going to be financially responsible starting immediately, and that he wasn't ever going to quit asking."

"In that order?"

"Yeah."

"That was decent of him."

"He's a decent man."

But not what Marcie had ever said she wanted. And not where her sister wanted, either. Marcie wanted to travel. And to meet new people. She wanted a busy life, social and involved in the world around her.

She didn't want to sit at home every night in Maple Grove and watch life go by on the television screen.

And that was all Hank had ever wanted.

Marcie wanted magic when she looked across the dinner table every night and woke up every morning.

Juliet understood. It was what she'd always wanted, too.

That was a part of their mother they'd both inherited. The part that, if they weren't careful, could kill them. Just as it had her.

ON FRIDAY NIGHT, one week after Blake's arraignment and two days before her sister rented a truck and drove from Maple Grove to San Diego, Juliet called Marcie.

"Hey, Jules, only two more days," Marcie said, out of breath from packing as she answered the phone.

She sounded energized, as though now that her decisions had been made, she was ready and hopeful about what the changes would bring.

"Mary Jane and I are spending all day tomorrow cleaning out the playroom," Juliet said from the beach outside her door. The child had talked of nothing else over dinner at the spaghetti warehouse that night. Assured that the key relationships in her life weren't going to change, she thought Marcie's moving in with them was the greatest thing that had ever happened. She had already planned which of her toys she could part with to make room in the small cottage for another adult.

"Hank still driving you down?" The man had taken a day off from the hardware store to help Marcie move.

"Yes."

Juliet didn't like that uncertain note in her sister's voice. "Don't get cold feet now, Marce. You've said a thousand times this is what you want."

"I know."

"The baby is just a catalyst making it happen."

"I know."

"And if you want to get married someday, San Diego has lots of men to choose from."

"For a woman with a newborn child?"

"For anyone."

They chatted for another couple of minutes about the logistics of the move. Juliet could see only good in Marcie's decision. They'd never had any difficulty living together. Marcie would finally begin the life she'd always wanted and Juliet could quit worrying that her sister was going to end up like her mother someday. And she'd have help with Mary Jane.

She'd never felt more in need of the latter than she did right then.

"How are things going with Blake Ramsden?" Marcie asked just as Juliet was starting to feel relaxed enough to sleep.

She kicked at the sand. Watched the moon's glow bob out on the ocean. Wished the waves would kick up enough of a breeze to cool her heated skin.

"As well as can be expected," she said, telling her sister about the plea agreement Blake had rejected. And that she thought he'd done the right thing.

"So," Marcie pressed, "you're doing okay?"

"I don't know." Juliet admitted to her twin what she wouldn't have told anyone else. "I think so, and then he'll say something and I get this horrible guilty feeling." She dug a little tunnel in the sand with her toes. "I think he's lonely, Marce. He bought this puppy...."

If she hadn't known all the reasons it would be a mistake for her to fall for Blake Ramsden, she might have been tempted when he'd been sitting there chuckling over the dog's having chewed a corner off the cupboard when Blake had locked him in the kitchen while he'd showered on Monday night.

"He got the dog from the pound. Named it Freedom because that was what they both needed. The puppy needed freedom from its cage and imminent death, and so does he...."

She had to stop before she did something stupid. Like start to cry.

"Sometimes I think it's cruel of me not to tell him about Mary Jane," she added when she could.

"How many days has it been since Mrs. Cummings called?" Marcie asked.

"Two. Mary Jane has failed three math tests in a row." It would be a cause for concern with any child. And with a child who could blurt out the answers to math problems in class before her teacher even had time to write them out on the board, it was especially worrisome.

"Is she doing it on purpose?" Marcie asked.

Juliet tried to concentrate on loosening the knot in her stomach. "Obviously," she said. "The question is why, and what to do about it."

"What does Mary Jane say?"

"That she's *not* doing it on purpose."

"She's never lied to you before."

The sky was black, with shades of navy and gray where the moon shone through. So much out there—unseen.

"I don't think she's lying now. She's somehow convinced herself she can't do the math," Marcie added.

"We had her talk to the school counselor and Mary Jane answered all her questions like a happy, normal, well-adjusted kid."

"What does Mrs. Cummings say?"

"That Mary Jane is troubled about something." Juliet had been trying desperately not to think of her most recent phone conversation with the elementary-school principal. She'd suggested that Juliet look into some kind of special-education class that worked with children one-on-one to determine the extent of Mary Jane's needs.

As if her daughter wasn't already segregated enough by her differences from the other children.

"And you think she's troubled about her father?"

Juliet didn't know what else to think. "School's always been a bit of a struggle, you know that," Juliet said. "She's too smart for her grade, too outspoken for her age, and she bores easily. But she's always taken that in stride. It never really seemed to bother her, until the past few months—ever since the first conversation about her father came up again. She seems to have lost, at least to some degree, her sense of security."

"Which is why you can't tell Blake anything about her," Marcie said. "Obviously Mary Jane comes first. And introducing a huge change into her life certainly isn't going to enhance her security. Besides, for now, Blake needs something else from you far more than he needs to know that you had his baby eight years ago. He's a client and should remain that way if you're going to do your job and set him free. You tell him about Mary Jane now, and there's no way you'd still be able to keep him on as a client. Things would be too personal.

"Think of it this way, Jules," Marcie continued. "It's not going to do him a hell of a lot of good to know he has a daughter if he's locked up and can't see her anyway."

"Yeah." She'd already told herself all the things that Marcie said. Still, the validation helped.

"Maybe after the case is over, and third grade is over, and I've been living there for a while, Mary Jane will be feeling secure enough for you to tell Blake about her."

Maybe. But that thought struck as much terror in her heart as anything else.

ON FRIDAY, two weeks after his arraignment, Juliet was back in Blake's office.

"I met Fred Manning coming up in the elevator," she told him, holding the back of her black silk skirt down as she took her usual seat on his couch. It was beginning to seem routine, all in a day's work, having her there.

She had a "usual" seat.

Careful, buddy, Blake warned himself. If there was one thing he knew, it was that it would be suicide to get too comfortable with Juliet McNeil. She was his attorney. Nothing more. They'd both decided to leave it that way before he even knew he *needed* an attorney.

"Fred's a good guy," he said now. "He's been with us for years. My father hired him straight out of law school."

"I know." Juliet smiled. "He told me. He thinks the world of you."

Blake shrugged, glanced around him at the mementos that were helping him more than his staff would ever know.

"Lee Anne does, too," Juliet added. "I get the feeling pretty much everyone around here does."

He took the chair adjacent to her, uncomfortable with the turn of the conversation. "They're a good group."

"It's important, Blake." Her gaze was dead serious as she looked him in the eye. "We're going to need every single one of them as character witnesses. I don't care if it takes six months to parade them all through court, we're going to paint a picture of you the jury will never forget."

Okay. He'd handle the embarrassment. It was a small price to pay.

"I have a list of all the things I'm going to need," she continued, pulling a typed document from her satchel. "This and anything else you can think of that might show any connection at all between your father and the other Semaphor board members, James, or any of James's other investors. The names are all there for you—you can do computer searches. I'm going to need bank accounts, with every single statement from the past six years...."

The list of documents was overwhelming. And he'd have every one of them in her hands before morning. Blake kept immaculate records, as had his father before him.

Unfortunately, there was very little he knew that might help her. To the best of his knowledge, Walter had never had any dealings with Eaton James, other than their time together on the board of Semaphor and the Eaton Estates investment.

"You know, it's odd that James waited until the end of his trial to expose all of this," he told her. More than anything, he kept coming back to this fact during the long nighttime hours.

"If what he says can stand up in court, then why didn't he come clean from the beginning? I know you said he was hoping for complete absolution, but forgery is a far lesser charge.'' Something else Blake had learned on the Internet. ''From what I read, since he'd never been charged before, he would've gotten off with probation.''

''I'm impressed,'' Juliet said. ''You've done your homework.'' And then she tilted her head. ''Of course, you're paying me to know that stuff. All you had to do was ask.'' Her smile took any sting out of the words.

''I wasn't sure you'd answer your cell at four in the morning.''

He hadn't realized quite how telling that statement had been until her eyes softened with a compassion he wasn't sure he wanted.

Juliet McNeil was his attorney, he reminded himself. He couldn't afford to need anything from her, other than legal services. Period. Too much was at stake.

''In answer to your question, it's very possible that there's something more in what James was saying, and it's my job to find out what that is.'' She paused, and then, her eyes narrowing, said, ''It's also possible that he was just so certain that he could fend off the fraud charges, he wasn't going to risk muddying his reputation if he didn't have to.''

So how in the hell did they find whatever James was hiding—especially when it might not even exist?

''I've got other questions for you, things to go over,'' Juliet said next, ''but first, we need to discuss your pretrial hearing.''

The mandatory hearing, thirty days after arraignment, was to discuss any issues that might hamper the trial—challenges of admissible evidence, for instance—to verify the trial start date, and to set probable length of trial. He'd read that the night after his arraignment. After a couple of whiskeys and a middle-of-the-night run with Freedom on the beach.

Juliet glanced up from a legal pad she'd been perusing, and when he nodded, she continued.

"This morning I received disclosure of the state's evidence, all of which we need to discuss, but at the moment, I'm concentrating on anything we'll want to bring up at your pretrial."

A part of Blake sat outside the discussion, watching. It had been weeks, and he still couldn't believe that this guy listening to the details of a potentially life-ending criminal trial was him. At the same time, his panic had subsided somewhat.

He had an attorney who was in complete control.

"First, there's mention of the Cayman Islands bank account," she said almost casually. "Schuster is submitting that document showing the opening of an account with your name attached."

Blake told himself it didn't matter. He didn't open the account.

"We won't have a problem getting that thrown out," Juliet said, slowing his heart rate once again. "There has to be real paper evidence—bank statements, letters addressed to you, anything official that proves the account was active in your name—and there is none."

And because the account was in the Cayman Islands, where an account number could not be traced, there was no way to get that evidence. One hurdle down.

Sunlight from the window caught the golden flecks in her auburn hair. Blake remembered being fascinated by strands of that hair covering silky white breasts...

"Second, Schuster's planning to use the testimony Eaton James gave at his own trial as evidence against you."

Blake slammed back down to reality with a painful thud. How could any human being fight a dead man?

"Can he do that?"

Juliet's eyes were warm, personal, as she glanced over at him. "It's possible, but that's where we're going to put our pretrial energies."

Watching her, listening, Blake's nerves calmed a bit. God she was beautiful. And smart. And determined. And on his side.

He'd known, that night nine years before, that he'd met someone special. He'd had no idea how special.

"If he uses the testimony, he's in violation of the confrontation clause." She spoke with respect, not down to him, not even like a teacher with a student. But as an equal. "That states all defendants have the right to personally confront anyone making statements against them."

"Is there a way around it?" he asked.

"Schuster has to prove that there was another opportunity for you to cross-examine or call James on what he said."

"I wasn't even in court!"

"I know. But Schuster will say you had opportunity after court that day to make a claim against James.''

''Schuster was the only attorney advising me then.''

''Which is a point I intend to make with the judge,'' Juliet assured him.

''I told Schuster the entire story was a lie,'' Blake said. ''I was his witness. We were on the same side. James was the opponent. I didn't think for one second anyone would actually believe my father would resort to blackmail. Nor did I see the point in pressing formal charges. James was going to jail, and I just wanted the whole thing over.''

''I know.'' Juliet set her pad aside, leaned over, her arms crossed on her thighs. ''I think we'll beat this.'' She didn't smile, but her expression reassured him. ''The fact that James...uh...did what he did...so soon after the testimony should be enough to show that you did not have ample opportunity for rebuttal.''

She was still bothered by James's suicide. Blake wished he could speak with her more about it. And knew that would be crossing a line he couldn't afford to cross.

At least not now.

So, okay. Concentrating on business, James's testimony was one battle almost down.

He wondered how many more hundred there'd be before this war was finally over.

And if, in the end, winning battles would matter.

It was the war he had to win.

CHAPTER FOURTEEN

AFTER SPENDING a couple of hours perusing Ramsden Enterprises' tax records and bank statements, Juliet left work early on Monday to take Marcie to her first prenatal visit. And then, when the doctor reported that, yes, Marcie was approximately six weeks along and everything looked perfect, Juliet and Marcie picked Mary Jane up from school and went for ice cream to celebrate. That led to a trip to the mall to look at baby clothes. A late dinner at the food court had to come next. And then, long after the sun had gone down, the threesome went home to the cottage.

Mary Jane skipped off to bed with a smile on her face.

Which made up for the time spent away from figuring out how to prove to a nameless jury that Blake Ramsden had nothing to do with the Cayman Islands bank account bearing his name. Lack of paperwork aside, if the prosecution found a way to bring up the account, he could play on the Cayman Islands confidentiality laws as the sole reason for the lack of paperwork. To make that stick, all he had to do was convince the jury.

Unfortunately, Juliet's time with her sister and daughter didn't take her away from other thoughts that continued to spiral out of control at unforeseen moments throughout her day. Thoughts of Blake as he'd been, naked in her arms, nine years before.

Of the man who'd laughed with her over drinks just weeks before.

And of the strong, ethical man who was attempting to stand against the lies and disasters plaguing his life.

A man she had no business thinking about.

THE PILE OF MAIL on her desk on Tuesday was twice as thick as usual, because she hadn't yet attended to Monday's stack. Going through the usual briefs, invitations and junk that just took up space and killed trees, she was surprised by a legal-size envelope toward the bottom of the pile.

For two reasons. The return address was Eaton James's. And there was something little and hard inside.

Staring at the envelope gave her an eerie feeling, raising all of the dark emotions her client's death had evoked several weeks before. How could Eaton James have sent her anything?

It didn't take long to find out.

The letter had been sent from James's attorney—a part of the distribution of his estate that no one but James and his attorney had known about. Other than the predated letter from James, telling her this, the only thing inside was a small key. And a post-office-box number.

THE BOX WAS IN La Jolla, not far from the address Blake Ramsden had given her. Juliet didn't get out that way often. She thought about driving around to see if she could find his place—just to see it.

And because she couldn't afford anything that was going to tie her to the man any more closely than she'd already been tied, she didn't.

It took her several minutes and a couple of conversations centered on the signed and notarized letter in her hand, but Juliet finally persuaded a supervisor at the post office to tell her who was registered to the box number and key she held. The answer sent chills down her spine.

The box had two registered users. Eaton James and Walter Ramsden. And inside were several recent bank statements from a bank account in the Cayman Islands.

The name on the account was Blake Ramsden.

"WE'VE GOT TROUBLE." On her cell phone in the post-office parking lot, Juliet used every calming technique she'd ever learned. The bright sun, which usually cheered Juliet, was giving her a headache.

If he was guilty, she wasn't going to be able to save him. And she couldn't fathom the alternative.

"Juliet? What's up?"

She'd found Blake in his office. He sounded preoccupied.

"I'd like to talk to you in person. Can we meet someplace?"

In the end, she agreed to wait for him in La Jolla, on a stretch of private beach not far from his home. As soon as he'd figured out that the news she had was not good, he'd opted for the ocean as a meeting place.

Juliet wasn't surprised. She'd made all of her toughest decisions by the ocean. Sitting on a beach late one night, letting the waves wash up around her legs, she'd decided to keep the baby she carried.

And not to tell the baby's father that he'd made a child.

She found the parking alcove and picnic table just as he'd described. She could drive right up. Take two steps to the table. No reason to remove her pumps and hose to walk in the sand. But she did, anyway. She couldn't pass up the feel of the sand between her toes and the scratching along the bottom of her feet.

Had Blake lied to her?

Juliet had left the jacket to her violet spring suit in the BMW, but it wasn't long in the bright sun before she was sweating anyway. Not that she cared.

Her ability to judge character had always been one of her strongest suits and was a significant factor in the success of her career.

Blake wouldn't lie to her. Or anyone. He was honest to a fault. If anything, his propensity to tell the truth proved the old adage that too much of anything was a bad thing.

Or was she just blinded by memories of sand and moonlight and the most incredible mind and voice and hands? And mouth.

She couldn't forget that mouth. It had done things to her body, aroused responses inside her, that she hadn't known were possible.

Responses she hadn't felt since that night.

And if he hadn't lied? What then? There was no way she was going to be able to fight a bank statement bearing her client's name. Some things really were black and white.

But there had to be some explanation. Blake would

be able to clear this up. She just had to wait for him to get there.

Down at the water's edge, she waited for the shock to come as the cold water lapped at her toes. Seagulls skimmed the edge of the ocean looking for prey.

What had happened to the days when being on the beach meant looking for shells and dreaming of sailing out to sea with a dashing captain? When had she lost those days, those childish dreams? At thirteen? On the move to Maple Grove? During law school? When she'd won her first case?

"I expected to find you back here." She hadn't heard Blake's steps in the sand.

She didn't turn. Not yet. She hadn't found the answers, the solid place to stand, she'd been looking for.

"I couldn't get this close and not feel the water," she told him, knowing he'd understand.

They'd discovered the night they met that they were ocean soul mates.

"Do you get to the ocean often?"

She looked over at him, squinting. "Every day. I live in a cottage on a private strip of Mission Beach."

His smile was small but genuine as he glanced down at her through his dark sunglasses.

"If I'd had to guess, I'd have had you living on the beach."

She'd left her sunglasses in the car. She needed to see the colors of the sky and the ocean and the golden glow of the sun on the beach in all its bright splendor.

"Do you own the place?"

It wasn't really a question for a client to ask his

lawyer. But perhaps it was one that an old lover might ask?

Or, probably more accurately, it was one that might allow him to avoid the reason they were there together in the first place. It would give him a moment to soak up a bit of the ocean's healing energy.

"Yes," she said. "It's not big, just three bedrooms, but I love it."

He'd removed his shoes, too, and rolled up the cuffs of his navy slacks and the sleeves of his white dress shirt.

"How long have you been there?"

"Four years." Just before Mary Jane had started at the first of a couple of private schools for gifted children. While academically they'd challenged her a bit more than her current situation, Juliet hadn't been happy about the rigid exclusivity. They were reputedly good schools but not the very best. Unfortunately the best had waiting lists ten years long.

"You live alone?"

They weren't here to talk about her. They were here to establish whether or not Blake Ramsden had lied to her, or to find the miracle that would explain the evidence sitting back in her car.

"My sister lives with me." She told him the truth, knowing that it wasn't the way he'd have presented the truth given the same circumstances. He'd have mentioned *everyone* who lived in his house.

Juliet tried hard to ignore the pressure in her stomach.

"Is she a lawyer, too?"

Hands in the pockets of his slacks, he started to walk slowly along the water's edge and she fell in beside him. The mail in her car was going nowhere. The facts would be the same later that night. And every night after as well.

"No, she's a hair designer hoping to get on with one of the studios here in San Diego."

Grinning, he started to walk again, leaving imprints to fill with water behind him. With a couple of quick steps, Juliet caught up with him.

"What's so funny?"

"Not funny," he said, still grinning as he looked down at her with an expression that was more bemused than humorous. "I'm just trying to imagine two of you in the same house."

"Marcie isn't like me," she assured him. "She's a lot more laid-back."

"You sound as if that's a bad thing."

"Of course it's not bad." She reached down to pick up a beautiful, luminescent shell. A rare find. "It's just like anything else, though. For every good side, there's a corresponding bad. Take me, for instance. I'm a go-getter, but I push too hard sometimes. I don't always know when to quit."

And take you. You're so caught up in telling the complete truth you aren't ever going to forgive me if you find out the truth I haven't told you.

"So what's the downside that brought that worried tone to your voice when you mentioned your sister?"

It had been like this nine years ago. Her urge to confide in this man—to tell him things she didn't talk to anyone about. Back then it had been dreams of the future and her need to prove herself.

That was how they'd started that long-ago night— drinking and confiding, partly because it had been so safe. They'd been strangers, with nothing invested in the relationship, who would never see each other again.

A couple of kids were throwing a Frisbee behind one of the houses above them. She couldn't make out what they were saying, but the innocence in their laughter carried clearly.

"Marcie has a tendency to settle for less than she wants. Our mother did that. And I saw how it ended. I will not see my sister die the same way. I don't think I'd survive."

"If your sister is anything like you, she has that core of inner steel we spoke about earlier. It would stop her before she took her own life."

Maybe. But then, Juliet had been fairly certain her mother had that same core. Where did Blake think Juliet had gotten it from? Certainly not from the weak and clinging man who'd fathered her.

She had to tell him about the bank statements, and then leave. Juliet smoothed her thumb over the soft inside of the shell in her palm.

Not that she had to hurry home. Tonight was Mary Jane and Marcie's night together.

"Marcie's pregnant."

He was the only person she trusted who would never know her sister. That was the reason she'd confided something that wasn't hers to tell.

"I take it there's not a husband who also lives with you?"

She shook her head, watching for more shells. "The father is in Maple Grove. They've been dating since high school but the relationship is more of a habit than a romance."

''He hit the road when he found out she was pregnant?''

''No.'' She should never have started this. There was no way he, or anyone else, would ever understand.

The waves lapped against the shore and Juliet heard other water. Saw again that tiny, plastic bathtub in the matching tiny bathroom in the trailer where she and Marcie had grown from girls into women. She'd been home for the weekend, preparing for her final exams in law school.

She'd come from Marcie's shop. They'd planned a surprise trip to San Francisco to celebrate their mother's birthday. They'd had reservations at a rooftop restaurant. Juliet had gone home to tell her mother to put on her best dress....

''Marcie hit the road. She's only been living with me for a little over a week,'' Juliet said slowly. ''She and Hank have had years to get married. Neither one of them has ever been motivated enough—or in love enough, she says—to make it happen. He works in the family hardware store and has no desire to be anywhere else. Ever. He's committed to his family and the store. She hates Maple Grove. Is bored out of her mind half the time. If she marries Hank because of this baby, she's going to get tied to that town just like our mother was. The reasons might be different, but the result will be the same.''

''A lot of people live very happy lives in small towns.''

''I know they do!'' Although a depressed transient town like Maple Grove didn't have a high percentage of them. ''But Marcie isn't happy there! She wants to travel. To see the world. To have a social life. All she could talk about while we were in high school was getting out.''

''So why didn't she?''

''She met Hank and got a job at the local beauty shop. She's always been into hair and makeup and stuff like that. She's really good. She drove an hour each way to take classes in San Francisco and got her cosmetology license long before I finished college.'' She ground her foot into the sand, comforted by the feel of it against her arch. ''Before she knew it, she had more than half the ladies in Maple Grove coming to her. In a San Francisco salon she'd still have been making minimum wage washing hair for some high-paid designer. A couple of years later, when she was talking about moving here to try for a job at a big salon—which had always been her dream—she was offered the chance to go into partnership in Maple Grove. The lure of her own place, and the safety of her relationship with Hank, kept her there. Dreaming.''

She'd never meant to say anything. Let alone so much.

''It's those dreams that kill you,'' she said a couple of seconds later. ''They eat at you until there's nothing left.''

If she thought for one second that Marcie would ever be happy in Maple Grove, if her sister had given any indication of wanting a life there…

''But they didn't this time.'' Blake's voice was soft. Empathetic. ''She got out.''

And Juliet went to bed every night worrying that Marcie wasn't going to settle in as quickly as she wanted to, that she wouldn't find a job right away, that she'd let the lure of security in Maple Grove call her back in a weak moment and put in motion the beginning of the end.

THE SUN WAS SINKING over the ocean by the time Blake turned around to head back toward their cars. Another mile or so and they'd have been at his place. He wasn't sure he trusted himself to have her there.

Especially not now, when she was becoming more friend than attorney. They were treading dangerous ground. And he couldn't afford any extra danger in his life at the moment. He was too aware of his aloneness to be sure he wouldn't do anything stupid. Like hit on his lawyer.

"I guess we've avoided the bad news long enough," he told her as they headed back up the beach.

He had to get home anyway. Freedom would be ready for his run on the beach. And then a nice ground-beef dinner. The little guy needed some fattening up.

As Juliet told him about the key she'd received in the mail, and more horrifically, the contents of the post-office box, Blake continued to put one sandy foot in front of the other. And that was all. The waves that normally called to him were no more than a roaring in his ears, drowning out all but the far-off voice of his defense attorney.

He ran every day. Several miles at a time. And came home barely winded. Now, just strolling the beach, his chest was so tight he could hardly pull in air.

There was a United States post-office box registered in Eaton James's name with his father as a co-signer. And a bank account in the Cayman Islands in *his* name, complete with bank statements addressed to him.

The voice fell away. Blake fought through the dark fog to focus on only one thing. The problem at hand. Not its ramifications.

"This makes the Cayman Island account admissible as evidence, doesn't it?"

They were walking more quickly and had almost reached the point where they'd turn up the beach to head back to their cars. The setting sun made it difficult to look out over the ocean.

"It could, yes."

"Could?"

"If we disclose the bank statements."

Blake slowed. "*If* we disclose them? Don't we have to?"

"It's not that clear-cut."

Here it comes, Blake thought. Those shades of gray he'd been worried about. As good as she was, as much as he needed her, he just couldn't let her do that. He really believed that his only hope of winning was to stand strong behind the values he'd sacrificed so much to find. If he wavered, if he lied, even by omission, he'd lose.

Blake removed his sunglasses, sliding them into the pocket of his shirt as they walked toward their cars.

"If the evidence is pertinent to the case, then, yes, we have to disclose it, but that's completely subject to interpretation."

"I think pretty much anyone would agree that Cayman Islands bank statements are pertinent to this case.''

She stopped, looked up at him. ''That account is yours, then? The card attached to it has your signature?''

''No.''

''Then, as far as your case is concerned, I interpret those statements as false documents, and therefore, not subject to disclosure laws. Ethically, I'm obligated to research them and, if I find evidence that they're legitimate, I have to disclose them.''

''And if they come up later and it's learned that we already had evidence of them?''

''I'll argue—and win—that they were subject to interpretation.''

She made sense. And yet...

''It's not right.''

''It's right then for us to hang you before we have a chance to figure out why James prearranged to have that key come to me? Or why, for that matter, there's apparently an account in the Cayman Islands with you as the principal signer? Because I can guarantee that if I turn these over now, Schuster sure as hell isn't going to try to find out. He's going to take them at face value and run with them.''

Was it a statement of his emotional turmoil that Blake could accept so much of what she was saying? Was he, when times got tough enough, just as capable as anyone else of selling out?

Juliet laid a hand on his arm. ''It's not an easy question, Blake. Both sides have perfectly valid arguments, but this one really is my call and I have to do what's in your best interests.''

In his best interests in terms of winning this case? Or in terms of being able to look at himself in the mirror for the rest of his life?

Of course, if he lost the case and went to prison, he probably wouldn't be facing a lot of mirrors.

"You could turn them over and still do the research."

He was disappointing her. He could read that in those expressive green eyes—and in her sigh.

"We only have two and a half months until the trial," she said, still calm, but not as gentle in her delivery. "What if I'm not able to find anything in that time that'll prove your name on that account was forged? It'll be your word against a dead man's, and the prosecutor is sitting there with paper evidence— bank statements that we've provided—that proves you the liar. What's the jury going to think, Blake? What would *you* think if you were sitting in one of their seats?"

What she was suggesting wasn't against the law. Things like this were done all the time. It was how the world worked.

And what if it somehow got out that he knew about those statements and his attorney hadn't disclosed them? No matter the argument, he'd look like a liar by default, and his integrity would take a legitimate hit.

Never in his life had Blake been up against a harder decision, or one less clear to him.

"I want you to disclose them."

Juliet lowered her head. But she didn't say what he knew she must be thinking. "You're making my job a lot harder than it needs to be."

"I know. I'm sorry." And he was. She was an angel there to save him and he'd always be grateful for that. Even from a prison cell.

"You understand that there's nothing illegal about what I'm proposing, correct?"

"I do."

"And you still want me to go ahead and send the statements to Schuster?"

"Yes."

"Okay." She started trudging through the sand again toward her car. "I've done my best, which is all I can do."

It didn't escape Blake that doing one's best was a form of honesty all in itself.

CHAPTER FIFTEEN

MARY JANE GOT A PERFECT score on her math test that week. She said it was because the boy in front of her quit chewing gum so loud and she could hear better. Juliet believed that Mary Jane believed this was the reason. To Marcie she dared to express hope that their new plan to give Mary Jane time alone with each of them, and to reinforce the partnership she shared with her mother, was working.

In less than two weeks' time, Marcie had applied to all the key studios in the San Diego area and had already received calls for half a dozen interviews.

And Juliet was busy systematically questioning every witness on Schuster's list, looking at year-end business statements, comparing accounts payable with credit card and checking statements and tax category credits. And trying not to think about the tall, athletic and ethically uptight man running on the beach with his new puppy. Eating dinner all alone. And going to bed that way, too.

He was a client. She could help him win his case. And as long as she was his attorney, she couldn't do anything about any of those other things.

On the last Friday evening in May, just a couple of days before Blake's pretrial hearing, Marcie and Mary Jane were off to see a traveling dinosaur exhibit that claimed to have one of the world's most authentic Tyrannosaurus rex specimens.

Juliet was planning to go home, give herself a facial and curl up in a blanket on the back porch with a reading light and a good book. A motivational book for women who wanted to live up to their potential. And if she finished that one, there was another about staying focused when life was in chaos.

And then, just as she was leaving the office, a letter arrived for her by local courier.

"Hi, Jason, how're the classes coming?" she asked the young law student who supplemented his scholarship by doing runs for a good many of the law offices in town.

"Hard." The tall, thin twenty-three-year-old grinned as he handed Juliet a clipboard to sign off on the delivery. "And long."

"You keeping up?"

"Always." With a nod and one last smile, he was off as quickly as he'd arrived, leaving Juliet in possession of a thick manila envelope from Paul Schuster.

With that almost perpetual knot back in her stomach, she dropped her satchel and keys, sank down to her desk chair and slit the envelope.

AN HOUR LATER, sitting in a quiet out-of-the-way bar not far from Mission Beach, Juliet waited for Blake Ramsden. Meeting for drinks might not have been the best idea, but she wanted Blake to have a glass of whiskey handy when she showed him what Paul Schuster had sent.

Besides, it was Friday night and they would've

been completely alone if they'd met in either of their offices.

In spite of all of her advice to herself, her heart fluttered the second he walked in the door. He'd said he was coming straight from the office, and while he'd pulled off his tie, undone the top button of his white dress shirt and rolled up his sleeves, he still looked every bit the successful professional that he was.

His dark hair, the exact color of his daughter's, was rumpled as though he'd either driven with the moon roof open on his Mercedes SUV, or run his hand through it more than a few times.

She hoped he'd driven with the roof open.

"Should we order first?" he asked as he slid opposite her into the back booth of the mostly deserted pub. It was still a bit early for the after-work crowd.

"Probably."

His eyes, when they met hers in the dim light, were warm. Concerned. "That bad, huh?"

Juliet nodded.

The older female waitress, who'd already been over twice, made a beeline for their table as soon as she saw Blake. She took their drink order, suggested an appetizer platter, and as Juliet and Blake nodded, smiled and said she'd be right back.

"We're either going to have to stop meeting like this, or start ordering dinner," Blake said with a half grin. "The carbohydrate count in those appetizers must be sky high. Not to mention the cholesterol."

"Probably not," Juliet responded, knowing that, if her stomach didn't settle soon, she wouldn't be eating enough of the appetizers for excessive carbs or cholesterol to be an issue. "Not that I pay as much attention to stuff like that as I should," she added.

"I have only since finding out about my father's heart condition."

She frowned, studied features that looked the epitome of health. "Are you at risk for heart problems?" The thought had never occurred to her. Somewhere, in the far recesses of her mind, she'd figured she had an entire lifetime ahead of her to tell him he was Mary Jane's father. Like maybe after the little girl was married. And he was a grandfather.

Or had she thought that she had a whole lifetime to find out if that magic night nine years before had been anything more than a figment of her imagination, glossed over and made more perfect by the passage of time?

"I'm healthy as a horse," he said easily. But his expression changed almost as soon as he'd said the words.

Was he wondering if longevity might not matter if his life was spent behind bars? She ran her finger along a scratch in the scarred maple table.

Blake took a long swig from his whiskey and soda as soon as it arrived. Then he set down the glass and looked over at her. "Shoot."

Juliet handed him the sheaf of papers she'd had on the table beside her.

"Eaton James's wife found these while going through his personal things at home. She sent them to Schuster, who's admitted them as evidence."

Blake remained calm as he glanced through copies of a checking-account register, paying particular attention to the items that had been marked with a yellow highlighter.

Had Schuster done that? Or Juliet?

There were copies of bank statements that corroborated the check numbers and amounts. Copies of canceled checks, both front and signed-off back, that also matched—numbers, accounts, dates.

It didn't take an attorney, or even anyone very intelligent, to figure this one out. What he had before him was irrefutable evidence that for at least the year before Blake's father's death, Eaton James had been making monthly payments to Walter Ramsden.

"Shit."

"That was my first response."

Her first. That meant she'd had a second. Blake's mind raced. "Is it possible James is a forger on a much larger scale then he admitted? Could he have forged my signature on that bank account in the Islands, forged my father's signature here, and on the post-office box?"

"It's possible." She handed him another cluster of papers. Bank statements from the Cayman Islands account.

With highlighted deposits matching the ones he'd just seen on James's personal account.

"That's good, right? It fits the theory. For whatever reason, James was writing himself checks out of his personal account and hiding the money in the account in the Cayman Islands."

"I'm not sure why he'd do that," Juliet said. The dim lighting prevented him from seeing the brown flecks in her eyes, but their warmth was evident just the same.

He wasn't sure he needed to see that warmth, though. It weakened him. Made him want things that weren't going to happen.

"If he was siphoning money from Terracotta..."

Juliet shook her head. "He wouldn't run it through his personal bank account."

"He would if..."

Blake had no idea what followed that "if." He just couldn't believe that his father had been blackmailing Eaton James. It didn't fit.

Juliet slid another statement across to him. He looked to see if there was anything else on the table beside her. There wasn't.

He glanced at the statement on top of his pile. Took another sip of whiskey. Read the damning words again. Skimmed the highlighted entries.

"My father deposited the money into his own personal account." There was no forging this one. The bank account had belonged to Walter Ramsden. Blake had turned over the information himself.

Sitting back while the waitress delivered their tray of wings and veggies, stuffed potato skins and nachos, Juliet just watched him, saying nothing.

He wished she'd speak and tell him it was over, that she couldn't help him. Or better yet, that she'd tell him she had a theory. That the evidence wasn't admissible. He wished she'd say she'd had a case just like this once before and it had all worked out fine.

The food between them went untouched.

"What now?" he finally asked.

"We keep looking." She took a sip of the wine she'd ordered, and then another. "While this might appear to substantiate James's testimony, we're planning to get that thrown out on Monday. Assuming we do, the onus will be on Schuster to tie all this together—to find witnesses or some other way to explain what all of this means. Based on what Eaton said, I don't think he'll be able to do that. The transactions that took place were kept completely private. Between two men who are no longer here to speak for themselves.''

Blake nodded, feeling a little less trapped. ''You said we keep looking? For what?''

''Anything that'll tell us what really took place five or six years ago. I didn't have time tonight, but over the weekend I intend to go over all of your father's payables, both personal and through Ramsden. We have a record of deposits into the Cayman Islands account, but no way of proving who made the deposit.''

''Unless my father's records show something?''

She shrugged and picked up a stalk of celery, but didn't take a bite. ''Even if he did, that doesn't clear you. Technically, that account is still yours and now that Schuster has evidence that'll hold up in court on that, we have to find a way to prove you didn't open the account.''

''You think my father opened that account in my name? That he's the one guilty of fraud?''

Blake felt her pointed look. ''Do you?'' she asked.

''No.''

She took a bite of the celery. ''And what happens if I find out differently?''

''Then you do.''

He'd be free. At least in a legal sense.

On an emotional level, he wasn't sure. Had his selfishness of almost four years cost his father not only his physical life, but his soul as well? Had he been forced to compromise the most important thing he'd given Blake—the only thing that sustained Blake at the moment—his sense of integrity?

Had the old man died a thief and a criminal?

As THE BAR slowly filled with Friday-night traffic, Blake and Juliet talked about other possibilities. Juliet was going to subpoena the records for the other businesses closely associated with Terracotta—the ones Schuster had claimed were false fronts behind which James hid Terracotta losses. She already had a private investigator in the Cayman Islands, questioning bank employees, showing pictures of James and Blake and Walter Ramsden to see if he could get any takers. The government was not required to cooperate. The banks weren't likely to either, since much of their business was based on the assurance that whatever happened there would go no further.

"Why are you smiling?" she asked just after the waitress delivered their second round of drinks. They'd made a very small dent in the appetizers.

"I didn't know I was." It was the truth. He grabbed a bean-and-cheese-filled chip.

"Well, you were."

"Hmm." Dipping the chip in sour cream, he took a bite, and then finished it off.

"Why? What were you thinking?"

Damn, the woman was persistent.

"About you."

"What about me?"

He always told the truth. So he could tell her the truth—that he didn't wish to answer her question.

Instead, he murmured, "That no matter how bad things appear, being with you makes them seem more manageable."

Face down, she ran a finger along the edge of her wineglass. Then she looked up. "Thank you."

"And I was wondering if it's something about you, something you bring to all of your...clients. Or if it's more than that."

"What more would it be?"

He took another chip. Broke it in half. Ate one half. "I don't know," he told her. "Something more personal."

"I don't get personal with my clients." The words were said with total confidence. And just a bit too quickly.

"I didn't think you did."

"It's completely unethical. I could be disbarred."

"I know."

He ate a wing. And then another. She toyed with a potato skin. He took a sip of whiskey.

"So, is this extra...nurturing or whatever it is something you offer everyone?"

She frowned and looked away, following the progress of an older couple as they left the bar.

"No."

She replied so softly, he wasn't sure she had, until that completely open gaze settled firmly on him. He read the truth there and was satisfied. He should leave it at that. Needed to leave it at that.

Wanted to leave it at that.

"When this is all over, will we be friends?" He

blamed the question on the whiskey, and a residual fear of being thrown in jail for the rest of his life that was making him needy in ways he didn't understand.

"As opposed to enemies?" She'd pretty much mutilated the potato, eating only a couple of bites and smashing the rest with her fork.

"As opposed to not seeing each other for another five or ten years, at which time we casually say hello when we bump into each other on the street."

Assuming he was on the street by then.

She peered over at him, eyes narrowed. "Do you want to be friends?"

"I think so."

Her eyes closed, her lips not quite steady.

"I..."

Reaching across the table, he touched her lips, barely, with one finger. And even that was a mistake. He wanted so much more.

"I'm not asking for a future, or even a relationship," he said. "I'm just asking if you'd like to keep in touch."

He waited a long time for her answer and was forced to realize how much it mattered.

"Yes." The relief was palpable when her response finally came. "I would like to be friends."

He chose to ignore the "but" he suspected he heard at the end of that sentence.

BLAKE'S PRETRIAL HEARING went exactly as Juliet had predicted. James's testimony was disallowed. The Cayman bank statements stood as evidence. The trial was confirmed to start on the morning of July twenty-third and expected to last a minimum of two weeks.

She and Blake met a few more times over drinks.
Now that Marcie was around, Juliet could get away
in the evenings and things just seemed more relaxed
for both of them in a bar than in either of their offices.

As the weeks wore on and Blake's tension grew,
she was eager to relieve any of it that she could.

Marcie finally landed a job in one of the larger San
Diego studios, which lessened one of Juliet's worries,
freeing her up to focus more completely as she studied tax records, company records and bank records,
and followed check trails, invoices, inventory, payables and receivables. She talked to every person on
Schuster's list—and Blake's. Slowly, systematically,
she was building a picture of the lives of Eaton James
and Walter Ramsden. And to a lesser extent, Blake.

All she could really do for him was build the
world's best character reference. There simply wasn't
any evidence of fraudulent activity between him and
his father or Eaton James. He'd been working in Honduras—and a couple of other countries—rebuilding
villages. She'd be flying a couple of key witnesses in
for the trial and had taken teleconference depositions
with many more who would testify to Blake's activities.

But none of that meant he hadn't also been in communication with his father. She just couldn't *prove*
that he hadn't been.

Schuster couldn't prove that he had been, either,
she assured Blake one Thursday night in late June.
They had bank statements but no matching check
numbers—no way to prove where the money in the
Cayman account had come from. However, as Blake
quickly pointed out, with those bank statements hang-

ing over him, complete with matching payments from Eaton James to Blake's father, Schuster might not have to prove anything else.

So far, nothing had turned up in any records anywhere to show monies leaving for the Cayman Islands. However, ironically, Juliet had found Ramsden contributions to a charity for homeless children in Honduras in amounts that perfectly matched the amounts of money—and pretty nearly the timing—of all the payments from Eaton James to Walter Ramsden.

Also ironic, and not lost on Blake when she told him, was the fact that the money was doing exactly what the Eaton Estates investment was meant to do— feeding poor and disadvantaged children in Honduras.

Blake had to cancel an appointment for drinks the last Tuesday in June. There'd been a fall at one of his sites and while the fault had clearly been a subcontractor's not working to safety code, Blake had gone immediately to the hospital to sit with the young man's pregnant wife.

Arriving home a couple of hours earlier than planned to find what she'd expected to be an empty house blazing with lights, Juliet pulled the BMW into the carport and hurried inside. Other than Marcie's morning sickness, life had been pretty glorious at the McNeil cottage now that school and Brownies were done, and Mary Jane could spend her days at home, at the studio with her aunt, at the office doing odd jobs for her mother and Duane Wilson, or with Donna Wilson.

There were still moments when Mary Jane worried about her mother spending time with Blake Ramsden.

Whenever the little girl knew Juliet had been with Blake, she'd crawled into bed with her mother that night. And Marcie had had some fairly alarming—to Juliet—moments of doubts about her decision to leave Maple Grove. Usually after a bad bout of throwing up. And Juliet—well, she was getting used to waiting out her own moments of doubt and guilt and secret longings, of which she was ashamed every time she came home to her single pregnant sister and sweet insecure daughter.

But all things considered, the McNeil women living together was a successful arrangement.

Mary Jane was sitting at the kitchen table, arms folded across her chest. She was still wearing the white shorts and yellow butterfly top she'd had on when Juliet left for work that morning and her curls were completely dry, which meant she hadn't gone swimming with Marcie as they'd planned.

Frowning, looking around for Marcie, Juliet set her satchel on the counter. "Hi, imp, what's up? I thought you and Aunt Marcie were going to the pool."

Since Marcie's schedule allowed her to be home fairly often during the afternoon, Juliet had bought a family membership to a community center with an outdoor pool.

"We were." Juliet couldn't tell if Mary Jane was hurt or angry, but something was obviously wrong.

"So what happened?"

"I didn't want to go."

Heart sinking, Juliet sat down opposite her daughter, reaching over to brush the curls behind her ears and watching as they sprang right back. Would Blake's hair be as curly if he allowed it to grow?

"How come?" she asked gently. "You love to swim."

"Because."

Mary Jane stared glumly at the table.

"Where's Aunt Marcie?"

"In her room."

"Why?"

"Because I don't want to see her ever again."

Juliet drew in a deep breath. Let it out slowly. She'd made it through almost a whole month without the constant panic and tension that had been riding her since Mary Jane had begged not to return to school number two after the Christmas holidays.

She'd complained that the school had had too many dumb rules. And Juliet had had to agree with her. But still...

"Why are you mad at Aunt Marcie?"

Please let this be something simple. Like Marcie eating the last chocolate snack cake.

Not that Mary Jane had ever let something like that upset her.

"She lied."

CHAPTER SIXTEEN

OKAY, SO IT WAS a miscommunication. That was relatively easy to fix. As soon as her daughter told her the whole story, she could bridge the gap in her understanding.

"To you?" Juliet waited for the nod.

Mary Jane looked up, her eyes filled with anger. "To you."

"Sweetie, Marcie didn't lie to me. We made a pact when we were young that we'd never lie to each other and we never have. Even when telling the truth has been hard and we've hurt each other's feelings."

Mary Jane's chin jutted forward. "She lied to you, Mom. I know she did. I heard her."

She'd never seen Mary Jane so angry and hurt and scared all at once.

"When?"

The little girl's eyes glistened. "When she told you she wasn't talking to Hank. He calls here."

Smiling gently, Juliet breathed a sigh of relief. "He calls, sweetie, but Aunt Marcie doesn't talk to him."

Marcie had told Hank that she'd call him when the baby was born and that she didn't want to talk to him until then. Juliet suspected that her sister was afraid she'd give in and go home to Maple Grove if Hank pressured her hard enough. Hank, who was turning out to be surprisingly determined, still called.

Where had all that determination been for the past fifteen years when Marce had sat home night after night, unhappy and going nowhere?

She watched for the doubt to enter her daughter's eyes, indicating that Mary Jane was considering another view than the one she'd held, followed by tentative hope and peace. She'd seen it happen many, many times in the little girl's life.

Mary Jane's arms were still clutched tightly to her chest, and her eyes remained hard, her expression adamant. "That's what she's telling you, Mom, that she's not talking to him, but she's lying."

Juliet didn't understand. Mary Jane had always been such a reasonable child. Even during her twos, when there were supposed to have been horrible tantrums, she'd usually been able to reason with the little girl.

"Did you hear Hank on the answering machine? Did he say something that makes you think Marcie's talked to him?" Words to which Mary Jane had given wrong meaning?

It's not that she doubted her sister for a second. She just wanted to fix whatever misconception Mary Jane was operating under.

The little girl shook her head, her full, angelic cheeks thinned with displeasure. "I heard *her* talking to *him.* And it wasn't the first time, either, because she asked about something he'd told her a few days ago."

It hadn't been Hank. Marcie would have told Juliet

about that. "Maybe it was Tammy. Or one of the other ladies she knew in Maple Grove."

"She said *our* baby, Mom." Mary Jane's voice dripped with unfamiliar condescension.

The little girl was positive she was right and growing more frustrated with Juliet by the second, giving Juliet her first doubts.

"You shouldn't have been listening to Aunt Marcie's private conversations, honey."

"She said that she was thinking about his questions," the little girl continued, ignoring her mother's admonition.

Questions?

"And that she really liked her job, but that it wasn't like the shop. She missed her ladies and all the talk. And she asked about his mom and the hardware store and then—"

"Okay," Juliet cut her off. Marcie had been talking to Hank. The rest of this she'd handle with her twin. "Enough. This isn't any of your business."

"Yes it is. She saw me."

"She caught you eavesdropping?"

"No." Mary Jane's legs swung harder under the table. "She thought I was outside on the beach and she was hiding in the pantry talking really soft and I came in to get some bread to feed the seagulls and when I pulled open the door she saw me."

"Does she know you're mad at her?"

Mary Jane nodded.

Something else occurred to Juliet. "You heard all that just when you pulled open the pantry door?"

Mary Jane turned her head.

"Look at me, young lady."

It took a long second before the child moved her head around, her eyes worried as they met her mother's gaze.

Juliet didn't say anything. She just waited.

"I got kinda scared when I came in and Aunt Marcie was talking in the pantry. I was afraid she was talking about me. Maybe to you. So I listened."

"Eavesdropping is wrong."

"I know." Mary Jane's full lower lip started to tremble.

Some pretty strong motivation must have propelled the little girl across that line.

"What on earth would Marcie and I have to talk about that would be so secret?"

"I don't know."

With a slight tilt of her head, Juliet silently gave the child a second chance to tell the truth.

"Blake."

Oh. So all wasn't as merry as she'd let herself think. On some level, she'd probably known that. Juliet never had been much of a Pollyanna.

"Mary Jane, you know I don't keep things from you, especially when they're about you. I've always been open with you."

The child's chin softened and sank to her chest. "I know."

With her index finger, Juliet lifted her chin. "I said I'd let you know before I told Blake about you, and I will. That's all there is to it."

"But what if he asks and you like him again and I'm just a kid and—"

"You mean more to me than anything or anyone else in this world, young lady," she said in a tone she seldom used with her daughter. "You come first. Always."

Mary Jane's eyes filled with tears and Juliet pulled the little girl into her arms, holding on for a long time. They'd been happy and contented for eight years. Why did it seem as if the world was trying to pull them apart now, when they needed each other most?

Or was it *because* they needed each other that circumstances seemed to be pulling them apart?

Something Mrs. Cummings had said back in March after the spitting episode came to mind, making Juliet uneasy. The woman had implied that her relationship with Mary Jane was too adult. Too open and equal to be natural. Juliet had completely dismissed her concerns at the time.

But could there possibly be truth to them?

Was that why everything seemed so hard? Because she expected more from a child than she should? Did she, because of Mary Jane's ability to understand beyond her years, expect too much from the little girl emotionally?

Or was it as with everything else of great value— the better it was, the harder you had to work to keep it?

She didn't know.

And that panicked her.

A lot.

BLAKE HAD NEVER DONE so much socializing. That last month before the trial, he accepted every invitation and hint of an invitation that came his way. Maybe, at least in part, he was driven by panic to get as much living in as he possibly could. Just in case.

However, he also wanted to see everyone he could, talk to everyone he could and meet everyone he could who might have known his father and Eaton James. Juliet had spoken to every single person on his list, turning up nothing of any substance, and he just didn't know who else might hold the elusive piece of evidence that would gain him his freedom.

As he sat at the hospital Tuesday evening, enveloped by dread while he waited with a young woman he'd never met to find out if her husband was going to live or die, he wondered whether no one could point to that missing piece. What if his father and Eaton James were the only two people who'd ever known what had really happened between them? What if Blake would never know the whole story? What if there was no possible way to prove his innocence?

What if the father of the unborn child across from him didn't live through the night?

"Do you have family in the area?" he asked the beautiful young Hispanic woman who hadn't said a word since the doctor had left them to take her husband in for emergency neck surgery.

She shook her head, her features striking even though her face was stiff with tension. "They're all still in Mexico. So far, Juan is the only one who got a visa to work here. They're all trying, though."

"Have you called them?"

With her hands slowly rubbing her belly, almost as though she didn't even know what she was doing, she shook her head a second time. "If I call my mama, she'll call his and I don't want them to know when there's no way for them to get here. No money."

"How about friends?"

"We really don't know many people yet. We haven't been here that long, and with getting ready for the baby and all…"

He glanced at her belly and away. "How long before you're due?"

"A month."

That was how long he had left to wait, too.

But while he had to wait alone, young Maria Gomez might not have to. Blake excused himself, made some telephone calls, and within the hour was able to tell Maria that her mother, as well as Juan's, had been wired money and—as was often the case in emergency situations—had been granted permission to spend a week in the United States. They'd be with her by the time Juan was coming out of recovery.

That was when the young woman started to cry. And as Blake sat there, holding a very frightened expectant mother, he prayed to a God he'd quit relying on sometime during his travels. He prayed for Juan and Maria Gomez. For their little baby. And for himself—a man ten years older than Juan Gomez, who'd never fathered a child and might never have a chance to do so.

Might the next month somehow find miracles for all of them.

Because, God knew, only a miracle or two would get any of them through the weeks ahead.

IF JULIET HAD ANY DOUBTS left about Mary Jane's story, they were gone by the time the child finally fell asleep half an hour after her bedtime. Marcie had yet to leave her room.

"You going to hide in here forever?" Juliet pushed open the door to her daughter's former playroom.

"No." Marcie sat on the floor, leaning back against the wall, a tissue in her fist. Her eyes were red and swollen.

"You want to tell me about the conversation Mary Jane interrupted?"

Marcie did, immediately, confirming what Mary Jane had already told her and more.

"I'd like to be able to tell you I understand why you lied to me, and that I'm not hurt," Juliet said, sitting on the edge of the bed. "But I can't. I don't understand why, if you really wanted to talk to Hank, you didn't tell me. The decision is yours to make. We've both always known that. And I am hurt. Really hurt."

Her twin's lips parted, trembled. Tears slowly filled her eyes. The sides of Marcie's hair were damp. She'd long since cried away any makeup she'd had on.

"I know."

The admission didn't heal the hole in Juliet's heart. She'd accepted many challenges in her life—met most of them head-on—and come through stronger. She was prepared to face whatever else life decided to hand her. She'd just never expected Marcie to be the one doing the handing.

They'd come through everything together. Everything.

"Why?"

"I—" Marcie broke off. And that, more than anything, scared Juliet. Even now, face-to-face, there was a wall between her and her sister. She had no idea what to do with it.

"What, I've imagined the bond between us all these years? Imagined the trust?"

"No."

She glanced at her sister's bent head and wanted to scream. Or cry. "Then what?"

"I'm not like you, Jules, so sure of everything all the time."

Juliet slid down to the floor, her knees up to her chest. "I don't know what you mean. I'm not sure of anything."

"Sure you are." Marcie smiled, but the expression held as much sadness as anything else. "You got pregnant, and you knew just what to do. Oh sure," she added when Juliet had been ready to interrupt. "You were scared, but you knew you couldn't marry Blake, knew you shouldn't tell him, knew you had to take the bar exam, and you knew that, eventually, you'd get what you wanted out of life."

Okay. Maybe. She supposed. So why, looking back, did she remember a different kind of feeling—the feeling that she was losing the opportunity to ever have what she really wanted?

"I'm not sure, Jules." Marcie's soft, teary voice brought Juliet's thoughts back to the bedroom.

And the fact that she was looking at the broken trust between her and the other half of herself. She and Marcie had always been able to talk to each other about anything. What had happened to change that?

"Okay, you're not sure. That's no reason to lie to me about talking to Hank. I didn't ask you not to. Or even ask you if you were talking to him. You're the one who came to me and asked me to filter the calls because you didn't want to speak with him again until the baby was born. And being not sure is a reason to talk to me. Haven't we always done that, come to each other, when we needed help?''

Marcie didn't say anything, but the conviction in her troubled blue eyes told its own story.

''What?'' Juliet asked. ''At this point you might as well tell me.'' She didn't figure there was anything else Marcie could say that would hurt her more. She'd never understood, until that moment, how one could hurt too badly for tears.

They'd come. She knew that. Later, when she was alone in her bed.

''I didn't think you could help me.''

''That's crazy!'' Juliet's defenses were up, a first for her with Marcie. It panicked her. She didn't know what to do. ''Who better than me, Marce? I was in the same position you're in right now. And I love you more than anyone in the world.''

''You don't know that,'' Marcie said. ''You have no idea how much Hank loves me.''

So that's what this is about. Two months ago, for the past fifteen years, Marcie had talked about the lack of fire between her and Hank, the lack of a feeling strong enough to get them to the altar. But now that she was pregnant, suddenly she was seeing things she'd never seen before?

Had it been that way with their mother, too? Had she known, before she got pregnant, that she and their father weren't in love?

Was Marcie just like her after all? Another believer in fairy tales? Another woman looking for a man to take care of her? Another dreamer?

Another gray body lying naked in a tub, waiting

for a daughter to come home? To dress it with shaking fingers to preserve an irrelevant modesty when the authorities arrived?

"It doesn't matter anyway," Marcie said, and Juliet stared, wondering for a minute what her sister meant. "Hank doesn't have anything to do with this."

"What does?"

She was pretty sure she didn't want to know, but something forced her to sit there and listen.

"Mom."

Marcie had read her mind, just like always. Under the circumstances, Juliet felt exposed.

"What about her?"

"You aren't rational where all that's concerned, Jules. You never got over it."

"Of course I did. I went to counseling. Got on with my life."

"You continued to live, but I don't think you ever moved beyond it."

Anger sped through her, giving her energy. Air to breathe. "You're somehow going to blame the fact that you lied to me on Mom's death?"

Marcie nodded and Juliet felt herself deflate. "You're so afraid I'm going to end up like her, Jules, that you can't see straight on this one. I know that. I understand. I love you for it. But I can't tell you how I feel about this whole thing with the baby and Hank and Maple Grove. You just don't get it."

Marcie was wrong. She had to be. Juliet was the strong one of the two of them. She always had been.

"Are you saying you think I made the wrong choice when I was pregnant with Mary Jane?" she asked, trying to find even a small part of the anger that had driven her seconds before and given her a sense that she'd survive. "Because if you are, then this is not the first time you've lied to me. You've often said you completely agreed with me."

"I don't think it was the wrong choice," Marcie said softly. "Not necessarily because getting married would have made you unhappy, but because you were so certain it would have. Because of that, there wouldn't have been any other option."

It was too much for her take in. After months of worry about Mary Jane, her renewed contact with Blake, the possibility that he could face life in prison, a case that was one dead end after another, and Marcie's pregnancy, she just couldn't process any more.

"What is it that I supposedly don't understand?" She asked a question she thought she could cope with.

"That I might be able to be happy in Maple Grove," Marcie said, her voice calm, growing stronger. "I hate the place. I have the same memories there that you do. But I do love Hank. All of this has shown me just how much."

Marcie stopped, her hands still in her lap as she glanced over at Juliet, and the momentary conviction in her sister's eyes gave Juliet more pause than anything else that had come before.

"I really thought that I wanted to move to San Diego," she said. "For years, I've thought that. I've been dissatisfied, unwilling to give Hank any indication that I was planning to hang around. That he was enough to keep me there. But I didn't leave, either. Didn't you ever wonder why?"

Juliet knew why. The same reason her mother and grandmother before her had stayed. Fear to believe in anything more. Fear of leaving what little security was guaranteed to find out what the world could bring.

"It's because I was too afraid *not* to want to leave," Marcie said, making no sense to Juliet at all. "I was afraid that if I wanted to stay in Maple Grove, I'd be just like Mom."

It made a very twisted kind of sense. Or was her sister merely justifying the very thing they'd both feared? That they *were* just like the two generations of women who had come before them.

"You expect me to believe now that you *like* Maple Grove?"

"No." Marcie shook her head. "But I love Hank. And he loves me, too. Probably even more. He's supporting me through all of this. He's willing to wait while I work things out because he knows I need to do this on my own. To know for sure. But his life is in Maple Grove."

"If he loves you so much, why can't he think about making a life somewhere else?"

"I asked him the same question."

"And?"

"He doesn't know the answer."

Life was never easy. And in the space of a few short hours, it had just gotten inexorably harder.

BLAKE WAITED at their usual booth in the little place out by Mission Beach for Juliet to arrive for their weekly meeting the first Friday evening in July—just three weeks before his trial.

Lucy brought over his whiskey as soon as he sat down. "Where's Juliet tonight?"

"On her way," he told the older woman. "She'll have the usual."

Lucy nodded, didn't bother with her pad. "You having dinner?"

"Probably."

"I'll just leave these then." She pulled a couple of worn black menus from the back of her waistband and plopped them down. "You don't look so good, son," she said as she was leaving. "Take that woman of yours on a cruise. You'll both come back rested and raring to go again."

Take his woman on a cruise. What an impossible thought.

But an intriguing one. A whole week alone with Juliet on the Mediterranean Sea. Fresh air. Sunshine. Cliffs older than time. History. Great food. And all night long for making love...

"Hi, sorry I'm late." He hadn't noticed her approach and she was already sliding into the booth before he could stand.

Probably not such a bad thing.

"Your drink's on the way."

Her smile was beautiful, as always, and mostly surface. He knew what that meant. The clock was ticking and answers weren't appearing.

"Might as well get it out of the way," he told her as soon as Lucy had brought her glass of wine.

She slid her arms out of the jacket to her suit. He hadn't seen the yellow one before and couldn't imagine many women looking good in it. On Juliet, with that fire-laced hair, the outfit was attention-grabbing. Or maybe it was just him. He seemed to find everything about her captivating.

"How do you know there's anything to get out of the way?"

Infuriating. But captivating.

"Your expression, Counselor," he said, bracing himself for whatever she might tell him. No matter how bad it got, he was not going to lose faith. It was about all he had left.

His faith, a room full of quotes that were daily reminders that the charges against him did not define him, and an attorney who was on his mind far more than was healthy.

Juliet took a pad out of her satchel. He'd noticed that while she always had that pad and a pen, she seldom used them.

"The worst news is there's nothing to report from the Cayman Islands." She looked straight at him. Pounded another nail in his coffin without flinching. He respected that about her.

"What else?"

Her smile was more genuine, if a bit sad. "We've been spending far too much time together if you know me so well," she said.

With both hands surrounding his whiskey glass, Blake watched her through narrowed eyes. "I don't think it's a matter of time," he told her.

In other circumstances he wouldn't have been so forthright. But faced with the fact that he might not have all that long, the normal rules of social interaction just didn't mean all that much.

She didn't say anything. But she didn't glance away, either.

"I think it's a matter of recognition. The first night we met it seemed as though I knew you."

She licked trembling lips, took a sip of wine.

"You think I'm nuts."

"No." She bit her bottom lip. "Not unless I'm nuts, too."

Blake needed to kiss that bottom lip. And the top one, too. He needed to feel those breasts against his chest. To lose himself inside her again as he'd done endlessly that night so long ago. To be free to have another night like that one…

"I found something else this week." Her voice cooled him off, though her eyes still bore that strange indefinable something that filled the space between them.

"What?" he asked. He'd had a long week, too, and didn't want to hear any more about things he could do nothing about. Yet he needed to know everything if the facts were ever going to come together to expose the truth.

"Interestingly enough, as I perused the records of a couple of other Eaton Estates investors, I noticed outgoing payables in the exact dollar amounts that James was paying your father and that were being deposited in the Cayman Islands. We don't know that the money was going there. It certainly wasn't recorded that way. Still, just as with your father's contributions to the Honduras charities, the coincidence is notable."

"You think there's a Ponzi scheme?" Had Eaton, like Charles Ponzi, used later investors to pay off earlier investors whose money he'd lost or confiscated?

"Possibly."

Blake sat up, his heart beating a little faster. If they could prove something like this, he'd be home free.

"If nothing else, it at least means the money in the Islands could have come from any number of sources."

"Yes."

"Why isn't this great news?" It meant there were other places to look for the missing clue—some kind of proof that someone other than him had deposited money in that damn account. Some record of those same amounts of money leaving someplace else with no known destination on just the right days.

"It might be great news, but it makes the pool of possibilities that much larger when our window of opportunity is getting smaller by the day."

Blake sipped his whiskey, in spite of the noose he felt tightening around his neck.

CHAPTER SEVENTEEN

THE SOUND OF CEREAL pouring into a bowl woke Juliet Saturday morning. Rolling over, she pushed the hair out of her eyes, trying to make out the numbers on the clock through sleep-blurred eyes.

Barely past six. If it were wintertime, the sun wouldn't even be up yet.

Yawning, pushing past the lethargy that had claimed her limbs during the long night, she grabbed the terry shorts at the end of her bed and slid them up under the spaghetti-strap T-shirt she wore to bed.

Something had to give soon. She couldn't afford too many more sleepless nights like the one she'd just had.

Worrying about Mary Jane. And Marcie. And Blake's case.

And refusing to think about the feelings he aroused in her. Desires she'd long since convinced herself had been the result of too much alcohol and a desperate need to feel something besides worry and grief.

She'd had nine years to escape.

And her body was so on fire for the man, she could hardly relax enough to fall asleep. She'd always thought it was only men who walked around all day with raging hormones.

"What's the rush, imp?" she asked, finding her

daughter at the kitchen table. Meandering over to turn on the coffeepot, she stopped to wipe up the puddle of milk spilled on the counter.

"I'm not rushed."

"You're up and at 'em pretty darned early. You have some big plans for the day I don't know about?"

"Uh-uh." The little girl spoke with a mouthful of cereal.

"You want to spend the afternoon on the beach? We could take the tools and molds and build another sand town like we did last year."

"Yeah." Mary Jane was already dressed in cotton flowered overall shorts and a matching purple T-shirt. Her hair, always a mass of unruly curls, had clearly not seen the hairbrush that morning. "If *she* doesn't have to come along."

"Mary Jane McNeil, that's enough." Juliet stopped, her arm half out of the cupboard with a coffee cup in her hand. She'd never spoken so harshly to the child.

Mary Jane was staring at her, mouth open. Her eyes were wide and glistening.

Setting the cup on the counter, Juliet pulled a chair up next to her and sat. "I'm sorry."

Mary Jane said nothing. Nor did she close her mouth.

"I was wrong to speak to you like that," she tried again, running one finger along the little girl's thigh.

The child's gaze moved, following that finger.

"Say something."

"You yelled at me like Mrs. Thacker."

The third-grade teacher who'd helped make life hell this past spring.

"I know." She couldn't believe it, either. She'd never felt that anger-filled tension toward Mary Jane before. "I lost patience and I'm sorry." She wanted to promise she'd never do it again, but she was afraid to. She didn't want to add lying to her list of sins, and because this was new territory for her, she couldn't be sure it wouldn't come again.

Mary Jane stared at her long and hard. And then nodded. "Okay."

Juliet couldn't leave it there. "It's just that what you're doing to Marcie, it's not right, sweetie."

"She lied."

"Yes, she did. But to me, not to you." Juliet was still trying to comprehend all the ramifications of her last conversation with her sister. "But she had good reason."

The little girl opened her mouth to speak and knowing that she wasn't up for a debate on the rightness of lying if the reason was good enough, she quickly said, "We all make mistakes, Mary Jane. You do. I do. Like I just did, snapping at you." She leaned down, arms on her knees, bringing her eyes level with the child's. "And think about how awful it would be if every time you made a mistake, I refused to talk to you or spend time with you. What if I didn't say it was okay when you said you were sorry?"

Mary Jane pushed her spoon around in the milk left in her bowl. "You can't do that. You love me."

"And you love your aunt Marcie, too."

The little girl looked over at her. "But lying is the worst," she whispered. "You always say so."

"I know." Running a hand around the back of her neck, Juliet struggled to focus, to find words to explain something that she was pretty sure she hadn't completely grasped yet. "But sometimes, there's more than one truth and the two truths don't go together and you have to choose which one to tell."

Mary Jane's legs swung under the table. She played with her milk. "That doesn't actually make much sense, Mom."

"Well," Juliet said, watching the little person who was as much a part of her as her own heart and bones, aching for her in ways she didn't really understand.

She couldn't tell the child much, couldn't involve her, but clearly some kind of explanation was necessary to calm her. "It's true that Aunt Marcie might want to go back to Maple Grove, but she knew that because I feel so strongly about the place, I wouldn't be able to understand what she was feeling. There's also another truth—that she hates Maple Grove as much as I do. Both things are true. But she just told me the one she knew I'd understand. The one about hating Maple Grove and understanding how and why I feel like I do about the place. She meant it when she told me she didn't want to talk to Hank, she just didn't tell me when she changed her mind because she knew I wouldn't understand."

Mary Jane let go of her spoon, scratched her nose, and then, reaching for her spoon again, accidentally knocked it aside, sending milk flying. Seeming not to even notice, she peered at Juliet, a sweet frown marking her forehead. "Kind of like when another girl has on a new dress and asks you what you think and you know she really likes it and you understand that, so you find something to say that's the truth, like the lace is pretty cool, when it's also true that you hate the dress?''

"Yes." Juliet smiled, the tension in her stomach easing for the moment. "I think it is kind of like that."

"So Aunt Marcie is still one of us?"

Juliet picked up the spoon and put it back in the bowl. "She'll always be one of us, no matter what," she told her daughter. "Just like you will be. Whether you lie or cheat or steal or grow up to be president, you'll always be my little girl, just like Marcie is always my sister."

"I know *that*," Mary Jane said, up on her knees. With her hands on each side of her mother's face, she put her nose within a couple of inches of Juliet's and stared. "I mean that we can believe her again."

"Absolutely," Juliet said, peace settling over her as she hugged her daughter tight.

FREEDOM WAS A GREAT DOG. Great at gulping down huge bowls of chow, great at chewing off the edges of cupboards, great at waking Blake up just about anytime he managed to finally fall into a fitful sleep. And great at being man's best friend. The puppy was already leash-trained—trained to know that he didn't want one. For that privilege, he'd quickly learned never to leave Blake's side when they ran on the beach.

To test his skills, and only to test his skills, Blake loaded the dog—and the leash, just in case—in his car on Saturday for a drive over to Mission Beach. He had no idea where Juliet lived and purposely did not try to find her address. Nor did he intend to watch for signs of her silver BMW. It was a long stretch of beach—a lot of it with private access, so not very crowded—and perfect for running with a new pup.

In his black running shorts, white muscle shirt and favorite running shoes, he wasn't ready to acknowledge that there was any comfort at all in just being close to the woman who'd become some kind of savior to him—and not just because she might be able to keep him out of jail.

She'd shown him a part of life he'd subconsciously been searching for and had given up on ever finding. The existence of something beneath the surface, beneath the endless fight for success. Juliet had shown him that he could find peace no matter how horrible the daily circumstances, just by being with the right person.

He stopped the car in a public lay-by, got out, walked around the vehicle and opened the front passenger door. "Let's go, Freed, and watch your manners."

The pup squealed, jumped down and wet the toe of Blake's sneaker. Patting the bouncing black head, Blake reached inside the black Mercedes SUV for a moistened towelette, wiped his shoe and tossed the towelette on the floor behind the seat.

"Come on, boy," he said, slapping his leg as he started down the side of a small cliff to the beach below. Freedom pushed through the weeds, prancing joyfully beside Blake.

There weren't any cottages on this section of beach and Blake ran easily, his mind wandering, as it always seemed to these days, to his beautiful barracuda defense attorney.

Now that he'd found her, he just had a few hurdles to cross so that he could do something about not losing her again.

A case to win. A jail sentence to elude. And a woman to convince.

The first people they saw weren't a problem for Freedom—a teenage couple lying on a blanket tucked into a cove along the beach. They were so engrossed, Blake suspected they didn't even know he and Freedom had passed.

Freedom must have sensed the same as, after a cursory glance, he ignored them, too.

So far so good.

At least if Blake was sent to prison, Freedom would have a better chance of finding a good home than he'd had when Blake got him. People preferred trained dogs to undisciplined ones.

He wasn't going to put his house on the market. He could afford to have Pru Duncan come in every day for the next forty years if he needed to.

She'd be somewhere in her nineties then.

So he'd hire someone else.

He'd even considered having Pru look after Freedom for him. But what kind of life would it be for the dog, having no family of his own, living alone with only daily visits from the hired help?

Hell, Blake had *chosen* to live that way and had ended up with almost intolerable loneliness.

Freedom barked at a bird that flew just in front of his nose. Blake chuckled. He couldn't ever remember a time of such innocence.

They passed a middle-aged couple walking along the beach hand in hand. After a quick sniff, Freedom

continued jogging along, sloshing in the water now
and then when he got too far ahead of Blake and had
to stop.

He'd sell the Mercedes. The thing would be ob-
solete twenty years from now. With a pang, he left
that thought behind. He'd only had the car a year and
wasn't anywhere near ready to part with it. They were
just settling in together.

He and the puppy ran for an hour in the July mid-
day sun along deserted ground banked by rocky
coves, and across sandy beaches bordered by distant
homes. Freedom was a friendly sort, greeting most
humans he passed, but a slap of Blake's hand against
his thigh told the dog not to linger. And when they
got hot, they dipped into the ocean just long enough
to cool down.

The pup rounded a corner up ahead and Blake
laughed out loud when he made the turn to find the
little guy with his nose buried deep in the sand.

"Freedom, get over here," he called. "You nut,
you're going to end up with a crab on the end of that
snout."

The dog barked and trotted on, as though proud of
himself.

Yeah, the dog was great.

Freedom barked again, and for a second Blake was
almost convinced the animal could read his mind and
was barking in agreement. He heard the voices ahead
just in time to see the pup tearing ahead of him. His
target—a young girl waist deep in sand amidst what
looked to be the most intricate sand village Blake had
ever seen.

"Freedom!" he called sharply, trying to avoid imminent disaster. The dog skidded to a halt just before galloping on top of a sand roof that somehow had the texture of tile. Whether it was Blake's call that had stopped the dog, or the little girl whose face was receiving a barrage of sloppy puppy kisses, he wasn't sure.

"I'm sorry," Blake said, only slightly out of breath as he stopped beside the little girl. And then his gaze moved to the two adults who'd been sitting in the sand with the child.

"Oh my God." Juliet McNeil jumped up, her face completely horror-stricken.

"I hardly think being caught in a very attractive pair of shorts and equally nice bikini top is reason for such horror," he said to her, pleased beyond reason to have run into her. Even if she was taking a little longer than he was to appreciate the chance to have their completely necessary professional distance breached for just a moment or two.

He hadn't looked for her. And here she was anyway, on the beach with a neighbor's child. And...

His eyes moved to the woman who was still sitting in the sand, staring at him with eyes that, while different in color, wore the same confusing expression of dread as they assessed him.

"You must be Marcie," he guessed, holding out a sweaty palm to take the sand-covered hand she offered almost as an afterthought.

The woman dropped his hand, nodded, stood. Juliet had not exaggerated when she'd said she and her twin had the same build. It was uncanny, looking at the two of them. One blond and blue-eyed. The other earth and fire.

"What's his name?" The little girl's question reminded Blake that it wasn't polite to stare.

"Freedom," he said. "Don't worry, he won't bite."

"I wasn't worried." Something about the child reminded him of someone, but he couldn't place who it might be. Her curly brown hair and chubby cheeks made her seem almost cherubic. The assessing look in those eyes could have been intimidating.

Blake smiled at her. "What's your name?"

"Mary Jane. What's yours?"

"Blake Ramsden."

The change in the little girl was instantaneous. Her face bright red, she spun in the sand to face Juliet. "You promised!"

"Mary Jane, I didn't tell him. Not anything."

Juliet's tone of voice was completely different, filled with a combination of authority and love that struck Blake.

"He knows where I live." The little girl's accusatory tone was unmistakable.

Confused, feeling as though he'd stumbled into some kind of inexplicable fantasy with nightmare overtones, Blake glanced over to see what Juliet would say.

Nothing shocked him more than his defense attorney's speechless—and helpless—stare as she faced the livid child.

"No, I don't," he offered, hoping it would help. "I don't know where you live." And then as more occurred to him, he added, "I guess Ms. McNeil told you the name of her newest client, but you don't have to be frightened. I'm not a criminal."

"You lied to me!" the little girl screamed, seeming not to have heard him at all. She didn't turn. Didn't spare him another glance. "I hate you," she spit at Juliet. "I hate you. And I'll hate you forever!" Without a look at anyone, including the pup who'd been trying to get her attention, she ran for one of the cottages in the distance.

"I'll go after her." Marcie spoke for the first time. At Juliet's nod, she ran after the little girl, catching up with her before they'd made it halfway to the house. Marcie's presence at her side didn't slow Mary Jane down at all.

"Pretty little girl," Blake said, floundering for conversation while he made sense out of what had just happened. He must have run farther than he'd thought, or it was hotter than he thought. He didn't usually feel so slow-witted.

"Yeah." Juliet wrapped her arms around her bare middle, her forehead creased as she glanced back toward the cottage. Marcie and Mary Jane disappeared inside what looked to be the largest dwelling in the row.

"Is she a neighbor?"

"No." Lips pinched, Juliet looked up at him. The expression in her eyes was strange. Hooded and yet full of something he wasn't getting.

"She's visiting you?"

"No."

Why did she look so hunted? And hurt?

And terrified?

"She's not Marcie's, is she? I assumed this was your sister's first pregnancy."

"It is."

He nodded then. Okay, so he was on solid ground there.

Freedom ran down to the water, plodding along the shore, pouncing on the waves.

"She's mine, Blake."

The sky was bluer than blue today. Clear and beautiful. Blake slid his hands into the pockets of his shorts, his fingers wrapping around the single car key he carried when he ran.

"You have a child," he said, nodding.

It didn't matter that Juliet had a child. He liked children.

Though perhaps, after all the time he'd spent with her these past weeks, he should have known something so important. They'd talked about being friends.

"Why didn't you ever mention her?"

He should probably wonder about her father. What part he played in Juliet's life. And the little girl's.

"I couldn't." Juliet's eyes were moist, as if she might cry. And they were pleading with him.

In some way, Blake realized something horrible was about to happen. He couldn't leave until it had played out.

Somehow, his life depended on it.

His neck was stiff. So was his chin. And lips. "How old is she?" It wasn't a question he'd have any reason to ask. The words came anyway.

"Eight." She held his gaze; he gave her that much. And really, based on how difficult this appeared to be for her, he supposed it was a lot.

"Born when?"

"December."

Eyes never leaving hers, Blake did the math. And

fought a swirl of emotion that threatened to consume him. His arms ached with it. His stomach knotted against it. Pain stabbed at his chest, making it difficult for him to breathe.

"She's mine."

Juliet slowly nodded.

And tears pricked at the back of his eyes. All those years lost.

Blake glanced back up at the cottage door through which his daughter had passed.

His daughter.

He had a child.

A girl.

Family of his very own.

And this woman who he'd thought was connected to him in some elemental way was a woman he didn't know at all.

He'd believed that she brought him peace. Instead, she'd robbed him of the first eight years of his little girl's life. Never mind that he hadn't been at all prepared for fatherhood back then. That seemed irrelevant now.

Blake rocked back, trying to stay on his feet as another onslaught of raw pain hit his chest. Mary Jane. He hadn't even had a chance to give her a name.

CHAPTER EIGHTEEN

"I HAVE TO GO to her." Juliet's voice was the barest thread of sound.

He couldn't allow it. Too many opportunities had already been lost to him. "I'll do it."

"Blake, no." He was surprised when she stepped forward.

"I have a lot of time to make up for." Another stab of pain. "And possibly few chances to do so." For the first time, insidious bitterness entered his heart. He'd managed to hold it at bay, but now…

He felt a nudge against his hand. Cold. Wet. Reassuring. Freedom. He'd actually forgotten the dog was there.

Thank God for Freedom.

"I'm not leaving," Blake said. He meant the words and would act on them, though the authorities would probably just haul him away for trespassing and zap more charges at him. Threaten more time locked away in a cell, waiting while life passed, taking with it all the opportunities he'd been born to find.

He was not going to die incomplete.

"I will see her."

"Okay."

Her compliance shocked him. With hair falling out of her ponytail, no makeup on her colorless face and droplets of sweat running down between her breasts, Juliet didn't look any better than he felt.

"Just let me go to her first," she said. And when he moved to argue, she held up her hand. "You can stay right here. I won't ask you to leave. But she's only a child, Blake. You have to think of her. She's going to need a minute to hurl hatred at me, if nothing else. And then, hopefully, she'll be able to listen. We have to make this as easy on her as we can."

That note of authoritative love he'd heard in Juliet's voice earlier came crashing back. It had been the voice of a parent.

He was a parent.

And as such, his daughter's needs came before his own.

"I'll wait," he said. And without another look in her direction, he turned, dropped down to the beach and stared out at one of his oldest and dearest friends—the ocean.

He might not understand it, but he could count on it to always be there. Steadfast. Unchanging. Living by its routine day in and day out, tide in and tide out, whether he was there or not.

Even after years away, the ocean had welcomed him home, same as always. Her shorelines might change. The boats upon her waters might change. But she did not. Ever.

And neither would he. For as long as it took, he was going to sit there.

"Freedom, come."

The dog came. Lay beside his master. Put his head down. And waited.

"JULES?" Marcie came running through the kitchen just as Juliet came in the sliding glass door from the beach.

"She's gone!"

"What?" Juliet, dreading the minutes ahead, deathly afraid that life would never be good again, stared at her twin.

"Mary Jane's gone!"

"Gone?" As fear tore into her, Juliet ran through the cottage. "She *can't* be gone. She just came in with you."

There was no sign of the girl in the living room.

"Mary Jane McNeil, you come out here right now!" Juliet screamed so loudly her throat stung. "I mean it, young lady. Come out here, now!"

Before this morning she'd never spoken to her daughter like that. Now it was twice in one day.

"She went to her room," Marcie was saying, running behind Juliet. "She shut the door and said she wanted to be alone."

That wasn't unheard of. Mary Jane didn't usually pout in public.

"I had to go to the bathroom and when I came out, her door was open and she was gone!"

Juliet burst into Mary Jane's room. "Mary Jane? If you're hiding under that bed, you'd better give it up. Now!"

The space under the bed was empty. And the room looked surprisingly normal. As though this was any other ordinary Saturday and they'd be leaving for the grocery store any minute now.

Until she noticed a bend in the blinds over the window.

And once she lifted them, the open window was obvious. So was a truth Juliet didn't think she was strong enough to withstand.

Mary Jane had run away.

HEARING FOOTSTEPS running in the sand behind him, Blake jumped up. He could hardly breathe as he turned around, ready to take his little girl into his arms for the first time.

He was thinking about how furious she'd been when he'd introduced himself, almost as though she'd recognized the name and had known who he was. It didn't make sense. But he was sure there'd be a logical explanation.

In the meantime…

He turned. His heart skipped a beat when he saw Juliet running toward him, alone, with a face so pinched it was almost unrecognizable.

By the time she reached him, the blood was pumping painfully through his veins.

"She's run away!" Juliet's terror was a horrible thing to see. And contagious.

A little girl out in the world alone. He shivered with cold and fury against all the unknown evils that could befall his child. And he was shocked at his own reaction—as though he'd been a parent far longer than this mere half hour.

"Call the police," he barked out.

"Marcie already is. And calling some neighbors and friends, too, to start a search."

He nodded. "Fine, but it'll take too long for them to get here. We can't wait that long."

"I know." Juliet swallowed. "I think she climbed out her window."

She pointed to the side of the cottage blocked from view by a little patch of trees.

He nodded and pushed aside any feelings he might at one time have had for her. "I'll take the beach. This direction." He pointed up the beach, where the child would have come out through the trees. "You and Marcie take the street. You go one way and tell her to take the other."

Looking like a lost little girl instead of the powerful defense attorney he knew her to be, Juliet nodded. "I'll take my cell phone. Marcie'll have hers, too."

"Mine's back in my car," Blake said. But he wasn't losing a second to go back for it. "Honk a car horn three times if someone finds her and I'll know to come back. Depending on how long I'm gone, you might have to drive up the road a bit for me to hear."

She glanced at him once more, and nodded. Blake refused to take the comfort she was offering. Or to give her what she needed, either.

He just didn't have it.

"Can Freedom stay inside?"

"Of course."

"Go, boy," Blake said, grabbing the dog's collar and handing him over to Juliet.

They hadn't even turned around before he was hiking up the beach.

SHE JUST WANTED to spit. And…and…anything else that would hurt her mother's feelings. Tromping along in the sand, making huge big footprints because she was so mad and stepping so hard, she stared at the ground. She wouldn't look at the water at all.

Mom always told her to look at the water. And to know that there was no end to what she could do with her life. And no end to hope. Or to love, either.

Mom was a stupid liar.

She almost stepped on a pretty, perfect shell. It was pink and all shiny with different colors in the sun. Mom's favorite kind. They always picked up and saved those ones. Mary Jane thought about stomping on it, but she didn't want some kid in bare feet to come later and step on it and get cut. She hated that.

Instead, she picked it up and threw it as hard as she could, far out into the water where Mom could never ever find it, even if she wanted it badly enough.

And then she trudged on, way farther than she was allowed to go—and after a while, farther than she'd ever been, even with Mom and Aunt Marcie.

So what? They said it wasn't safe for her here alone, but who cared? They were both liars.

She turned some corners and walked really fast. She sweated a lot, too.

If she got too hot, she'd go in the water. Mom didn't want her to do that, either. She was just going to do everything Mom didn't want her to do. Mom deserved it.

Sometime after she'd passed some people on a blanket—a man, a woman and some boy—Mary Jane thought about how tired her legs were. She'd forgotten how tired the sand could make her feet when she walked in it a long time.

So she moved closer to the water, letting the waves come up over her new white tennis shoes.

She loved them most when they were brand-new white. Mom did, too. And she'd be really sorry when she saw them all dirty.

Not that she was going to see them. Mary Jane wasn't ever going home again. Who could live with people who lied to you?

She heard a dog bark and jumped back, kind of scared. Mom said stray dogs were dangerous sometimes and they could bite and give you rabies, which could make you have some pretty bad shots or die. She'd never been alone around a stray dog.

But when she looked around, there wasn't one too close. She was kind of thirsty, though. And the ocean water was bad for drinking because of salt making you even thirstier. She shoulda brought her thermos from school. And a sandwich, too. Because it was going to be dinnertime and she hadn't figured out where she was going to live yet.

Still, she was away from the liars. And that was all that mattered.

A man was by himself, up ahead by the water. Mary Jane slowed down. She wasn't scared or anything, but everyone knew men were sometimes bad and she didn't want to have to run away fast. She just wanted to be left alone. And quit being lied to.

Just then she heard the dog bark again. It ran to the man. And then a lady was there, too, and Mary Jane said hi as she walked past. They said hi and smiled. She probably could ask them for water if she had to. And if they fed a dog, they might feed her. A lot of adults thought dogs and kids were a lot alike. And besides, she wasn't a picky eater and didn't eat much either.

So she'd be okay.

But she was tired. And she needed to find out where she was going to live before it got dark and she had to go to bed.

Mary Jane ran into a wave, laughing as the water came up to get her shorts wet. And then she did it again.

Pretty soon she was all wet. It wasn't really funny when you were all alone and no one could see.

She wasn't going to be scared of the dark. She just wanted to get her bed made before she couldn't see what she was doing. Lumps in beds made her kind of grumpy.

Mom had teased her about that one time when they'd camped out in a sleeping bag on the beach. Mary Jane kept punching at the lumps in the sand and finally Mom got a sand shovel from the house and dug Mary Jane a perfect oval to sleep in.

She could dig her own oval, though. She knew how. She'd use her new white tennis shoe and get it even dirtier.

When she stubbed her toe and fell down, Mary Jane didn't really care. Her knee was scraped, but only babies cried over stuff like that. And she wasn't a baby. She was big and strong and didn't need any father.

Slopping along at the water's edge, she thought about Blake Ramsden's dog. He'd licked her. And his tongue was rough and kind of tickled. And was gross wet.

She'd always wanted a dog but Mom said they couldn't have one because they weren't home enough and who would feed it and train it to go potty outside and clean up on the beach when it made a mess.

Mary Jane said she would, but Mom still said no.

But so what? Mom was a liar.

And then she thought of Blake Ramsden. He'd

smiled at her before she knew who he was. She'd liked him then. She'd felt all warm inside when he'd smiled, like she could have run to him if the house was on fire and he'd climb a ladder and save her mom *and* her dog.

Even when he'd asked her name, she'd liked him. He probably made good sand villages, and maybe would've let her play Frisbee with his dog on the beach. If she had a Frisbee. She'd lost hers.

Then he'd said his name. Mary Jane hated his name. And she hated him, too. Because Mom didn't want him to be her dad—or he didn't really want to be her dad. How did she know which it was?

She stumbled again. And fell on the very same knee. And got wet sand in with the skin.

It stung a lot. But that wasn't why there were tears in her eyes. She just felt like crying. That was all.

Pretty soon, she felt like crying a lot. And it was going to get dark. She wasn't afraid of the dark but bad men came out more at night. The ocean meant dreams come true, though, so she'd stay close to that.

Wondering what she was going to do next, Mary Jane wandered farther up the beach.

BLAKE DIDN'T KNOW *how* to have an eight-year-old daughter. He'd never been a father.

Striding up the beach, eyes straining to see every movement, focused on any movement, he revised his last thought. He'd been a father. He just hadn't known about it.

He couldn't walk fast enough, look carefully enough. He couldn't do enough. Ever. He wasn't going to recapture eight lost years. And he might not have eight more weeks to get to know the child who was flesh of his flesh. His family.

The only family still alive.

As he passed a man and woman on a blanket with their little boy, asking if they'd seen a little girl, and moving on as they shook their heads, he wondered if he even wanted his own child to get to know him. Did he want his daughter to meet a man on trial for more crimes than she had years on earth? Did he want her to learn that her father might be spending the rest of his life in jail?

He wanted her to know he wasn't guilty of those crimes. He wanted her to know that if she had nothing else but her integrity, it would be enough.

He wanted her to understand that he loved her without even knowing her. That he'd give his life for her.

About her mother, he thought not at all. He couldn't afford to.

The beach was relatively deserted. Blake wasn't sure if that was good or bad. With fewer people out, the percentages were less that a twisted jerk would find a little girl strolling alone on the beach. And yet, with fewer people around, a twisted jerk would find that girl easy prey.

Sick to his stomach, he walked on, moving rapidly, missing nothing. There were indentations in the sand, but too many to be distinguishable as a little girl's footprints.

Or there were no footprints, which was why he was only seeing footprint-like indentations. She might not have come this way. She might be somewhere in the village of Mission Beach, wandering streets where all kinds of weirdos could be watching her—a beautiful little curly-headed angel all alone.

No. He couldn't think that way. She was out here on the beach, pouting, drawing shapes in the sand somewhere with a twig, maybe even on the verge of running back home.

Was she smart enough to walk on the edge of the waves so her prints would be washed away? Or smart enough to stay away from the water so that she wasn't unexpectedly sucked under?

The familiar dull stabbing in his chest struck again as he considered that he knew nothing at all about his own child. Was she good in school or did she struggle? Did she laugh at cartoons?

Could she keep herself safe?

Blake had thought, when he'd been face-to-face with the reality of possibly losing his freedom for the rest of his life, that the emotions consuming him were the absolute worst he could ever experience.

He'd been wrong.

He walked. He searched. Under every bit of brush, in every cranny of every cliff bank, in yards. He talked to the few people he passed on the beach. He knocked on cottage doors, asking if anyone had seen an eight-year-old girl with dark curly hair and sweet chubby cheeks. He could hold up a hand to show them how tall she was. But he didn't have the actual statistic.

He didn't even know the color of her eyes.

And when people shook their heads, again and again, he resolved not to lose hope. He'd find her.

He had to find her. To know she was safe. To get to know her.

And when he did find her, he was going to spend every waking moment with the child, listening to everything she had to say, telling her about her grandparents. Showing her his home. He was taking no chances. If he went to prison, his daughter was at least going to have these weeks. She was going to know that she came from good, hardworking, honest people.

He had a lot to do in very little time.

The sun was starting to sink and Blake had covered more than a couple of miles of beach, with still no horn sounding from the road above. Worry was starting to override every positive effort he made. If they didn't find her by nightfall, the entire situation changed. His daughter would no longer be an upset little girl pretending to run away. She'd be an endangered female child.

A young couple with a dog had seen a little girl pass by, although they couldn't really describe her. A couple of teenage boys with new surfboards and no idea what they were doing were sure they'd seen her. But they didn't even know the color of her hair.

He should turn back. The police would be there, and a search party would have gathered by now. Maybe Marcie or Juliet had found her and sounded a horn and he just hadn't heard it.

She'd probably run back home as quickly as she'd left.

But still he plunged on. That little girl had been furious with her mother. She thought she'd been lied to.

He stopped himself just short of determining that her running was justified.

Did he seriously want his little girl sacrificing her life because of a lie?

God, no.

Truth wasn't worth that.

He almost missed the sound as he walked. A quiet, animal-like moan coming from between a boulder and a cliff in a spot where the beach narrowed to almost nothing.

Heart pounding, Blake focused on calm as he slowly rounded the boulder, not sure what he'd find. An injured squirrel? A dog?

A child.

Sitting hunched over, knees pulled up to her chest, her head buried in her thighs. He'd only seen her once, but one glance at the curly brown head and Blake knew he'd found his daughter.

There was dried blood all over her.

The sound came again. A tiny moan followed by a dry sob, as though she was still hurting but was all cried out.

Keeping his emotions in check, when he wanted to grab up that tiny body and run for the nearest phone, Blake kneeled down a few feet away. He didn't want to scare her, but he had to know how badly she was hurt.

"Mary Jane?"

She jumped, her eyes wide and glazed with fright. And then, seeing him, she hid her swollen, tear-and-sand-stained face.

"Honey, are you hurt?"

Dumb, Ramsden. Really dumb. Of course she was hurt. It hurt to bleed. And it hurt to think that the one person in the world you could trust had been lying to you.

When she continued to ignore him, Blake tried again. "Mary Jane, I understand that you need to be alone, but you're bleeding. At least let me make sure you don't need a doctor."

"I don't." The voice was surprisingly strong.

"Can I please see where you're hurt, just to be sure?"

A skinny little leg popped out, showing him a severely scraped shin and knee. While the cuts weren't deep, there wasn't much skin intact.

"Is that all?"

While she kept her head lowered, the other leg came forth. And then two palms and an elbow. From what he could tell, she was right. She probably didn't need a doctor. But she would if those scrapes weren't cleaned up.

"What happened?"

"I fell." She was talking to her chest, but the words were full of energy. And anger.

"Where?"

She glanced up at him then, her little face puckered with irritation. "On the beach and here." She pointed to the cliff.

Blake glanced up. And swallowed. "You tried to climb up there?"

"I saw a cave."

She saw a cave. The kid had walked for miles. Been gone for hours. Missed at least one meal. And she hadn't been planning on coming home.

And suddenly his years of not being a father were extremely evident. He had no idea what to do next.

CHAPTER NINETEEN

THE ROAR OF THE WAVES was so loud he could hardly hear himself think—not that he was having any thoughts worth hearing.

"I'm a klutz," the child announced suddenly.

"What?" He watched her, his heart filling, breaking, and filling some more.

"I'm a klutz," she repeated in a matter-of-fact tone that lost some of its effect with the residual sob that accompanied it. "You might as well know, I knock things over and fall a lot."

The condition didn't seem to upset her much.

"Okay."

"I don't need a father."

The words might have hurt, if he'd had any room for any more emotion. But he'd figured out, somewhere during his trek as he'd replayed that scene on the beach between her and her mother, that Mary Jane would not have chosen to see him.

"You know who I am."

Green. Her eyes were green with little brown flecks, just like her mother's.

"You met my mother one night a long time ago."

Well, that just about summed it up.

"I..."

"You can go now. We're just fine without you,"

she said, and then, as he digested that, as he told himself he couldn't possibly feel more pain, her face screwed up as if she might cry again.

"I'm sorry," she said. "That was mean."

"A little."

"But it's true, and this is one of those times when someone asks if you like her dress and you have to say no, you hate it."

In spite of all the heartache and frustration consuming him, Blake smiled. He couldn't help it. The little girl intrigued him, and not just because she was his daughter.

But she was. He'd only just met her and suddenly felt as though he'd known this child all her life.

"You are your mother's daughter," he said.

"Yeah." The derision was back. "But I don't want her, either."

"You don't mean that."

She studied him for a minute, her red-rimmed eyes serious beyond her years. "Pro'bly not, but I'm really, really mad right now."

Taking a chance that she wouldn't close up on him, Blake settled in the sand in front of her, his legs stretched out so his white tennis shoes were almost touching hers. Huge and so small. The contrast made his throat tight.

"Why is that?" he asked when he could.

Those wide green eyes hardened. "She lied to me. She promised me she wouldn't tell you about me. I knew when she took your case this would happen, but she promised and promised and I believed her and she lied to me."

Mary Jane knew he was Juliet's client. And that

he'd been with her mother once, a long time ago. What else did this precocious child know? The extent of his crimes? Why her mother never told him that she existed?

"She didn't lie to you."

Mary Jane didn't believe him, not that he blamed her. He knew what it felt like to be lied to.

"I didn't have any idea you existed until I saw you with your mother on the beach," he said. "I knew she had a cottage somewhere on Mission Beach, that's all. She'd never told me where. Freedom needs practice being around people. Mission Beach is a little busier than mine, but not *too* busy, so it seemed like a good choice." It struck him that he was a grown man, sitting on the beach, confiding in an eight-year-old child.

He'd thought earlier that this child's mother had brought him something he'd been searching for his entire life—a sense of peace that could be found with the right person.

Not with her—never again with her. But perhaps with the daughter she bore him.

IT WAS GETTING DARK. Pacing between the front door and the back, the beach and the street, with Freedom alongside her, Juliet watched frantically for anyone who might show up with her baby girl in tow. Duane and Donna were out, Marcie was out, some of the neighbors were out.

Blake was out.

The police had full descriptions and pictures, and had put out an alert.

Juliet was home in case the little girl returned on her own, and to answer the phone.

She was doing that, and slowly losing her mind. This morning she'd been relatively happy. She'd managed to patch things up with Mary Jane and Marcie. And she had Blake Ramsden on the periphery of her life, wanting to be her friend.

This morning she'd held her daughter in her arms.

Tonight, Mary Jane was gone. And two of the three people who owned her heart hated her.

Freedom whined, shoving his nose into her palm. She rubbed his black head almost unconsciously.

God, please let her be okay.

The eight-year-old had been gone for almost four hours. At best, she had to be getting hungry. At worst…

Juliet couldn't even think about it. Not and stay standing.

That look in Blake's eyes when he'd realized Mary Jane was his child tortured her. Over and over again. She'd lost the respect of the one man whose regard meant more to her than her independence.

And the worst part was, she'd deserved that look. She'd robbed a father of eight years of his daughter's life.

Just as she'd robbed her sister of the confidante she'd needed at one of the most critical times of her life.

And at least partly because she had this contrary habit of believing that she knew what was best for everyone. How in the hell had she developed such an ego? And without knowing it? No, it had taken seeing everyone she cared about in pain before she'd recognized that little fact about herself. It had taken these hours of being utterly alone.

She'd meant well. And that fact didn't do anyone one bit of good.

Her gaze stretching so far her eyes ached, Juliet took in the beach for at least the hundredth time. Where was he? Had he found her?

She looked and saw nothing. Her vision blurred as tears filled her eyes again. She'd fallen apart a couple of times since Marcie had announced that Mary Jane was gone.

For once in her life she felt completely powerless. There was no way she could fix this one. She just didn't know what to do.

Except check out front again to see if anyone was coming.

No one was. Juliet's head dropped against the front window as sobs shook her shoulders.

"Oh God, Mary Jane. Please come home. Please, baby. I didn't lie to you. I didn't tell him about you. I love you, baby. Please come home…"

At first the words just played over and over in her mind. But eventually, as she stood there, a dead weight against the window, she started to talk to her daughter out loud. The words were sometimes indistinguishable, broken up by almost animalistic moans of pain, but she continued to talk to Mary Jane. Maybe the little girl would feel the power of her need.

Or maybe she was losing her mind.

"I didn't lie to you, imp. I'd never lie to you…"

"I know."

Juliet froze, her forehead wet and sticky against the window.

"I know you didn't lie. Blake told me."

She spun around and then, with huge, gulping sobs, grabbed up the child who had miraculously appeared in the room behind her. If she was demented, so be it. She didn't want them to ever bring her out of it. Freedom was barking like crazy.

"Mary Jane?" She couldn't let go long enough to look at the child's face. But she knew the heart beating against her own. "Thank God. Oh, thank God."

She had no idea how many minutes passed before she noticed the man standing behind their daughter, watching her. No matter what happened from there on out, how much he hated her, how horrible he was to her, she would always be grateful to him. Blake had brought her baby back to her.

The irony in that didn't escape her.

IT WAS ANOTHER TWO HOURS before Juliet had a chance to be alone with Blake. Once she'd assured herself that, while Mary Jane might look a mess, she was none the worse for her escapade, Juliet had the wherewithal to call the cell phones of the other searchers and tell them that Mary Jane had returned. She owed them all more than she'd ever be able to repay.

And she called off the cops.

Everyone, including the pair of officers she'd spoken with earlier, stopped at the house, just to see for themselves that the little girl was fine. They all wanted to hear the story of how Blake had heard her whimpering behind a rock several miles from home, and then carried her all the way back.

Sitting at the kitchen table eating a peanut butter

sandwich after her bath, with Freedom sleeping under the table at her feet, Mary Jane held court with her visitors, telling them about her adventure. The little girl would have to be punished, Juliet knew that, but not yet. Not tonight. Tonight she was home and safe, and needed all the nurturing she was getting.

It wasn't every day that, with no warning, a girl came face-to-face with a stranger who also happened to be the man who'd fathered her.

And when Mary Jane's eyes started to droop, everyone except Blake said their goodbyes.

The neighbors had given the tall, good-looking man several curious looks. Duane Wilson was going to be grilling her like crazy when she got to work on Monday, asking why her client had been on her beach in the first place.

"It's past your bedtime," Juliet announced as soon as the front door closed. She needn't have bothered. Mary Jane was already off her chair, hugging her aunt Marcie good-night. Juliet waited to walk with her down the hall and tuck her in. Tonight, of all nights, she wasn't going to miss that.

She had to blink back more tears when Mary Jane stopped in front of Blake.

"Thank you for finding me," the child said solemnly, staring up at him.

His eyes glistened as he gazed at his daughter, as though enraptured. "You're welcome."

"And I've thought over what you said and it's okay for you to see me again. But I still don't need a father."

He bowed his head, whether simply to accept her

offer, or because he was hiding emotion he didn't want them to see, Juliet didn't know. "Thank you."

Mary Jane reached out one small hand and patted his. "Good night."

Hands on the table in front of him, Blake said, "Good night, sweetheart."

Juliet had a feeling he'd have given his life for a hug, and felt her heart break a little bit more when he didn't push the little girl.

HE WAS WAITING alone in the kitchen when she returned from the bedroom.

"I'm so, so—"

"Don't." He held Freedom's leash. "I don't want to hear it. I just stayed to let you know I intend to see her as much as possible over the next couple of weeks."

There was no softness in his voice, and no warmth in the eyes staring back at her. Cold and withdrawn now that Mary Jane was gone, Blake was more of a stranger than he'd been the moment she'd first met him nine years before.

"As long as it's okay with her, it's fine with me."

"You don't really have much choice in the matter. You owe me eight years and I'm not aware of any way you'll ever be able to pay that back."

She could feel the tears filling her eyes again and could do nothing to stop them. She didn't blame him for his anger and wouldn't blame him if he never spoke a civil word to her again.

"If you're ever ready to listen, I'm here and will tell you anything you want to know."

He tapped his leg for Freedom. Put the dog on his leash.

"Would you like me to drive you to your car?"

His eyes were hard as he glanced over at her. "I'll walk," he said. "I need the air."

And being in the same car with her would be far too confining, she read between the lines.

He opened the back door and was halfway through it before she spoke.

"Blake?"

He turned.

"Do you want to find a new attorney?"

He frowned, gave a derisive sigh. "There's hardly time, is there?"

Probably not. The paper trail was too extensive for anyone to have time to come in cold and get up to speed.

"I'll do my best."

He nodded. Walked out. And closed the door behind him with obvious finality.

OVER THE NEXT TWO WEEKS, Juliet saw Blake but spoke to him only briefly, to make arrangements for his visits with his daughter and to update him regarding his case. She tried a couple of times to speak with him about the past—and a future. Each time, he reminded her that he was her client and any kind of personal interaction between them would be unethical.

They both knew his words were more a slap in the face than a demonstration of concern over legal ethics. While they certainly couldn't embark on a relationship while she was representing him, they'd already had some highly personal conversations.

Mary Jane was still claiming she didn't want a father, but after her first dinner with Blake—a dinner she almost backed out of—she agreed to see him every time he asked. She didn't say much to Juliet about what they did or where they went, or even what they talked about. For the first time, her daughter wasn't sharing everything with her.

Juliet tried to talk with Mary Jane about her growing feelings for her father, whatever those feelings were, wanting her to know that she supported them, but Mary Jane wouldn't discuss Blake with her. Nor did she seem to want to talk about Blake's upcoming trial.

Until the day the trial began.

"You're not wearing red," Mary Jane said that morning, her voice almost accusing as Juliet came into the kitchen.

"It's not my turn yet, you know that," she said, pouring herself a second cup of coffee. She'd taken the first one into her bathroom with her while she got ready for a day she was dreading.

Marcie had come into the bathroom and talked with her while she put on her makeup and did her hair, but, not feeling well, she'd gone back to bed for another half hour rather than follow Juliet out to the kitchen.

"But this case is special. You should wear your power suit every day."

If she'd had more than one red suit, she would have changed. "I can't wear the same suit every day of the trial," she told the little girl. "Besides, it loses effectiveness if you wear it all the time."

Mary Jane dug into her bowl of cereal, spilling some of it over the side of the bowl onto the table. "You'll wear it the first day it's your turn, though, right?"

"Right."

"And you're going to win."

"I'll do my best." She couldn't give the girl the promise she wanted.

Eight years of love and trust had seen them through this crisis with Blake. Neither of them had ever mentioned Mary Jane's mistaken assumption that Juliet had lied to her. But she couldn't risk having Mary Jane accuse her of lying a second time.

JURY SELECTION TOOK ten days. The prosecution only took four to present enough evidence to put Blake away for life. Much of it was circumstantial. The bank account was not.

Juliet had a few tricks up her sleeve, but even with those, things didn't look good for Blake.

"We're up first thing in the morning," she told him as they left the courtroom the second Wednesday in August. Dressed in a navy suit and sedate navy and cream tie, Blake walked beside her out of the building and toward her car.

It was the first time he hadn't taken his leave of her at the first opportunity.

"For what it's worth," he said, hands in his pockets, "I have complete faith that you'll do the best job that can be done. I won't blame you if things don't go well."

He blamed her for robbing him of his daughter, but she got full marks for her legal ability.

Juliet wondered if that said something about her priorities. She hoped to God it didn't, and was scared to death it did.

SHE ASKED HIM to go for drinks, to talk over the questions she'd be asking him on the stand the next morning. He figured he already knew the drill. They'd been discussing the case for months. But for some reason, he agreed anyway.

Probably because Mary Jane was out with Marcie that evening and Blake didn't want to go home to a house empty of her sweet voice. He'd had her for dinner every night since the day he'd met her. She wouldn't let him get too close, wouldn't discuss her feelings and interrupted him or pretended not to hear any time he tried to tell her how he felt. But she was friendly and generous with her thoughts on any number of topics. And she had hundreds of questions. Blake attempted to answer every one of them. He tried to be patient, although the days were passing far too quickly—days that might be his only chance to establish a relationship with the daughter he'd lost.

Juliet had been completely generous with the little girl's time; he had to hand her that.

Or not. So she'd given him a couple dozen nights. She'd taken eight years.

He'd have preferred to meet Juliet downtown, some bar with a lot of people and enough noise to make conversation just difficult enough to keep the meeting short. They ended up at their usual bar out in Mission

Beach, but only because Blake wanted to stop in and see Mary Jane before she went to bed.

As soon as Lucy had served them, commenting on their absence in the past weeks, Juliet got right to the point, outlining the questions she'd be asking—about his time abroad, his relationship with his father, certain business dealings that revealed him as a man to whom integrity came first. She didn't acknowledge the possibility of losing, only of giving a win their best shot.

He'd been right to think he had it all down. There were no surprises here. He nodded. Sipped his whiskey. And nodded some more. Until her voice trailed off.

And then there they were, with half a drink apiece, and nothing left to say.

Had Lucy been close, he would've motioned for the check. She was across the room, her back to them as she waited on a group of guys in another booth.

"I was wrong."

He considered pretending that he hadn't heard Juliet speak. He looked at her through half-lowered lids, instead, saying nothing. But listening.

Not because he believed she had anything to say that he wanted to hear. Or because there was anything she could *ever* say that would make him okay with what she'd done.

Perhaps what he felt was morbid curiosity. Or maybe just the simple fact that anything was preferable to being alone the evening before he took the stand in his own defense.

She toyed with the stem of her wineglass, her eyes focused somewhere between it and the table.

"I didn't figure it all out until just recently," she said. He couldn't tell if she was talking to him or just taking out loud to herself. Somehow that made him pay more attention. "I had this conversation with Marcie…"

She looked over at him. "She lied to me."

"Must run in the family." Blake regretted the words as soon as they were said. Not because she didn't deserve them, but because they were beneath him. He'd never deliberately hurt another individual in his life.

"I told you my mother committed suicide," she said, her eyes narrowed and tired-looking as she peered at him through the dim lighting. "What I didn't mention was that I was the one who found her."

Shit. She'd been what? Twenty-three? Four?

"I came home to help her get ready for a surprise birthday dinner in the city. I'd brought a new outfit for her to wear—a silk dress just like she'd worn when she was married to my father. I even had pumps to match…"

Blake swirled the whiskey in his glass. She didn't have to tell him this. He didn't need to hear.

"She was lying faceup in the tub. She'd only been in there a couple of hours, but already her skin was gray, her body bloated and wrinkled."

He wanted to down the rest of his glass and order another. He couldn't make himself lift it to his lips. Couldn't be that present in the moment.

"I called 911, and then got obsessed with the idea

that she'd be mortified if perfect strangers came in and saw her naked. She'd want to be seen in that new dress..."

He was still watching her. Couldn't pull his gaze away from hers, even when her eyes filled with tears.

"So I hauled her out, dried her as quickly as I could, struggled with underwear. And panty hose..."

Juliet's voice trailed off and Blake breathed a sigh of relief that she was done. Even though he knew she wasn't. He waited.

"I had her completely dressed, shoes and all, by the time they got there."

She shook her head and smiled, as though trying to pretend that she hadn't just been talking about dressing her dead mother's naked body.

"You should never have had to go through that." He hadn't meant to comment. "Especially not alone."

With a half shrug, Juliet picked up her glass, swallowed the remainder of the contents.

"Yeah, well, the thing is, I thought I'd dealt with all of that. I went to counseling. I understood the phases of grief. I went through them and got on with my life."

He wanted to hold her in his arms. Just for a second.

"I learned from the experience, used it to catapult me to success. My mother got pregnant just before she was due to start college. She gave it all up to get married and have Marce and me. I wasn't going to do the same. I was going to make her sacrifice worthwhile by not repeating the same mistake."

No. He wasn't going to let her make sense. Wasn't

going to understand. Her choice had cost him too much.

"But you know what?" She looked as innocently lost as their daughter had that day he'd found her huddled behind a boulder on the beach.

"What?"

"I wasn't over it at all. Instead of learning from my mother's life, from her choices, I let her death rule me."

Eyes narrowed, Blake sipped his drink, and motioned to Lucy for two more. "How so?"

"When I first found out about Mary Jane, when I first knew that I was pregnant, what I wanted more than anything was to tell you."

He might have thought she was lying, but she didn't seem to care whether he believed her or not. She was telling him what she knew without any apparent interest in his response. She was confessing, not convincing.

"I wanted to believe in the fairy tales and magic my mother had always talked about. The stuff she'd read from those storybooks from the time we were toddlers."

She stopped as Lucy brought their drinks, and then, without touching hers, continued.

"I let my fear of being too much like her, my fear of making the same wrong decision, my fear of believing in love at first sight distract me from the truth."

It made perfect sense. But so much had happened between then and now. So much had changed.

"There wouldn't have been a way for you to contact me," he heard himself saying. The pain of losing so many years of Mary Jane's life had been easier to bear when he could blame it all on her. "When I first left, even my father didn't know how to reach me."

There was always later, though.

"Would you have come back if you'd known?"

And that was the million-dollar question. Blake would like to believe, unequivocally, that he would have.

He just wasn't sure.

"And what about five years ago? You were married to an unhappy wife, disoriented yourself, thankful that you didn't have children."

Mary Jane would have been three. Still a toddler. Too young to remember that he hadn't been around from the beginning.

"I would've taken responsibility." He meant what he said.

But how could he have managed that? As she'd already said, he'd had an unhappy wife. He'd been filled with guilt and grief. Disoriented.

She nodded. Stood.

"See you tomorrow," she said, and walked out, leaving him there with her untouched drink.

CHAPTER TWENTY

THE DEFENSE SPENT a week bringing in witnesses who testified to the character of the defendant. Employees, clients, even friends from Egypt. Juliet built a solid picture for the jury, a picture of a man incapable of defrauding anyone. A man who'd spent his time in the Cayman Islands living like the young married and financially modest man he was, not a man in possession of more than a million dollars. A man who was on the Islands only occasionally in between volunteering for weeks at a time in third world countries. Eaton James had sent money to help feed homeless children. Blake Ramsden taught them to feed themselves.

And still, the jury looked doubtful.

"It's that damn bank account," she told Duane late on the third Thursday in August. The trial had been going on for almost four weeks. If she didn't win them over soon, Blake Ramsden was going to prison.

"What I know," Duane said, lounging back in the chair across from her desk, "is that I've never seen you so emotionally involved in a case."

She didn't like his tone. "And your point is?"

"Nothing, Juliet." He sat forward. "You're like a daughter to me, you know that."

She did, and acknowledged his statement with a nod. "But?"

"I just wonder if maybe your emotional involvement with this man is clouding your judgment."

"You think he's guilty."

"I have no idea." The older man ran a hand over his balding head. "What I do know is that you have a talent for finding the truth and for some reason, that talent isn't helping you out on this one."

Her friend and partner had never asked her why Blake, her client, had been at her house that day. He'd never asked why the little girl had run away. But she knew he was hurt that she wasn't telling him.

If she had any idea what to say, she would.

But she didn't.

ON THE SEVENTH DAY of testimony, when the defense was due to rest, Mary Jane insisted on attending court.

"He's my dad, Mom," she'd said over breakfast that morning. "He needs me there."

Juliet might have replied if she hadn't been choked up with tears that she couldn't let fall. It was the first time the child had acknowledged that she *had* a dad. Until then, Blake had been a father in the biological sense. And, maybe more recently, a friend. Blake seemed to be capturing his daughter's heart as surely as he'd captured Juliet's. When Juliet said nothing, Marcie jumped in, offering to bring the little girl to the afternoon session.

Had there been any chance the jury would deliberate and deliver their verdict that day, Juliet would never have allowed Mary Jane to be there. As it was, she couldn't justify keeping her away.

Blake had already lost eight years of sharing life with Mary Jane. And she was right. He did need her there.

All morning in court he was restless, and growing more tense as the minutes ticked past. Like her, he could probably see the writing on the wall.

And there wasn't a damn thing he could do about it except sit there and wait to be hanged.

She offered to take him to lunch, or to have sandwiches brought in to her office. He opted to drive out to the beach instead. She hated to picture him there, all alone, but couldn't very well stop him from going.

She went to her office alone, instead. And spent the hour and a half poring over numbers and reports and statements that she'd already committed to memory frontward and backward.

BLAKE TOOK HIS SEAT for the afternoon session of court with more peace in his heart than he would have expected. He'd rather die than spend time in prison, but somehow, over the past weeks, he'd come to understand that there was one thing that mattered more than time, or prison, or even life or death. It had finally hit him an hour before, at the beach.

It was the obligation to be true to oneself.

He'd been true to himself when he'd stayed away three years longer than he'd planned—and when he'd come home, despite the difficulty his wife had had adjusting to life in one place.

The obligation to be true to oneself was why Juliet had had to have her baby on her own terms, by herself.

After weeks, months, years of searching, it had

taken one walk on the beach with his back completely against the wall to show him what he'd known all along.

Real honesty meant following the dictates of one's own heart.

He was already seated in court by the time Juliet arrived. She'd been planning to wait outside to walk Marcie and Mary Jane in. He didn't turn around to see if she had.

But he did try to catch her eye as she slid into her seat beside him. She didn't give him a chance. Something had happened.

Tight-lipped, she shifted in her seat as they waited for the call to rise. She shot up the second Judge Lockhard asked if she had any further witnesses. He knew that she had not. She'd already presented every piece of evidence she'd disclosed.

"May I approach the bench, Your Honor?"

Eyebrows raised, Lockhard glanced toward Paul Schuster, motioning both attorneys to come forward. There followed a rather lengthy consultation, during which Blake found it hard to keep his hold on the peace he'd brought in with him. One way or the other, he was ready for this to be over.

He could feel Mary Jane back there somewhere behind him. He suffered warring emotions knowing she was there. Her presence gave him a strength he didn't know it was possible to have—a need to survive, just so she'd be okay. But it hurt him, knowing that his little girl was watching him like this, accused and on trial.

Finally, following something the judge said, both attorneys turned. Schuster, with eyes serious and mouth unsmiling, sat. Juliet nodded to someone behind him.

"The defense calls Private Detective Richard Green to the stand."

Blake frowned, turned, watched a man he'd never seen before step forward.

To his defense?

The man took the stand. Agreed to tell the truth.

Coming back to the table, Juliet pulled a sheet of what looked to be mug-shot photos out of her satchel.

"Detective Green, can you explain what I'm holding here?"

"Yes, ma'am, that's a printed copy of parts of a videotape taken at the National Bank in the Cayman Islands."

The bank where Blake's supposed account was housed.

"And can you tell me what's significant about these particular photos?"

"That is the portion of film taken the day and time when Blake Ramsden opened his account."

Juliet turned to the judge. "I'd like this admitted as evidence, Your Honor."

Judge Lockhard glanced toward Schuster. "No objection, Your Honor."

The judge nodded.

That was when Juliet turned, looked straight at Blake and smiled.

"Mr. Green, do you recognize the man in those photos?"

"Yes, ma'am."

"Would you tell the jury if that man is in this courtroom today?"

Blake held his breath.

"That would be impossible, ma'am. The man in these photos is dead."

Blake's head swam.

Eaton James had opened the account himself, forging Blake's name. Just as he'd forged Walter Ramsden's name on the post-office box, and forged various other documents and investment agreements, as well as the names of principal signers of companies that did not exist.

Blake had figured all along that Eaton had opened that account. He'd had no idea of some of the other things the man had done.

And didn't particularly care at the moment.

He listened, trying to focus on facts being revealed by Green, who'd just flown in from the Cayman Islands. It seemed James had taken the secrecy of the Cayman Islands a little too seriously. First, he'd thought he could hide his ill-gotten gains there in an account that could not be verified by anything other than a bank statement, which he'd manipulated to point the finger at someone else. And second, he'd thought he could shoot off his mouth there, too. Once Green had found James's watering hole, just the night before, the truth had come pouring out, validated and verified by witnesses over and over again. It had taken him hours—and probably money—to get his hands on the tape.

James hadn't lost money on Eaton Estates, he'd banked it. He'd purchased the land for less than a tenth of what he'd shown in the investment agreement, for less than a tenth of what he'd charged his investors. True, the original investment had gone sour, but Eaton had that extra money no one knew about. And when Walter Ramsden had started to ask questions, James had offered to prove his integrity by paying the man back every cent he'd invested, to keep Ramsden from nosing around.

That explained those checks James had written to Blake's father. Payoff, not blackmail. James must've had a great laugh at Ramsden for turning around and sending every dime of that money to Honduras to feed those hungry children—who were the first and only children to have benefited from the Eaton Estates deal.

Blake tried to pay attention to the rest, to focus on the answers that had nearly driven him insane with their elusiveness. But they just didn't seem to matter anymore.

He wished Juliet would finish up with her witness and come sit beside him.

She did, and the moment her gaze met his, when that old connection flared between them, was as sweet as any he'd known.

Until, two minutes later, when he heard the words, "Case dismissed."

He felt like jumping up, whooping and hollering like a kid, but he couldn't seem to move. Afraid he might do something really stupid, like cry, he sat there, his arms heavy against the arms of his chair, and blinked a couple of times.

It was all the time it took for Mary Jane to come hurtling forward and fling herself on top of him.

"We did it!" she cried, hugging him.

It was the first time he'd ever felt those tiny arms around him.

Tears slowly dripped down his face.

JULIET STOOD and watched while the courtroom quickly cleared out, reporters following Paul Schuster through the back door. She tried not to watch her daughter in Blake's arms. Tried not to be jealous. Tried not to need to be there, too.

Marcie, who'd come forward behind Juliet, nudged her. "I guess this is as good a time as any to tell you I'm getting married."

Juliet had suspected as much, and was scared to death of what Marcie's future would bring her.

She pulled her twin into her arms and held on. "Be happy, Marce."

Marcie hugged back, tightly, and then leaned back to look Juliet square in the eye. "I am, Jules. For the first time since Mom died, I feel genuinely happy."

"Did you tell her?" Mary Jane piped up from her father's arms. Blake had risen and held the little girl high on his suited hip, as though she were little more than a toddler. The sight took Juliet's breath away. Her daughter had a dad. And seemed to be perfectly happy about it. Mary Jane might be tough, but Blake was tougher. Her mother could have told her that.

"Yes," Marcie said, the smile on her face going on and on. She rubbed her stomach and though she wasn't really showing yet, Juliet felt another twinge of envy. Marcie was going to have it all. Mary Jane was going to have it all. Blake was going to have it all.

And Juliet had robbed herself of everything she'd ever wanted.

"So then." With one arm hooked around her father's neck, Mary Jane pulled her mother over to them in the now deserted courtroom. "Now that Daddy knows everything about the bad guys, aren't you guys going to quit lying and just admit that even if you're mad you really love each other and want us to be a family?"

Juliet choked. And tried not to cry. Her emotions were on overload.

"If I have to have a father, that'd be okay, but there's no way I'm going to be a split."

"It's not that easy, sweetie," Juliet said, hating the fear she heard behind Mary Jane's attempt at confidence.

Blake looked at her, at their daughter, and then back at her. "I think it might be."

She stopped. Stared. Afraid to believe.

"You did what you had to do," he said, his gaze intent while his daughter looked from one to the other. "You were being true to yourself, and that's integrity at its core."

Her eyes filled with tears then, even though she was still in court. "What are you saying?"

He glanced from the child to Juliet again. "Our daughter said it's time to admit that we love each other."

She tried to speak. And couldn't.

"I always tell the truth," he finished.

"So does Mom," Mary Jane asserted.

Marcie laughed out loud.

"So I guess this means it's official," Mary Jane said. "We should get married before school starts so that I can finally quit getting so mad every time someone says something about dads."

MUCH LATER THAT NIGHT, on a blanket on the beach behind Juliet's cottage, Blake lay with Juliet beside him, his arm cradling her head, while they looked up at the stars.

"I want to know everything about her."

"I have scrapbooks with pictures and journal entries for every major event," she told him. "I told myself I'd send them to you when she turned eighteen."

He couldn't get upset with that. He understood that those books were Juliet's way of keeping him with her when her fear was forcing him away. Her fears, her life's experiences and conditioning—his choices—had forced her to raise their daughter alone. But her heart had insisted that she share the time with him anyway.

"When does school start?" he asked.

"In a couple of weeks."

The cool breeze coming in from the ocean felt glorious on his heated skin.

"Doesn't give us long to plan a wedding."

"Flights go from San Diego to Vegas every hour."

"Can you get off work tomorrow?"

"At the moment, I just lost my biggest client," she told him, sounding as if she was grinning. "How about you?"

"I'd already cleared my calendar in case of an extended vacation."

Juliet didn't say anything and he wondered if she'd come up with some other challenge to block her trip to happiness. Whatever it was, he wasn't going to let her do it twice.

"I know we said we'd wait, but I can't," she finally said, her voice fraught with pain.

He turned to look at her. "Wait for what?"

"This."

With a heavy groan, she rolled on top of him. "I just can't wait anymore." Very slowly she lowered her head to his, opened her mouth and took them both back nine long years—to a beach and a night and a moment that they had never forgotten.

No one had ever been like Juliet, nothing like the way he felt in her arms. Or she in his.

"Mary Jane," he muttered when he could form a coherent thought.

"Is a very sound sleeper."

Blake didn't stop for another thought until the dawn was coming up over the ocean.

"We've done it again," Juliet said, sitting beside him on the blanket with her recently donned clothes skewed and wrinkled.

He hoped so. God, he hoped so. Including the very same consequences they'd had nine years before.

Only this time, Daddy would know.

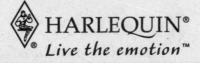

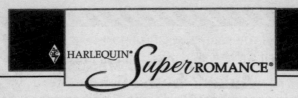

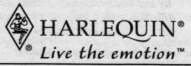

HARLEQUIN *Super*ROMANCE®

A new six-book series from Harlequin Superromance.

WOMEN *in Blue*

Six female cops battling crime and corruption on the streets of Houston. Together they can fight the blue wall of silence. But divided will they fall?

The Partner by Kay David
(Harlequin Superromance #1230, October 2004)

Tackling the brotherhood of the badge isn't easy, but Risa Taylor can do it, because of the five friends she made at the academy. And after one horrible night, when her partner is killed and Internal Affairs investigator Grady Wilson comes knocking on her door, she knows how much she needs them.

The Children's Cop by Sherry Lewis
(Harlequin Superromance #1237, November 2004)

Finding missing children is all in a day's work for Lucy Montalvo. Though Lucy would love to marry and have a family of her own, her drive to protect the children of Houston has her convinced that a traditional family isn't in the cards for her. Until she finds herself working on a case with Jackson Davis—a man who is as dedicated to the children of others as she is.

Watch for:
The Witness by Linda Style (#1243, December)
Her Little Secret by Anna Adams (#1248, January)
She Walks the Line by Roz Denny Fox (#1254, February)
A Mother's Vow by K.N. Casper (#1260, March)

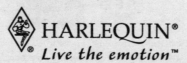

HARLEQUIN®
Live the emotion™